The Curious Case of
Sidd Finch

GEORGE PLIMPTON

The Curious Case of Sidd Finch

G.K. HALL &CO.
Boston, Massachusetts
1988

A signed first edition of this book has been privately
printed by the Franklin Library.

Published in Large Print by arrangement with
Macmillan Publishing Company.

G.K. Hall Large Print Book Series.

Set in 16 pt. Plantin.

Library of Congress Cataloging in Publication Data

Plimpton, George.
  The curious case of Sidd Finch / George Plimpton.
      p.   cm.—(G.K. Hall large print book series)
  ISBN 0-8161-4452-4 (lg. print)
  1. Large type books.   I. Title.
[PS3566.L5C8 1988]
813'.54—dc19   88-11931

Introduction

The publishers have made the mistake of calling this book a novel. It is not, of course, as anyone who turns the pages will realize. A chronicle might be a more apt description—since it details the career in the National League of the Buddhist scholar, Sidd Finch, who caused a considerable and memorable stir during the 1985 baseball season. The author, Robert Temple, whom I barely know, has asked me to write a short introductory note to his book. I am flattered to be asked. As only a part-time viewer of baseball—though I have a deep affection for the game—I know that other authorities from the sports media are far more qualified to put Temple's opus, and thus Finch's impact on the game, in a proper perspective.

I suspect I was asked because I wrote the first piece on Sidd Finch that attracted public attention. In mid-winter 1985 Mark Mulvoy, the editor of *Sports Illustrated,* called me in to offer me two projects. One was to follow up on a report about a Japanese distance runner in the London Marathon who, newly arrived there, had apparently got things confused and thought he was to run not for twenty-six miles but for twenty-six *days.* He had disappeared into the English countryside. According to the story, which appeared in the *London Observer*, his wife had called from Osaka, worried; she had commented on her husband's determination. He had been spotted running by a petrol station in East Anglia, etc.

"What's the other one?" I asked Mulvoy.

He began describing the rumors drifting up from Florida about a superphenom pitcher—"We think he's a converted cricket-bowler from Pakistan"— who had turned up in the Mets training camp in St. Petersburg. That was the story I picked. The "cricket-bowler" turned out to be Sidd Finch.

Because of various deadlines ("We must get this in by the April First issue"), my piece ended with the question still unresolved whether Sidd Finch, who indeed was possessed of the most wondrous arm in baseball history, would actually ever play in the big leagues. In retrospect, I wish Mulvoy had been a lot more patient. Or at least allowed me to follow up on the story when it became evident there was much more to come.

In any case, Robert Temple has picked up the cudgel. His book provides many of the answers we would like to know. By all accounts Sidd Finch is a terribly shy bird. Temple got to know him. So that was fortuitous.

I never actually saw Sidd Finch pitch that summer. At the time I was in the Orient looking at firework factories and preparing a book called *Fireworks: A History and Celebration* which I might suggest (in passing) even the layman will find of interest. Indeed, on August 5th, 1985, an extraordinary day in baseball history—the day Finch first pitched in the majors—I was recovering from watching a million-dollar fireworks show put on just outside the little Japanese town of Tondabayashi. Both events, on opposite sides of the world, paralleled each other as galvanic happenings.

Osaka is only thirty miles from Tondabayashi. If I'd had my wits about me I could have moseyed around Osaka to find out whatever happened to the Japanese marathon runner who disappeared into the English countryside. It is not good practice to let these opportunities slip by.

—GEORGE PLIMPTON

Acknowledgments

I am indebted to the New York Mets, of course, especially the front office people—Nelson Doubleday, Frank Cashen, the general manager, and Jay Horwitz, the publicity director—who, whether willingly or not, got me involved in the Sidd Finch affair. They were all extremely helpful, though I could have done without being asked to be Finch's spokesman—especially the frightening morning at Huggins-Stengel Field when I found myself talking to the assembled press about yak dung. Of the Mets staff, Davey Johnson, the manager, and Mel Stottlemyre, the pitching coach, were of considerable assistance. The officialdom of baseball was very gracious with its time, in particular the Commissioner of Baseball, Peter Ueberroth; the president of the American League, Bob Brown; and Bill Deane of the Hall of Fame Library at Cooperstown. I am grateful to my friend, Pat Jordan, for his reminiscences about Steve Dalkowski, the speedball pitcher in the Orioles chain, and also to Mike Marshall, the Cy Young Award winner, for allowing me to reprint part of his treatise on Sidd Finch's pitching motion. *Sports Illustrated* is to be acknowledged for extracts from their April 1st story on Sidd Finch. Among the authorities who analyzed and were helpful about Sidd Finch's religious background I am thankful to Peter Matthiessen, Dr. Robert Thurman of Amherst College, Barry Bryant of the Samaya Foundation, and, of course, Dr. Timothy Burns of Florida State University. Gay Talese was my authority on the Mob; Bob Johnson of the New York Philomusica helped me with the French-horn material. My gratitude to both.

For pulling all this together I am in great debt to Sarah Dudley whose perceptions and help in preparing the manuscript were inestimable.

I am also grateful to the following: Dominick Anfuso, Edward T. Chase, Jonathan Dee, Laurie Lister, James Linville, and Jeanne McCulloch.

Lastly, I would not have undertaken this book (or "opus" as the introduction has it) without the approval of Debbie Sue and Sidd Finch. They sent me a postcard congratulating me on getting "unblocked" and wishing me success. They supplied (not at all surprising) a Zen koan: *Ask yourself: who is the writer?* Debbie Sue encircled this puzzling question with a heart drawn in a pale lipstick.

I suppose I should also thank the author of the Introduction, though frankly I detect a hint that he regrets—having broken the story originally— not having followed it to its conclusion.

—ROBERT TEMPLE

For Freddy, Medora, and Taylor

The idea is that you simply can't understand the secret of our existence by using logic. There is a wonderful Zen metaphor for the futility of such understanding . . . that it is like playing a flute which has no mouthpiece or openings while a mosquito is biting an iron bull.

—DR. TIMOTHY BURNS

Give me a Presbyterian any old time.

—DAVEY JOHNSON

The Curious Case of
Sidd Finch

Part
I

I

THE PHONE RANG. I could barely hear it. I happened to be strolling by in the dark hall of the bungalow. The instrument has a device at its base to tone down the buzzer, or the bell, whatever is inside, and I keep it at the lowest pitch possible without turning it off entirely. My sister, who has a rather overdramatic way of putting things, complains that if I shut off my phone completely I am throwing away a lifeline to society, normalcy, and so forth. So I placate her, though she lives two thousand miles away. That does not mean I must answer or use the thing. Very often I let it go on ringing, a pleasant low intermittent buzzing that keeps up for a while. It stops. Then I can spend fifteen minutes or so in the mildest kind of conjecture—wondering who had been trying to reach me and what they have in mind.

No matter. If it is urgent, they can always write me a letter. I open about half my mail and read about a quarter of what I open, stopping if it turns out to be a request to write an article. "We would be most interested if you would . . ." That sort of thing. There was a time when I would open letters with a kind of desperate urgency, very often tearing what was within—notice of a clearing-house sale! I would snatch phones out of their cradles almost before the first ring died away, scared that whoever was on the line would hang up before I could find out what they wished. "Hello? Hello?"

Now it was different. My sister said that I myself was like a phone with the volume dial turned way down, almost off, so that I was just about out of it. Dead in the water. When she peers at me with her hard intelligent eyes, gray-green and beautiful, I know she is thinking about giving me a good stiff kick.

This time I picked up the phone. Perhaps I thought it *was* my sister. Perhaps it was because I just happened to be close by, indeed looking down at the phone when it went off. As it was, I let it ring six or seven times.

"Hello?" Captain Leroy T. Smith was on the other end. "Smitty" everyone calls him. I had met him in Vietnam, where he was a helicopter pilot, flying—or "muscling" as they called it—a two-rotor-bladed Chinook up into the hills to the fire camps with supplies.

Just this year I had run into him by chance on one of the St. Petersburg beaches—Madeira Beach it may have been, or Treasure Island out by the Aquarium. No matter. I remember two college kids in jams throwing a red Frisbee, tossing it half speed so that a golden retriever they had with them could run along underneath, leaping up from time to time to snap at it.

4

Smitty and I shook hands and we remarked on the coincidence of meeting on a Florida beach in such pleasant circumstances. He told me he had left the military but was still flying. He was the pilot of the Goodyear blimp *Enterprise*, stationed in the Tampa area. I saw him from time to time after that. He even came around to the bungalow in Pass-a-Grille. He was easy to be with—a big man, amiable, and my silences did not seem to bother him in the slightest. He would mix himself a drink or get something out of the refrigerator. Sometimes he would pick out a book from my sister's library, settle back, and read. "Listen to this," he might say, and read a passage to me that had interested him. Once, I said aloud that he reminded me of a large peaceful animal—an elk. That didn't seem to bother him at all. He never left without asking me if I would like to go flying with him in the blimp.

Indeed, that was why he was telephoning. "Bob, it's such a nice day. I'm taking up a couple of people from the Mets. Their club trains here in St. Petersburg, you know. They made the request a couple of days back. Plenty of room, Bob, and the air's so clear I'll guarantee you'll be able to see across the Gulf to Mexico!"

Ordinarily, I would have turned down such an invitation. It involved so much preparation—worrying about the right directions to the airfield, wondering if the car was low on gas, even concern that I might get airsick. So what I usually say in such circumstances is that I am sorry but I have committed myself to go fishing.

"Smitty, I've committed—"

"Come on, Bob. It'll do you good."

I have an aversion to people who say things like "It'll do you good." They feel something is wrong with you—a sentiment delivered with hearty, yet unctuous, sincerity. But in the case of Smitty, his concern was legitimate: he knew I was hardly functioning. He was very matter-of-fact about it. He said, "Kid, come on. It's a fine day for a ride. We'll just drift above the fields."

"The Mets?"

"It seems odd, doesn't it. The bigwigs. Nelson Doubleday, Frank Cashen, the general manager. And you. The surprise guest."

"Okay," I said abruptly. "Just this once."

It took me a long time to start the Volkswagen. Almost everything I need is within walking distance in Pass-a-Grille. On occasion I drive into St. Petersburg to see Amory Blake, the psychotherapist. The car sits at the end of the driveway under a thatched shelter that leaks badly. Its engine coughed into life and I backed out across the palmetto fronds, which crackled sharply under the tires; I never seem to have enough energy to go out there and sweep them clear.

The blimp seemed enormous moored in the field. A grid panel of light bulbs was set along its vast flanks to flash messages at night—"The Super Skytacular." As we walked out Smitty told us that in the old days the blimps carried loudspeakers through which advertising slogans were *shouted* down—discontinued, finally, because people were startled and didn't cotton to being bellowed at by "voices in the sky."

Counting Smitty and his copilot, whose name I've forgotten, seven were in our group. I recognized Nelson Doubleday and Frank Cashen of the Mets management, and Davey Johnson, the manager. Their pictures appeared regularly in the St. Petersburg *Times*. With them was a thin, athletic-looking gentleman wearing a Mets warm-up jacket and a baseball cap with its orange *N.Y.* Smitty whispered to me that he was Mel Stottlemyre, the Mets pitching coach. He was carrying a large leather bag.

The Mets contingent got up in the front of the gondola, lugging the leather bag with them. There were six passenger seats. I sat myself down in the rearmost. No seat belts. Behind me was a panel-sized reproduction of an old-fashioned dirigible with a grid of sails to direct it. The cabin was done in gray-blue. The seats were upholstered. The windows, big and bay-sized, had a slight overhang, so one could almost look straight down. A dozen men were below us, hanging on to guide ropes and running alongside. The ground fell away. Three ropes hung down off the bow, streaming back as we picked up speed. The racket of the two engines on their pods made conversation difficult. Above the front windshield was a large mirror—presumably so the pilot could keep an eye on the behavior of the passengers. I caught Smitty glancing at me. He winked. Alongside his seat was a big wheel that directed the pitch of the blimp. He leveled us off at about fifteen hundred feet. We were heading inland. The big windows were open at the top so that the warm breeze off the Gulf poured in on us. The gondola seemed outdoors . . . like an open gazebo on a summertime lawn. The wind was fresh, and I was glad I had come.

We spent about fifteen minutes easing above the patchwork country east of the Bay region, passing over cattle meadows bordered by drainage ditches. I heard one of the Mets people up front sing out, "There they are!"

Far below I could see a small contingent stand-ing in the middle of a field looking up at us, their faces pale against the green background. Two vans were parked off to one side; their roofs glistened in the sun.

"I don't think we need to be quite so high up," I heard Nelson Doubleday saying. "I'd bring her down to about a thou. We've calculated that's about the right height."

I could distinguish that the group below was composed mostly of baseball players. I could see their peaked baseball caps. Two or three men were wearing blue field jackets; I took them to be coaches. The propeller blades were feathered. We hung above them.

"Can we get this window open?" Cashen was calling.

Stottlemyre had a walkie-talkie with which he was in communication with the group on the ground. The instrument squawked and Stottlemyre said into it, "We're close to dropping one. Is everyone ready down there? We're about two minutes away."

The leather bag was hefted into position by his seat. Stottlemyre reached in and produced a baseball. Suddenly it was perfectly evident what he was going to do: lean out the blimp's window and drop the ball down into the cluster of ballplayers far below.

He spoke into the walkie-talkie. "How's our position? You got Reynolds directly below?"

Stottlemyre leaned out, his head and shoulders over the bay windowsill; I could see him sighting his target and letting the baseball drop. Distinct, it seemed to hang off his fingers for just a second before it bore down toward the meadow, quickly infinitesimal, and I could see one of the Mets standing in the middle of a wide circle start tottering around, his minuscule glove up—a catcher's glove it was evident to me even from that considerable height—as if he were shading his eyes from the sun.

From up in front of the gondola Nelson Doubleday, craning to see out one of the windows, called out, "How'd he do?"

The walkie-talkie murmured by his ear and Stottlemyre looked up. "Apparently Reynolds muffed it. He backed away and missed the ball by ten feet. The ball stuck in the meadow almost out of sight. They tell me it's kind of boggy down there. Reynolds is not having a good time."

Cashen said, "Let him regain his composure and we'll try again."

Stottlemyre said into the instrument, "Wait'll he regains his composure. We're going to try again."

I have always enjoyed dropping objects from high places. I was raised in a tall apartment house in New York City, fifteen stories above an interior courtyard, into which, during my adolescence, I dropped a steady barrage of objects—water bombs, tennis balls, an occasional golf ball, filched from my father's golf bag, which would crack alarmingly against the concrete far below and soar back up an amazing height toward me, reestablishing its properties as it hung at its apex before falling away again. What else? Stones from Central Park, pencil stubs, paper gliders by the dozens, and the detritus that should have gone into a wastepaper basket often going out that window. Best of all, I had a wooden bomb-shaped projectile with feathers at its tail to steady it in flight. It was equipped with a nose cone that sprung back on rubber bands so that pistol caps could be inserted. It was the ultimate object to drop from an apartment window. Down the long cliff of the building it would go on a direct line from the fingertips and explode on the concrete far below. Heads would emerge from various windows. Later I would venture down to retrieve it for future use.

All of this came to mind as I watched Stottlemyre reach into the leather ball bag and lean out of the blimp's window to let another baseball loose.

"May I drop one?" I found myself saying from the back of the gondola.

Up until then the small Mets contingent had paid almost no attention to me. They must have assumed I was an employee, a member of the blimp's crew. They looked surprised, but one of them—Nelson Doubleday, I believe it was—motioned me forward. I moved up the aisle. Stottlemyre said, "Give it a slight spin as you drop it out. Otherwise it'll flutter down like a knuckleball."

I leaned out. The blimp had turned so the open window faced west and in the distance I could see the blue slate of the Gulf stretching to the horizon.

Once again I felt the exhilaration I remembered from childhood—starting the ball on its swift progression to the BB-sized thing disappearing into the cluster of Mets below.

Mel Stottlemyre's walkie-talkie squawked and we heard a burbled voice announce that Reynolds had caught one.

"Great!" Nelson Doubleday exclaimed. "Now we're getting somewhere! Tell him he's got the record. Gabby Hartnett caught a ball from a blimp eight hundred feet up. We're at a thousand. He's in the books."

Mel Stottlemyre repeated the message into his walkie-talkie and reported that Ronn Reynolds did not seem particularly excited. He wanted to know if since they had the record, they could all go home.

Nelson Doubleday said, "Let's have just a few more and then we'll call it quits."

"That's quite a coincidence about Gabby Hartnett," I said. I told them that Gabby Street of the Washington Senators had once tried to catch baseballs tossed off the top of the Washington Monument. As a joke the last thing thrown out from the top was a small grapefruit. It had burst in Street's glove, a frightening spray of seeds and pulp, and he had cried out, "I'm dead! I'm dead!" The Mets contingent did not seem especially amused.

I was allowed to drop a few more. We stayed above the field for about fifteen minutes. After a while Nelson Doubleday called out, "Well, they got a taste of it, okay?"

I went back to my place in the rear of the gondola. On the way to the landing field I came under a certain amount of scrutiny. Heads turned and I was inspected over the backs of the uphol-stered seats. Frank Cashen talked briefly to Smitty and then he came down the aisle. I could see Smitty's face looking a little grim in the big mir-ror.

Cashen sat down opposite me. He seemed slightly embarrassed. His bow tie bobbed as he swallowed. "How did you happen to know about Gabby Street?"

"I've forgotten. Research, probably. It was in-teresting that they were both Gabbys."

"Do you mind me asking what you do?"

"I do very little," I said. "I'm a reporter originally, but I've been recuperating."

Cashen looked shaken. "What kind of a reporter?" he asked slowly.

"A kind of free-lance writer," I said.

"Would I know your name?" he asked.

I told him. Robert Temple. He nodded.

"I know your name," he said. "Look here," he continued. "I feel awkward telling you this, but there's been a grave lack of communication. You're not supposed to be up here in this gondola. What's been going on here is a . . . secret . . . a kind of closed practice."

I said I was sorry I had intruded. I told him what had happened—that the invitation had come from the blimp's captain that morning. I was sure neither of us had any idea that we would be meddling in some private affair, especially anything as mysterious as dropping baseballs into a field from a dirigible!

"I wouldn't have come if I'd known. I simply came along for the ride."

"Would you mind if we kept in touch with you about this?" he said.

I shrugged. "That's fine with me, Mr. Cashen."

When I got back to the bungalow the phone was ringing. For the second time that day I answered it. A record, it occurred to me. Smitty was on the other end.

"I'm in Dutch," he said.

"What's wrong?"

13

"I shouldn't have invited you along. When they found out you were a writer those guys really got heated up about it."

"I know. Mr. Cashen talked to me," I said. "Well, what *was* that all about?"

"Damned if I know," Smitty said. "If I'd known we were going to be throwing baseballs out the gondola, I wouldn't have taken them up. Hell, I'm going to be in trouble with the Federal Aviation Agency if they ever find out. It's against the law to throw *anything* down from a blimp."

"I won't say anything," I said. "My lips are sealed."

"You're going to get a call from Cashen," Smitty said. "I gave him your number. I'm sorry. I didn't know what else to do."

"No problem. Did you notice they let me drop a few of those baseballs?" I asked. "I was really in the spirit of things. I had a good time."

He told me it had been the strangest assignment of his career as a blimp pilot. When the *Enterprise* was up in the New York area for the summer months, he took up photographers. "I take them out to photograph the Statue of Liberty. They lean out the windows. They click away. They don't throw things, though. Jesus! Baseballs!"

Sure enough, the next morning I got a call from the Mets office. I answered the phone quite quickly for me. They asked if I would come down and see Mr. Cashen at Huggins-Stengel Field. I told them

14

why not. It was a pleasant spring day. I had nothing really to do until the afternoon.

My days were carefully structured. I kept a master chart, marked out on the back of a cardboard box, listing various tasks to keep me occupied and my mind off things. That afternoon I was scheduled to stroll down to the marina to look at the yachts. Kids fished there in the black water that sluiced and sucked slowly back and forth between the piles, and sometimes they'd catch a big drum, a fish with large scales and striped black and white markings. Elderly fishermen turned up there, too, with exact rituals, a collapsible stool that they snapped open and settled their haunches onto, precariously perched it always seemed to me, and they gazed at the tips of their poles, waiting for the quiver of the line. Close by the stool they kept live shrimp in a galvanized pail; sometimes they opened up a fishing box and, rummaging among its trays, pulled out a sandwich wrapped in cellophane. It was comforting to spend a couple of hours among them.

But that morning I was only supposed to water the little plot of grass behind the bungalow and put some feed in the fish pond at the back of the property. It was the least interesting morning during the week, though I had learned to pass a pleasant hour or so slowly revolving to direct the spray from the hose and feeling the cool of the water against my thumb.

So I skipped the morning schedule and I drove out to Huggins-Stengel Field. I knew the way. I had done a couple of stories that had taken me there. Huggins (the players drop the Stengel when they refer to it) is where the varsity, or the "A" squad, moves over in early March from the Payne Whitney complex on the other side of town. It's their home base until the big tin equipment trunks are packed and everyone moves north. Huggins is comparatively small—two baseball diamonds set down in a pleasant suburban area of St. Petersburg, with an artificial lake that once had alligators in it beyond the chain fence. In one corner of the complex is a giant pale-blue water tower with a circular staircase rising in a curl around the supporting pillar. Up on the vast bubblelike water container various slogans are painted, and when I arrived a crew was painting out a message that *Mary Lou Loves Duke*—a stirring thought since one had to assume that a *girl* had been up there at that dizzying height doing the letters. They had just started painting over the *ar* of Mary.

The clubhouse was a stablelike one-storied building. Frank Cashen had his office in one corner. I was ushered in. Ruddy-faced, wearing a seersucker jacket and the same bow tie he had worn the day before, Cashen smiled and motioned me to a chair. His office was almost barren—an ugly potted plant in the corner and two baseball trophies on a side table. A corner window looked out on Huggins-Stengel, where a few players were shagging flies.

After we chatted a while Cashen asked, "Well, what did you make of yesterday?"

16

"You mean that business of throwing baseballs out of the blimp?"

He nodded.

"I thought it was very entertaining. It's not something you see every day."

"No."

"It's better being *up* in the blimp, isn't it? I wouldn't care to have a baseball suddenly drop down out of the sky, much less try to catch the thing."

"You saw the ballplayers down there?"

"One or two," I said. "Yes, I didn't recognize anyone, if that's what you mean. We were pretty high up. But I saw their gloves, big ones, catcher's gloves I had to assume."

"Do you have any idea why?"

I paused a second. Then I said, "At the time I thought you had picked a very unusual way of training your outfielders. But then I wondered what had happened to the good old fungo bat, and of course there was the question of the catcher's mitts . . . why were they all wearing them? And besides, what kind of fly ball would be coming down from a height of a thousand feet? So my theory didn't make much sense."

I did not mention a curious fancy that had occurred to me the night before as I was trying to get to sleep—that the Mets had devised a weird kind of punitive practice . . . that was if a player missed a bed check, or got into a fight in a bar, made too many errors in the field, or committed

17

some major kind of indiscretion, he was sent out early in the morning to face the blimp!

The scene was clear in my mind. Davey Johnson would say, "All right, kid, it's the *blimp* for you!" And whoever he was pointing his finger at would groan and call out, "No, no, not the *blimp!*"

Cashen had put his fingertips together. "Mr. Temple, you're a writer, aren't you?"

"I *was* one," I said quickly. "I haven't really done anything in some time."

"I remember your stuff. Those dispatches from Vietnam. I remember an article about athletes' autographs. Some boxing articles. Another on Sadaharu Oh, the Japanese slugger. I'm an admirer. Especially the Vietnam pieces."

I began feeling nervous. I felt a tic in my cheek developing and I put my hand up to check.

"Now we have a problem here," Cashen was saying. "The last person in the world we wanted in the gondola yesterday morning was a journalist. It really confounded us."

"I'm sorry," I said. "You *did* seem very upset. I wouldn't have gone up if I'd felt I was going to confound anyone."

Cashen said, "It wasn't your fault. But the fact is that you were there." He leaned forward. "I'd like to make a bargain with you. It's our feeling that any good reporter would keep digging until he found out why all this was going on, wouldn't he?"

I shrugged.

Cashen said that he knew something of my

reputation. If I wanted to, I'd be sure to track the story down and it would break in a newspaper or a magazine. That would do it: they'd lose Finch for sure.

"Who's Finch?"

Cashen said carefully, "Look, if I give you some idea of what was going on up there, and I lay it out for you, can I get you to hold the story?"

I was about to explain that a bargain wasn't really necessary, that his story was safe however much I knew, when Cashen, who must have taken a slight, somewhat bewildered nod of mine as acquiescence, began to say, "In the old days we spoke about phenoms. Well, we have a pitcher coming into camp who's a kind of *super*phenom, to put it mildly. The scouting report on him is that he's the fastest pitcher the game has ever seen—a kind of freak."

"How fast is he?"

"I'm talking about a guy who can throw the ball half again as fast as it's ever been thrown!"

I did a hasty calculation that made me shake my head in disbelief. "You talking about someone who can throw the ball at *one hundred and fifty?*"

"Around there somewhere," Cashen said. "Not only that, he apparently throws with unerring control. He's learned to do this in the Himalayas somewhere. Mind over matter. We understand he's a kind of monk—a Buddhist monk. His name is Sidd Finch," he went on. "Sidd with two *d*'s, which I understand is to honor Siddhartha, the Buddha."

Cashen looked down at a page of notes. "He's English. An orphan. He was adopted by a famous anthropologist named Philip Sidney-Whyte Finch when he was about six. He was given the first name Hayden. The kid grew up in a rather grand house in London. His father was a widower, an expert on the mountain tribes of Nepal and Tibet. Out there somewhere he was killed in an airplane crash. At the time the kid was in his last year at the Stowe School—one of those English public schools—where he must have done very well because he was accepted into the Harvard Class of 1980. When he got the news about his father, the kid dropped out of school and spent a couple of months in the summer of 1976 in the Himalayas looking for him. No one actually saw the crash; the plane just disappeared. That's quite something, isn't it?—this kid wandering through those mountains looking for his father."

I nodded and wondered if the mystery had ever been resolved.

Cashen said he didn't know. "That same fall he came out of the Himalayas and entered Harvard. He dropped the 'Hayden' and 'Whyte' from his name, and changed Sidney, which he changed to Sidd with two *d*'s. Maybe he didn't like hyphens. We got all this stuff from the alumni records up there at Harvard. They didn't have very much on him, frankly."

"Did he play baseball up there?" I asked.

"Nope," Cashen said. "He didn't stick around long enough. He's not even in the freshman directory. He dropped out after just a couple of months there. *Really* dropped out. He went back to Nepal, Tibet, somewhere out there, and continued his studies, or looked for his father, whatever, wandering from one monastery to another, for almost eight years. That was where he learned to throw a baseball. Don't ask me how."

"Doesn't everybody in baseball know about this guy?" I asked.

"Well, that's the point," Cashen said. "We'd know all about him if he'd come up through the high school system here. Or the Sally League, or the Triple-A. The first scouting report came in from Bob Schaeffer last year. He's one of our people—the manager of the Tidewater Tides, one of our Triple-A farm clubs. The Tides were playing in Old Orchard Beach in a series against the Maine Guides. Schaeffer called us from the Friendship Hotel in Old Orchard. He asked for me personally. I remember him saying that they'd just had an autumn cold snap; a lot of the leaves had turned, so the team was out there playing in this crazy football weather.

"I knew that wasn't why he had called me—to talk about the weather in Old Orchard—so I said, 'Yes, Bob, yes?'

"So he tells me this. After the game he decided to walk back to the hotel from the ballpark, which, incidentally, is actually named The Ballpark. It's about a two-mile walk, but the Tides had played badly and Bob apparently wanted to get the game out of his system. About halfway, this kid—tall,

21

gangly, clean-shaven, wearing blue jeans, a back-pack, and a big pair of woodsman's boots, starts walking alongside. Very shy but obviously wanting to say something. Clears his throat a lot. 'Ahem, ahem!' What Schaeffer thinks is perhaps the kid wants to ask for an autograph, or maybe to chat about the game. But no, this kid says, 'Sir, may I be allowed to show you the art of the pitch?'—some odd phrase like that, in this kind of sing-songy English accent.

"Something about the kid's voice—maybe the politeness, the self-assurance—makes Schaeffer stop. He says, 'Sure, kid, I'd like to see the art of the pitch. We coulda used it this afternoon,' refer-ring to the fact that the Tides had just been bombed for fifteen hits.

"So the kid points out a soda bottle on a fence post. Maybe seventy feet away. Green markings on it. An empty bottle of Sprite, Schaeffer thought it was. The kid skins off his pack, sits down on the ground, and unlaces this big hiker's boot he's wearing. He pulls it off so that one foot is bare. 'For balance,' he explains to Schaeffer. Then he reaches into his knapsack and takes out a baseball. He stands up, he kicks that bare foot of his way up into the air, and he flings the ball.

"Schaeffer tells me the bottle on the fence post out there explodes, just *explodes*. It disintegrates like a rifle bullet had hit it—just little specks of vaporized glass. *Puff.* Schaeffer told me that he could follow the flight of the ball only after it had hit the bottle. He could see it bouncing across the grass and stopping about as far as he could hit a three-wood golf shot on a good day."

Cashen leaned back in his chair.

"So what Schaeffer says, very calmlike, is, 'Kid, would you mind showing me that again?'

"He did too. They found a beer can, or something, and he sent that thing *flying*. Schaeffer told me it was the damndest thing he'd seen in all his years in baseball. He told me over the phone he was going to send in a scouting report. It was going to be a weird one because the guy had no record in organized baseball. He kept telling me to invite Finch to spring training here in St. Pete. I'll always remember what he said—'This guy can change the face of the future.' "

Cashen shuffled through his papers. "I've got the scouting report here," he said. He told me I could have a copy for my files. He passed it over the desk.

Cashen waited for me to inspect it. "What would you do if you got a scouting report like that?"

"Irresistible," I said.

"Exactly. So we invited Finch. Why not? No guarantees. No contract. Just a look-see. We sent off the invitation to a post office box in Old Orchard. I didn't think much more about it until a month ago when a letter came in—postmarked Old Orchard—from Sidd Finch."

Cashen showed me the letter. It was written in a curious formal hand with large characters, as if a quill had done the work—a miniature of a proclamation one might find tacked on a monastery

NEW YORK METS
FREE AGENT PLAYER REPORT

First Report ☐
Supplemental ☐

OFP #

Player: **FINCH** (LAST NAME) **HAYDEN** (FIRST NAME) (MIDDLE NAME)

Date of Last Report

Nickname **SIDD**

Home Address: **GENERAL DELIVERY OLD ORCHARD BEACH ME.** STREET / CITY / STATE / ZIP   Home Phone ( ) AREA CODE

School Address: STREET / CITY / STATE / ZIP   School Phone ( ) AREA CODE

Position **PITCHER** Bats ⟋ Throws **R** Hgt **6'4"** Wgt **170** DOB **1956 ?**

Team Name **NONE** City ⟋ State ⟋

Date Eligible: MONTH / YEAR   Regular ☐ Secondary ☐ Grad. Date

Total Games Seen to Date ☐ **0**   Total Innings Pitched ☐ **0**   DATE LAST GAME SEEN ⟍

RATING KEY	POSITION PLAYERS	Pres	Fut	PITCHERS	Pres	Fut	NON-PHYSICAL QUALITIES (2 to 8)	
8 — Outstanding	Hitting Ability			Fast Ball Vel	8	9²	Aggressiveness	
7 — Very Good	Raw Power			Fast Ball Mvmt	8	9⁸	Drive	
6 — Above Average	Power Frequency			Curve Ball	?		Self-Confidence	DON'T
5 — Average	Running Speed			Slider	?		Mental Toughness	KNOW
4 — Below Average	Base Running			Change-Up	?		Pressure Player	
3 — Weak	Arm Strength			Other			Courage	
2 — Poor	Arm Accuracy			Overall Control	8	9⁸	Dedication	
	Fielding			Command	?		Coachability	
	Range			Poise	?		Work Habits	
Use Major League Grading Standards. Do Not Use Plusses or Minuses.	B B Instinct			B B Instinct	2	4	Off Field Habits	WEIRD
	(TYPE OF HITTER)			DELIVERY ✓			OVERALL MAKEUP GRADE	
	Pwr ___ Linedrive ___ Slap ___			OH ___ HL ___ LH ___ SA ___ UH ___				

PHYSICAL DESCRIPTION & INJURIES   Glasses ☐   Contacts ☐   Married ☐ Yes ☒ No

GAWKY STRING-BEAN-TYPE. NO VISIBLE INJURIES

STRENGTHS **UNBELIEVABLE(!) FAST BALL AND CONTROL YOU GOT TO SEE THIS.**

WEAKNESSES **NEVER PLAYED (NO JOKE)**

OVERALL SUMMATION **COULD BE THE PHENOM OF ALL-TIME. CALL ME VERY HARD TO FIGURE**

SIGNABILITY DATA   Asking for $ **0?**   Actual Worth $ **?**   Agent Involved ☐ Yes ☒ No

START AT WHAT LEVEL **MAJORS**

PROSPECT CATEGORY   Excellent ☒   Good ☐   Average ☐   Fringe ☐   Org ☐   N.P. ☐

SCOUT'S NAME _____

Date **JULY 28, 1984**

WHITE - Office Copy   YELLOW - Supervisors Copy   PINK - Scouts Copy

24

door. I remember the salutation was "My dear Sirs. . . ." The language was stilted, and very polite. Finch wrote that he was grateful for the invitation and would turn up in the training camp at St. Petersburg but he was not sure he actually wanted to join the team. He wrote apologetically that great mental adjustments had to be made in the shift from being a monk to pitching baseballs . . . and that he was not sure, frankly, about certain aspects of the game that did not adhere to what he called "tantric principles."

"What does that mean?" I asked.

"I have no idea," Cashen replied. "I suppose we'll find out."

I went back to the letter.

He did not want to sign any contract, or be involved in team practices, or have a locker, or talk to the press. He did not want to stay with the rest of the rookies. Any old room in a boarding-house would do. He wanted to pitch *in camera,* as he put it, in some kind of enclosure where no one except a few representatives from the Mets management could watch. The reason for all this was that he did not want to raise anyone's expectations, much less those of the fans. If he decided he didn't want to play, hardly anyone would be the wiser.

"So you agreed to all this. . . ?"

Cashen said, "At first we all thought it was absolute nonsense. The reason we didn't throw Sidd's letter in the wastepaper basket is that we kept remembering what Bob Schaeffer had told us. 'This guy can change the face of the future.' So we agreed. We got him into a boardinghouse. Mrs. Butterfield . . . she's over on Florida Avenue."

"What about the other requests?" I asked.

"Well, here at Huggins-Stengel we put up a kind of tarp-surrounded enclosure for him to pitch in so no one can see. You can spot it from the corner of the window."

"Doesn't everyone wonder what's going on in there?"

"The word is out that irrigation machinery is being installed. That's for the press. They don't bother checking. Not much of a story in a new irrigation system. Some of the players must know something's up. Anybody who looked in there, lifted up the corner of the tarp, you know, would find a pitcher's mound and a plate . . . hardly items associated with irrigation machinery."

"No."

"We began getting our catchers ready—"

"So *that* was what the blimp was about," I said.

Cashen nodded. "It was Nelson's idea. He tends to be impetuous—quick decisions. To get our catchers ready for Finch, we needed a ball going that fast. We couldn't get the pitching machines cranked up to anywhere near that speed. So the idea was to throw a ball out of something way up in the sky and let gravity help us out. A blimp! Eureka! Why not? So we get a blimp. That's the way corporate America works!"

26

"How fast does a ball go dropped out of a blimp?" I asked.

"We got someone to work on it," Cashen explained. "It depends on the height. They told us that from five hundred feet or so that a baseball will get up to about a hundred and thirty miles per hour by the time it reaches the ground. From a thousand feet a ball comes down at one hundred and seventy, just about what Finch throws . . . close enough to give the catchers some idea."

"So you're prepared."

Cashen leaned forward again. "Finch is here in camp. He came in yesterday afternoon. We took him to Mrs. Butterfield's boardinghouse. Today we brought him out here to Huggins. We went out to the enclosure to watch. It's all absolutely true."

II

A WEEK WENT by. I heard nothing from the Mets. The phone in the bungalow rang on occasion. I picked it up more often than usual—my curiosity naturally piqued by the goings-on in the blimp and how Sidd Finch was doing at Huggins. On the other end were not the Mets, but a friend or two, including my sister. She was so startled to hear my voice actually answering the phone that she temporarily forgot what it was she was calling about.

I thought about my morning in the blimp and

about the conversation the next day in the Mets office with Frank Cashen. What was odd about the meeting was that he felt he had to strike a bargain with me. If he had taken the time to check it out, he would have discovered that I was not capable of writing a paragraph, much less a line of copy. I was a completely defused member of the communications industry.

Still, I was pleased Cashen knew my work. At one time I had indeed been making a comfortable living as a freelance writer. The editors at *Esquire, Playboy, Sports Illustrated, Rolling Stone, Life,* and so on, knew my name, and when I called I could get through to them. Often an editor would call me—"I have an idea I'd like to talk to you about." He would add, "Let's have lunch," and we would go to The Four Seasons, where half a dozen editors I knew from other publications would be leaning across the wineglasses to plot with their writers of the moment, most of whom I also knew. At the end of lunch I would usually say, "Well, let me think about it for a day or so." Sometimes it took two lunches. At the end of the ritual I would usually agree to do what had been suggested.

My "pieces"—as everyone called such things— tended to be long, imbued with a flair that was mostly a kind of irreverent whimsy. Editors took this to be thoughtful analysis. More important to them, I got the pieces in on time. The variety was far-ranging. I wrote portraits of politicians, labor leaders, athletes, publishers. I used a fold-back notebook and wrote a self-developed shorthand in it. I wrote travel articles. I prided myself on finding pegs on which to hang the subject. I wrote pieces about bubblegum cards and autographs.

I did a few stories for *Sports Illustrated*. One of them was on bicycle polo—a sport played during one of our recent recessions and mostly by Argentinians who temporarily could not afford strings of ponies. They pumped furiously around the lovely manicured lawns of Southampton on fat-tired dirt bicycles. They wielded sawed-off mallets. Silver trophies shone in the late afternoon sun. The girls who came to watch wore designer jeans and ballet slippers. I knew a lot of them. Farmington. Garrison Forest. They asked after my sister. They lolled on the grass as if posed there by fashion photographers. Many of them wore large straw hats. The players were completely serious about what they were doing on those little bicycles, as solemn as owls—helmet-clad, rugby shirts with big numbers on the back, the little mallets held aloft as they churned about those ocean estates. There was an entire league as I recall—Westbury, Purchase, Meadowbrook . . . all those posh polo centers. Elaborate dinners and dances were given for them in the evening. Everyone knew that things were going to get better and it was only a matter of time before the players were off those little dirt bicycles with the fat tires and back onto their ponies, kept for them somewhere, Texas probably, in the interim.

I had an interesting enough life, full of the unexpected that came up with each assignment. I traveled. There always seemed to be a half-empty suitcase on the floor of my little one-room apartment in Manhattan. I enjoyed being with the people I wrote about, and in the company of my fellow writers. I spent too much time getting down to the Lion's Head in the Village, and coming back so boozy on one occasion, I slept past my stop and ended up in the Bronx.

Then, in 1971, after three lunches in The Four Seasons with an editor who thought I would have a "fresh" eye on the "human" side of things there, I went to Vietnam. It turned out to be a grave mistake. I know writers—a lot of them my friends from the Lion's Head—for whom that place was like walking into a candy store. It was as if they had been waiting around for a story that finally came. My own ability, which was to find little mockeries—like Argentine ex-millionaires pumping around on bicycles playing polo—was overwhelmed by the scale of the buffoonery going on there.

I liked the helicopters. When they tilted flying at a couple of hundred feet, the jungle canopy below seemed as harmless as a thick carpet of grass, almost beckoning, like a pillow, and I got so used to being up there that I felt I could unbuckle my seat belt and step out the open door into the slipstream and float above all that like a balloon. Some journalists who enjoyed helicopter flights called them "joy pops." I even liked the night flights. The enormous clatter of the blades took me through the cottony comfort of the darkness.

Even ground fire, rising up in slow orange balls, seemed ethereal and harmless, ornamental rather than deadly.

I wrote a number of pieces from Vietnam—especially about the helicopter people. But what I put down became increasingly frantic, garbled, opinionated, finally unprintable I would have guessed (I have never checked to see) and then suddenly some internal capping took place within my head and the torrent of words stopped.

Officially, I was suffering from something quite novel among journalists, but common enough among the field soldiers—what the Veterans Administration called "post-traumatic stress disorder." The symptoms were identifiable enough: paralyzing depressions, a sense of shame, even guilt; abrupt fits of anger, suspicion, and so forth. In the First World War the affliction was called "shell shock"—a fine description that suggested the incessant shelling of trench warfare, the great range of sounds from the violence of shell explosions to the patter of dirt on the iron of the helmet as one cowered in the trenches. All this simply unhinged one after a while, and he had to be removed to the rear areas. In the Second World War the phenomenon was given a more euphemistic name—"battle fatigue" . . . as if what had happened was nothing that a few *zzzzzz*'s wouldn't solve. The victims just got awfully tired.

Now it had a grander name you could really get your teeth into. "Post-traumatic stress disorder." It not only brought my writing to an abrupt stop—

a truly astonishing case of writer's block—but I could not get it going again. I was hard-pressed to write out a laundry list. Letters, even to my family, were impossible. I stared at the blank pages of my fold-back notebook.

I stayed on in Vietnam until almost the very end. I hung around. I was like a street person. The magazine disconnected me as their correspondent. Finally I came back home—that swift impossible conversion by jet plane from life in a rice paddy to the Oakland Army Terminal—in a kind of bum's rush with very little preparation for the transition. I did not feel I could survive without straightening things out for myself. I called my sister and told her what I was going to do. I leased a little log cabin in the pine forests of the Olympic Peninsula and hunkered down there.

I do not know how you measure bad times. By terms, perhaps, as in "prison terms." My first term was a couple of years—living in a strange niche in the American post-Vietnam War culture: in the still, pine forests of the Olympic Peninsula with the Pacific on one coast and Puget Sound on the other. In there with me, though I rarely saw them, were others. We were known as "trip-wire veterans"—all of us suffering from "post-traumatic stress disorder." We were called trip-wire veterans because that was how we guarded our solitude—setting out wires around our abodes so that an intruder would trip an alarm device of some sort.

I put a few trip-wires out myself. They were wired to little bells, the kind that ring in antique shops when you open the door. Other people out there in the pines did much more to protect themselves in this savage kind of isolation—huge deadfalls, homemade mines as big as garbage can covers, tiger traps, booby-trap systems, all of these connected with wires stretched thin across the ground like a vast trellis, and there were tunnels into which they could duck, and fox holes, and in the pine-log and tin cabins they had built—like World War I redoubts—they sat staring out across the invisible networks of wires, often with a Winchester in their laps.

When I took walks through the pines I moved carefully, because if I saw the horizontal lines of a log cabin or the glint of tin I knew I could be coming up on someone like that. It was very quiet in the pines. Once in a while the sounds of ships' horns drifted in from Puget Sound, an odd seasound amid the tree trunks. Twilight was the frightening time. The sunlight, filtering through the pines, gave way to shadow. The French have a phrase for this time of day—*le temps entre le chien et le loup* . . . the time between the dog and the wolf. . . .

From time to time I'd walk through the forest to the firebreak and from there to the blacktop highway, about ten miles away, maybe more, to thumb a ride to Forks, which was the nearest place for supplies.

Out in the pines the people usually ate what they could catch. They smoked the salmon brought in from the Sound, and there were brook and steelhead trout from the streams. Rabbit and squirrel were all right in stews. I fished almost every day; the noise of a gun made me shake for minutes after firing it, so my fish diet was supplemented by packets of dried food I toted out from Forks in my backpack. Beef tetrazzini was my favorite. Once I had beef tetrazzini for a week.

The magazines kept in touch with me for a while. My sister forwarded the mail. I picked it up when I went in to Forks. It was easy enough to read the letters, but the idea of putting words to paper even to answer the editors was too formidable an exercise. The letters seemed communications from another planet—packets that had dropped down through the tops of the pines. The editors wanted stories on vacation spots—the "Hotels of Bermuda," "Polo in Jamaica," "Fishing the Lochs" . . . as if their way of getting me back on track was to combine the assignment with the pleasures of a spa.

Actually, I mended in there. It was the kind of therapy that comes from living from one day to the next, not expecting too much. Others in the pine forests set up structured programs for themselves. One of the few trip-wire veterans I met out there (when he came to see me the sudden knock on my door made me jump . . . not *one* of my antique-store bells had jangled) said he had been able to collect his wits by days of spying on a herd of elk. He crept up on them buck-ass naked, a long crawl from his log cabin on his elbows, infantryman style, to an orchard-like clearing in the woods where the elk liked to spend their days and bed down in the evening. In the early morning there was always a thick ground mist, about two feet deep, through which he crawled, the moisture cool on his bare skin. He would rise up slowly from time to time to see where he was, and then submerge into the cottony gloom, like a submarine, and move ponderously forward across the forest floor. He told me that the elk family never did anything that was surprising, or really very interesting. They grazed, lay their gray bulks down in the meadow grass; they turned their great antlered heads; their jaws moved sideways, and they looked aimlessly into a bovine middle distance. It was their undisturbed life that was so soothing for him to watch; a large ear flicked at a horsefly; he could hear the sound of their breathing, the sound of grazing. The suck of their hooves in the meadow grass. The slow, dull tempo, just about somnambulant, of their easy lives. Even spying on them made him feel good, because he felt he was a part of it. He used to tell me that it gave him assurance that the whole world wasn't caving in.

I was even tempted to ask him if I could creep down through the mists with him. But the suspicion crossed my mind that I would not find the peace he did . . . that the size of these great pronged horns would frighten me.

Actually, the guy never really understood why I was *in* the pines. I was a writer, after all; I was an observer. I had not done any of the things in the paddy fields and the fire lines that had put him in there.

I went to the telegraph office in Forks to wire my sister for money to come home. I think the thought of creeping down on those elk made me realize that my therapy had to take place elsewhere. The girl behind the counter shoved a pad of yellow message blanks toward me. I glanced at the pen, which was attached to the counter by a bead chain. I told her that I could not write. I was an illiterate. Would she mind writing down my message for me. "No problem," she said brightly, as if illiterates were a common phenomenon in her office. I dictated to her. "Dear Sis . . . "

I never went back to the cabin.

My sister met me at the plane. We embraced and she told me I smelled of the woods.

"We'll go down and pick up your baggage."

"I don't have any baggage," I told her.

"You've been gone for three years and you have nothing to show for it?"

"I guess not. I should have brought a gift."

In New York I found very little serenity. I spent far too much time in my apartment. The phone was disconnected. I could barely hear the sounds from the street. I thought about taking the subway down to the Lion's Head, but not seriously. I ate beef tetrazzini. When my sister came she brought the food and cleaned up the kitchen afterward. The income from my family trust was enough to keep me going. I had very few expenses, after all.

I went up and spent some good times with my family—my parents lived in Marblehead—but after a while I left, knowing that they were scaling down their social activity on my account. I did some aimless traveling. I went to Africa and took a trip on the Senegal River. I was urged to take notes, which I didn't. By mistake I left a little suitcase in Dakar and once again I arrived in New York with only the clothes on my back.

"No gifts?" my sister asked as I came up the ramp.

"I'm sorry," I said. "Perhaps next time."

I spent a bit over a decade in this kind of shiftless fog—nearly a castaway life . . . vegetating (a word my sister dropped on me from time to time). I shipped out as a deckhand for two years on a freighter. We put in at the Seychelles, the island archipelago in the middle of the Indian Ocean—great granite rocks that rise out of the azure sea as if the coastline of Maine had been transported into the tropics—and I went back there and spent two years living in a small thatched-roof house on stilts set back in a palm grove just up from the sea. The chickens clucked and dusted under the floorboards. The view, down between the palms, was rarely changed by weather shifts. I was frozen in aspic.

An English schoolteacher lived with me for a while. We had interests but very little sharing of them. A patient sort, she was a bird-watcher—the Seychelles being an ornithologist's paradise—which led me to think she didn't mind my long silences. On occasion I worked on a sportfishing Bertram that went out into the Indian Ocean. At supper I would say we had caught two bonita. After a while she would allow that she had spent the day looking for the Black Paradise Flycatcher, but hadn't seen any. I would sink into my curious reveries of the time, and she into what I assumed were hers. I didn't think she minded this sedentary domestic kind of existence, but one day she said to me, "We are the oldest couple we shall ever know. I believe I am now at least eighty," and she left.

I moved myself—west to the African coast to the old slave port of Lamu at the mouth of the Tana River. There was one car in Lamu, the mayor's jeep, and the lamplights were gas. It's a place you can reach only by dropping into the tiny airstrip, or by dhow. There are less than a dozen Europeans in Lamu, at least when I was there. One of them was a famous professional hunter. When the full moon was out he took me down to the water. He said the elephants walked out and stood in the sea, the small rolls of surf washing past their flanks. We were never fortunate enough to see such a sight. I got malaria in Lamu, which didn't help, but I loved the place. I often dream of the wide white beaches, especially the elephants coming out across the sand dunes to the sea.

On the way back home I remembered just in time and in the Dar es Salaam airport I bought a souvenir spear. Its feathers were as bright as new paint and it would not have surprised me to discover it was made in Korea. My sister saw me coming down the ramp with it and she called out, "Oh, Robert, you remembered. Just what I wanted!"

My favorite place was my sister's bungalow in the Pass-a-Grille beach area of St. Petersburg. The artistic hangout of the area, it was a community at the tip of the peninsula with the Gulf on one side, the Bay on the other, and good beaches popular with the young crowd, who at night frequented the little restaurants perched along the canals off the Bay.

The bungalow had a backyard with a frog pond at the far end, which smelled of sulphur. In front was a large stone bird bath on a pedestal. Vegetation had piled up around the side of the house. The sunlight filtered through fitfully, dappling everything within. I walked barefoot on stone floors through a kind of goldfish-bowl hue. The house smelled pleasantly of wet leaves and mildew. A fan turned in the ceiling of each room. The place was larger than I needed—a large living-dining room, a kitchen off it, three bedrooms, a screened porch with a wicker writing table set up with a portable typewriter with a blank piece of paper, curled from the humidity, in the roller, and a large porch out back with comfortable sofas in bright Palm Beach patterns, one of them hanging from chains, and a sliding door on runners that opened out on the yard with the frog pond.

Our parents had given the bungalow to my sister when she got married—a honeymoon cottage. Her new husband was an Army fighter pilot. His face was so boyish and finely sculpted that it seemed age could never affect it—as permanent as Cellini's Perseus, whose features it resembled quite astonishingly. It was the kind of face you see in grammar school and can never imagine seeing it turn adult; age would seem as silly on him as a mustache on a child at Halloween. His name was Thorvald. Everyone called him Toby, thank goodness, including my sister, except when she was mad at him.

Occasionally, in the bungalow, I would find evidence of their lives together. In the master bedroom was a large sketching pad . . . with designs on it for an oil she was going to paint of him as an aviator. Plane fuselages. A sketch of an undercarriage. She was apparently planning on a portrait of Toby in an old-fashioned flying helmet with ear flaps and in the background what looked like a World War I Sopwith Camel with American markings.

Naturally, I never told my sister about my love of flying—those "joy pops" in Vietnam. In that part of the world, looking down at those green puffy hills from the helicopter, I had on occasion wondered if I was looking at the one on which Toby had "bought it" as they liked to say. He was one of the first pilots killed in Vietnam.

Our parents lived in Marblehead. When my sister visited from New York, where she had a little studio, my parents took her out in *Salty IV*, their yawl, and she wrote me about lying in the sun up on the foredeck, the warm teak wood against her cheek and listening to the swells crack against the bow and gurgle back along the sides of the yacht. It was then she understood my absorption with isolation.

Everyone called my father Salty. He vaguely resembled Leverett Saltonstall, the craggy-faced New England senator; the nickname also reflected his obsession with the sea and sailing. When we were younger my sister and I crewed for him. He affected a pipe when he sailed, often upside down after he quit smoking, and he was adept at calling out orders with the pipe stem still in his mouth. We never saw the pipe except when he was on the water. It stayed aboard the *Salty IV*. My mother made a wall bracket in which it rested just off the companionway.

When my father retired from his investment counseling firm, they sold the apartment in New York City and the country home with the tennis court and the rose gardens in Cold Spring Harbor. They moved up to Marblehead into a smaller house because the country life by the water was what they truly craved and the summer cruising was better. Also, it was easier to get down to Narragansett Bay for the America's Cup trials and the races. It just about killed my father when the Australians took the Cup to Perth.

I don't know what my parents made of the two of us. We followed in their academic footsteps (Amherst and Smith). My sister's determination to paint, and her skill at it, and especially her refusal to be influenced by the abstract artists, delighted them, but my decision to write unnerved them, I suspect. They hoped my writing was an interim period, like being a ski bum for a couple of winters, or joining the Peace Corps, and that I would go on to something sensible and secure—at the very least into publishing. My father knew one or two publishers and felt they were sensible, even "top-drawer"—a description he used for people he truly admired.

I make him sound like a snob. He was not. He felt that given the advantages (family background, security, and good education), a certain obligation existed to follow a proper pattern, as solid in his mind (the right jobs, clubs, marriages, and so forth) as if he were a Brahmin, a "top-drawer" Hindu.

During my convalescence both of them wrote long letters to keep in touch. They knew their chances were slim that they could reach me by phone. Their letters were impersonal. They never mentioned my troubles. Always financial matters. Gossip. The Davisons ("You remember them, of course") had run their Columbia 32 into Execution Rock in a fog. "Your sister has been traveling . . ." In the bungalow in Pass-a-Grille I kept their letters in a packet fastened with a rubber band. They always ended their letters with the unintentionally mocking postscript "Do write."

How possessed they must have thought me. I read with envy about authors who professed how little trouble it was to write—Robert Frost, who could write anywhere, take his shoe off in a railroad car and turn it over to use like a little desk in his lap. My sister took me once to hear Archibald MacLeish lecture on poetry at Columbia not long after my return. He stood in a heavy woolen suit that looked as though he had woven it himself and he said that poetry is the art of understanding what it is to be alive. I took my sister by the elbow afterward and I said, "Well, that's my problem, isn't it? I'm not really alive. I'm perhaps a quarter alive."

"You're coming along," she said.

In Florida I lived by what I called my "master plan of idleness"—the cardboard with a daily schedule marked on it. Monday morning—the visit to the marina. In the afternoon—the trip to the mangrove swamps. Tuesday—fish day. That sort of thing.

Fishing became an obsession—bait fishing with a red and white bob in the quiet mangrove-flanked channels, off an ancient gray-planked dock that swayed eerily under me as I ventured to its end, easing myself down, legs dangling toward the water. The mangroves formed a small amphitheater, closed off from the traffic of the deeper channels. Sometimes I could hear the slow puttering of a skiff trolling on the far side of the trees. The bob moved slowly in the tide. Sometimes the blue crabs, swimming up from the silt of the bottom, would collect the bait, pulling the bob down so that it was half submerged, the current flowing slowly past it. There were times, I am willing to admit now, when I did not even bother to bait the hook; at the end of the line the silver shaft and barb hung harmlessly in the murky water. I felt the sun on my eyelids; car tires would occasionally thunder on the wooden bridge beyond a turn in the line of mangroves. It helped to wear dark glasses. I found a pair smoked almost black, so that even the sunlight was removed from the brightness of the Florida afternoon. I stirred in a cocoon of darkness.

III

"I THOUGHT YOU'D like to hear what's been going on with Sidd Finch."

Frank Cashen was on the other end of the phone.

"Yes, sir," I replied. "I have been curious."

"First of all, I want to thank you. Nothing's leaked out so far."

"I'm surprised," I said.

Cashen explained that hardly anyone had noticed Finch. He arrived in the Mets car (he was chauffeured by a local kid named Elliot Posner) around noontime when the playing field was closed down for the midmorning break. He only pitched in the enclosure for about five minutes. Other than Mel Stottlemyre and, on occasion, a couple of the Mets top brass, no one was in there with him except the catcher.

"Who's the catcher?"

"Ronn Reynolds," Cashen said. "Kid from Kansas."

"He was the guy under the blimp?"

"He's the one." Cashen laughed. "After his day with the blimp he's one guy who's never going to worry about camping under a high pop foul!"

"Well, how's your boy?" I asked.

"Finch? Well, he's an odd one. First time I ever heard a British accent out there on the grass. He plays a horn. Did I tell you that?"

"No."

"We're having a little trouble with that. Mrs. Butterfield, his landlady, called to say that he's a French horn player. She hadn't been told that. She says the sound seems to come from everywhere at once. Sometimes she thinks all the radio clocks and her TV set have gone on simultaneously. I'm not sure she can take it. You wouldn't mind taking in a boarder, would you?"

I thought he was joking.

I asked Cashen how fast Finch was. Cashen hemmed and hawed, but then he said that, well, the Mets had brought in a radar gun.

"It's called a JUGS, after what everyone in the old days used to call a big curveball—a 'jug-handled' curve. Black with a big snout. Weighs about five pounds. It's usually pointed at the pitcher from behind the catcher's position."

"Who handled the thing?" I asked.

"Mel Stottlemyre. He took the gun out to the enclosure. It has a glass plate in the back that

45

shows a pitch's velocity. The figure at the top of the gauge is two hundred miles per hour."

"Well, what did it show?" I asked.

"I'd just as soon not tell you on the phone," Cashen said. "I'll tell you when you get here."

"I beg your pardon?"

"That's why I'm calling," Cashen said. "I'd like to see you. Can you come around?"

I put the phone down and went off to look at my master chart. I was scheduled to wander down to one of the marinas and then see Amory Blake, the psychotherapist. I came back to the phone and said, "I guess I can fit it in."

I drove down to Huggins. Cashen's secretary told me that he was busy with an appointment, but that he was expecting me. I was free to wander around. I watched the players shag flies out on the field. I looked in the locker room—wood-paneled in mahogany with toilet stalls that had doors shaped like the swinging doors of cowtown saloons. The carpeting was wall-to-wall and blue, a kind of Astroturf material. To my surprise, Sidd Finch had a locker. It was between George Foster's and Darryl Strawberry's. His name and his number, 21, were painted in white block letters on a blue board. There was no evidence of his presence. A cluster of coat hangers was bunched together at one end of the cross pole.

Down the line the cubicles were cluttered by comparison—clothes, jackets, inevitably a half dozen pair of baseball shoes, gloves, tape, an occasional handgripper, strips of Bazooka gum, packets of sunflower seeds, and bundles of mail. Strawberry's had a long rectangular yellow-metal street sign a fan had wrenched off its standard (STRAWBERRY AVE, it read) jammed in at an angle.

Cashen's secretary appeared and said he was ready to see me. He motioned me to a chair. "I'll come right to the point," Cashen said. "I think you're in a position to help us."

He summarized what had happened since I had talked to him last: the front office had made no headway with Finch. "We haven't signed the guy. He's only here at Huggins for ten minutes or so. We can't persuade him to stay around for lunch. He comes dressed in a baseball outfit which he puts on in the boardinghouse. He doesn't bother with a shower. He hardly pitches long enough to work up much of a sweat. Though we put his name up and everything, to my knowledge he hasn't visited his locker stall. So we don't have much time to persuade him of the virtues of a baseball career. He's gone before we can lay a hand on him."

"Where does he go?"

"We drive him down to the beaches—sometimes near where you live . . . Pass-a-Grille. Sometimes the driver leaves him there. Sometimes he waits and drives him back to Mrs. Butterfield's. Apparently Finch sets up targets in the sand dunes—beer cans and stuff—and throws baseballs at them. He watches the Windsurfers."

"Why can't you talk to him on the beaches?"

"We think he'd bolt from anyone he knew was from the Mets organization. It's part of our agreement. He wants to work it out for himself."

"What about the driver?"

"The kid who drives him? Elliot Posner. They talk about religion. Posner is going to study comparative religion at Brown University. Sometimes Finch gives him a koan, one of those Zen word puzzles, just for the fun of it, to work on. Posner gets back here. We rush out. 'Did he say anything? What's the word?' "

"Posner opens up a notebook. He reads from it. 'When your mind is empty like a canyon you will know The Power of The Way.' The kid walks around here in a daze."

Cashen paused and readjusted his bow tie slightly. "So that leaves us with Mrs. Roy Butterfield, his landlady. *She's* not your idea of a baseball nut. They tell me she collects dolls and little things made out of coquina shells. She's not comfortable with Finch in her house. 'Why didn't you guys send me some normal guy from Arkansas?' This gentleman, well, *startles* her. He bows a lot. He always seems to be behind her. His feet don't make any sound on the floor. She whirls around a lot. '*Namas-te,*' he's always saying, which apparently means 'hello' *and* 'good-bye.' He talks to himself. She hasn't the slightest idea what the languages are. Sometimes he calls out in a loud voice, 'Moo!' Sometimes 'Om!' which—according to Elliot Posner—means 'the roar of eternity!' She comes around the corner and there he is meditating in the hallway, staring at the wall, his legs tucked under him. He has his own rug, a small little thing. Mrs. Butterfield has never had a boarder who brought his own rug. He has this soup bowl. Mrs. Butterfield thinks he sleeps on the floor—his bed is always as neat as a pin."

Cashen leaned back in his chair. "Couple more things. Finch has this uncanny knack of imitating sounds. He will hear a sound—oh, a very common one like a tin wastepaper basket going over, and he'll *echo* it. It's an incredible skill. Mrs. Butterfield thinks her house is a kind of echo chamber. In the kitchen she closes the refrigerator door and a few seconds later the *ker-thunk* sound echoes back from upstairs, from Sidd Finch's room. So you can see why Mrs. Butterfield thinks Sidd is 'off-putting' as she says. She's asked us to find Sidd a new place to stay."

I nodded. "Not the easiest sort of boarder."

Cashen said, "He's sort of like a furtive bird. Frankly, we, uh . . . thought *you* could relate."

"What's that?"

Cashen's ruddy complexion seemed to deepen. "There's a real problem with Mrs. Butterfield. We've put you . . . uh, down on a list of options for him. We've told him something about you. Southeast Asia, all that. We called your friend Captain Smith of the blimp for info about you. He says it's a great idea. He thinks you need company."

A Buddhist monk? Gee, thanks a lot, Smitty, I was thinking.

"Don't worry," Cashen said. "It's a long list. I don't think it'll come up."

"Well, I hope not," I said. "I'm hardly in the boardinghouse business."

Cashen nodded. "We know that, of course. But if you're ever going to follow up this story, it'll give you an excellent opportunity to get to know something about Finch himself." He stood up from behind the desk. "Of course at the same time you'd be in a good position to make a pitch for us."

"Have you tried to get him to sign a contract?"

"I got Jay Horwitz to come into the office as witness, and I pushed one across to Finch. He looked at it for a while. He gave us one of those koans. He said, 'A pair of monkeys are reaching for the moon in the water.' "

"Not what you hoped to hear."

"He sounded like an agent. He's no dummy."

"What makes you think he'll make the move into my bungalow?"

Cashen shrugged. "It may never happen."

I changed the subject. "How fast does he throw? You said you'd tell me."

Cashen sat back down again. "All right. The fastest pitches ever recorded were thrown by Nolan Ryan and Goose Gossage. An All-Star game in St. Louis. Both were clocked at a hundred and three miles per hour. This guy Finch throws sixty miles an hour faster! We thought something was wrong with the measuring gun. But the fact is that it showed a hundred and sixty-eight! You can barely see the ball—just enough of a blur to know that it's not a magic trick."

"What's his motion like?"

"It's a sort of convulsion, one bare foot high in the air, and then the terrifying whip of the arm coming through."

"I'd like to see it."

"No reason not to. We hope," he said pointedly, "that an awful lot of people will come to see him pitch."

"What about the catcher?"

"Ronn Reynolds? There's a kind of explosion of sound when the ball hits the pocket of his mitt. Then a little yell. Who can blame him? He hasn't got time to move the glove an inch. Finch has to be right on target. He has been, so far. It's uncanny. But we haven't got him on board. We're all scared we might do or say something that'll make him take off."

Cashen paused before continuing. "So we've given Sidd your number and address. We've told him you're not connected with the Mets in any way. You happen by accident to know of his skills. You might be someone he'd like to talk to about his future." Cashen shrugged. "Who knows? He may not do anything about it. Sometimes I think this whole damn business is a pipe dream."

I drove from Huggins-Stengel to the marina and puttered around there, watching the elderly fishermen with their slow procedures, until it was three o'clock and time to see Amory Blake. As I drove

51

into the parking area behind his condominium it occurred to me that I was having one of the busiest days I'd had in years.

My sister had recommended Blake. She said that he didn't exactly have *official* credentials as a therapist (that is, he didn't have a diploma from the University of Rochester or anything like that hanging from the wall) but he had a large clientele who simply *trusted* him. He had a commonsense approach—his notion being to find some practical way to instill confidence in his patients.

In my case his hope was to get me over my writer's block by trying to compile a notebook of strange facts. "Odd occurrences" as he sometimes referred to them. "We've got to get you putting words to the page," he had announced. "I would ask you to start a diary, but that tends to be traumatic for beginners."

"What sort of facts?" I asked.

"Strange ones. The stranger the better."

"You mean like Ripley's *Believe It Or Not?*"

He must have sensed an edge to my voice. "What we're working on here is trying to get you back into the process of writing."

"Do you do this with other patients?" I asked. "Is anyone else doing strange facts?"

"Two," he admitted. "They're not really writers. One is an advertising executive. The other is a chauffeur. It's working out very nicely for them. It gives them something to put their minds to. Before you know it, you'll be off and winging. . . ."

"How do I start?" I asked.

Blake said, "I would recommend the reference shelves in the public library. Browse around in there. Four or five good, strange facts a week is your assignment."

So I would drive across town to the public library to pursue my therapy, collecting strange facts for Blake. It was pleasant and quiet. The sunshine streamed through the tall windows. The spaciousness of the reading room was a relief after the low-ceilinged confines of the bungalow. I often felt it was a fine therapeutic practice simply to be there, the empty notepad in front of me, the reference books dutifully removed from the stacks in a neat pile. Sometimes I wondered if one of my fellow researchers on strange facts was one of the occupants of the cubicles opposite—the advertising executive or even the chauffeur. An hour or so browsing would produce one or two items I thought would be appropriate. I never wrote anything down. I memorized the items and rehearsed them just before going into Blake's office.

He motioned me to the chair opposite. We talked for a while. He asked me how I had been doing on strange facts. I thought of telling him about throwing baseballs out of the blimp's gondola, but instead I gave him one from my library research.

"It's about Beau Brummel, the famous dandy," I said. "He kept a special man to make only the thumbs of his gloves."

"Yes?"

"Well, that's all there is to it."

"Well, I suppose that's all right," he said after a moment of reflection. He made a note on a three-by-five card. "In fact, it's very nice. Any more?"

"Here's one of the ones I found," I said. "Near Louisville, Kentucky, a rabbit reached out of a hunter's game bag, pulled the trigger of his gun, and shot the guy in the foot."

"Come on!"

"It was verified in *The New Yorker*, May 1947."

"Sensational!" the therapist said. He wrote the facts down. "Mr. Temple, I'm very pleased with you." He looked up questioningly.

"No, I'm afraid that's all I have this week. There were others that I thought marginal."

"I don't mind a clinker from time to time. Do let me be the judge."

"All right."

"I think we can do more than just two."

"I will increase my efforts."

"I notice you have memorized your 'odd occurrences.' It's very important that you write them down. After all, that is why you are here."

"I will try."

"Can you draw?" he asked.

"Yes," I said. "I can draw hats. . . ."

"Do you draw figures, either male or female?"

"I am not very good at them," I said. "Sticklike. The animals, being four-legged, tend to look more . . . rotund. I should be better at it. My sister—"

Blake said, "I'd like you to create some figures and draw a line up from their heads into balloons, right?"

I nodded. "You'd like me to be a cartoonist?"

"What I want you to do is try to put little snatches of conversation in those balloons." He paused. "Of course this doesn't mean you should give up your research on strange facts."

"Okay."

I was tempted to tell him one more strange fact—that the Mets had an English-born Buddhist monk in their organization who could throw a baseball 168 miles per hour with unerring accuracy. I thought of his pencil poised above that yellow legal pad on his knee and the sight of his smile fading.

He would have said, "These odd occurrences have to be absolutely accurate, *truthful* . . . I mean, that's the whole point!"

IV

I BELIEVE IT was the day after. The Mets office called and asked me if I would like to come around to Huggins-Stengel Field to hear a specialist on Eastern religions talk about Sidd Finch. His name was Dr. Timothy T. Burns. I guess the idea was that they had found out so little about Finch that an examination of his religious background might give the management a clue as to how best to keep him content and in camp and finally to sign a contract.

About eight of us were on hand, crowded into Cashen's office. Cashen, of course. Nelson

Doubleday, who had come in from Palm Beach. A couple of coaches. Jay Horwitz, the publicity director. Davey Johnson, the manager, looked in a couple of times, and then crept out. I suspect Dr. Burns' manner not only put him on edge but his analysis of Sidd Finch constructed a portrait so foreign to the manager's concept of a baseball player that, quite simply, he was discomfitted. It was as if he were being asked to insert a weird, otherworldly freak into his lineup, someone who would cause no end of dissension and ill feeling among the others. He didn't want to hear about him.

Dr. Burns had started as follows: "Everything I've heard about Sidd Finch leads me to believe that what we have here is almost surely a *trapa*, or aspirant Buddhist monk."

A grunt, perhaps more of a *moan*, emerged from Nelson Doubleday.

"Technically," Dr. Burns continued, "it is more likely he is a *gaynyen*, who is a kind of ordained layman."

Dr. Burns, who had come down the peninsula from Florida State University, was wearing a dark double-breasted blazer with four large polished gold buttons on each sleeve. He looked like a retired sea captain. On his wrist was a large double-faced watch with a red second hand that moved in little jumps in its cycle across the complexity of dials on the watch face.

Dr. Burns went on to say that though he had not spoken personally with Finch, from what he'd seen out in the enclosure, the pitcher was almost surely a disciple of Tibet's great poet-saint Lama Milarepa, who was born in the eleventh century and who died in the shadow of Mount Everest.

"The sect is called the Karmapas," Dr. Burns told us. "They were the first to establish any kind of influence with the Chinese Emperor Kublai Khan. In Marco Polo's journals there's a marvelous account of a competition between teachers of Christianity, Islam, and Taoism to convert the Emperor to their particular faith. The Karmapases' representative won out by causing a cup to rise to the Emperor's lips of its own accord. Quite something, eh?" Dr. Burns rolled his eyes. "The extraordinary thing about Milarepa and his followers," he went on, "is their ability to perform astonishing phenomena like this. Milarepa himself could produce 'internal heat,' *tumo*-heat, which allowed him to survive blizzards and the intense cold of the Himalayas wearing only a thin white cotton cloth. That is what Milarepa means—'cotton cloth.' He could walk through boulders and come out the other side as if he were walking in and out of a room. He once turned himself into a pagoda."

"A pagoda?"

"On another occasion he came down among his disciples in the form of a shooting star. People who can do this are called *lung-gom-pa*—someone who has learned the dynamic nature of the physical self and is able to exert a direct influence upon any part of the body . . . in the case of Sidd, of course, the arm and the wrist. What he has been able to achieve is a parallelism of thought and movement . . . a kind of astonishing rhythm that has gathered a tremendous amount of cosmic force into its service."

He sat forward in his chair and raised his finger.

"Gom . . ."

"How do you spell that?" It was Jay Horwitz who was taking notes, presumably to put together a press release one day.

"G-O-M. Gom means the meditation, the contemplation, the concentration of the mind and soul upon a certain objective—namely, in the case of Finch, the desire to throw a ball with absolute accuracy to a specific target. This requires a gradual emptying of the mind until it is supplanted by an absolute identification of the baseball and what one wishes to do with it. Lung—which is spelled L-U-N-G—represents the energy or psychic force that is physically generated by Gom. So the two words together represent what Finch has done— namely that he is a person who understands the body as an expression of the mind and is able to control directly any part of the body. Pa, of course, is someone who can do this. So what we have in Sidd Finch is a lung-gom-pa."

"Does that last word, pa, have an *h* on the end?" Horwitz asked.

"No. Pa. They say the really good, the great lung-gom-pas after years of practice no longer touch the ground and they glide on the air with great speed. Those who do this," Dr. Burns went on,

58

"are called the *kang gyog ngo dub*, which means 'success in swiftness of foot.' " I saw Jay put down his pencil in exasperation. "You might ask what it feels like. It's apparently as if the runner were anesthetized. He can bump into rocks or the trunks of trees and it doesn't affect him. He can't feel the weight of his body. It has been described as being the faint euphoria you get when you drive a car at great speeds.

"As he goes the lung-gom must neither speak nor look anywhere else than at a distant object—a star at night, for example, watching it so intensely that if a cloud crosses it, it will remain in his mind's eye. He must concentrate his thoughts, his steps in time, not only to the cadence of mystic incantations known as *ngags,* but to the in-and-out breathing. That is very likely what Finch is doing when he winds up and throws the ball."

Nelson Doubleday interrupted. "Can he teach other guys how he does it? Our pitchers?" He produced a small hollow laugh. "Can he teach me to hit a golf ball four hundred yards?"

Dr. Burns paused to let the murmur of laughter die away. Then he said, "Breathing, to produce inner heat, or tumo, is important. One must clear the lungs of pride, anger, covetousness, sloth, stupidity, and then inhale in the five corresponding wisdoms. After a while one imagines that a golden lotus exists in one's body, just below the navel. In this lotus is the syllable *ram,* and just above it, the syllable *ma.* These two are called *bija* mantras and some Tibetan authorities believe that these words, carefully pronounced and chanted, can produce a glow of warmth, as if the person were a kind of Franklin stove, even set things ablaze! In fact, in extreme cases this heat can be emitted through the navel like a blast from a blow torch. Quite a spectacular—"

"For Chrissakes!" Nelson Doubleday exploded.

Dr. Burns raised his hands. "I can assure you that Sidd Finch is incapable of doing such a thing. But what he does undoubtedly is to imagine his body as a vast enginelike sling. He recites ngags— these incantations—to himself. They could be dangerous, these exercises. Tibetans worry about overdoing them. It is possible to kill oneself 'by one's own imagination.' Indeed, I should remind you that *all* of this is quite fragile," Dr. Burns said. "It is dangerous to break the concentration necessary to perform. It is something you will have to consider in your treatment of Sidd Finch."

Frank Cashen asked him to explain.

"Well, if you made the mistake of stopping a lung-gom-pa clipping along at forty miles an hour, skimming the ground, to question him, or offer him a sandwich or something, that could very well *kill* him. What they say is this—the god who is in them escapes if they cease to repeat the ngags, and that in the process of leaving, the god shakes them so hard that the lung-gom-pa simply succumbs from the trauma."

"There's a god inside Finch?"

"Perhaps. It is more accurate to say that a lung-gom-pa is in a kind of trance. If you shake someone out of a trance, it can be quite an assault on the nerves—that would be the Western way of looking at it."

"Are you suggesting," Cashen asked, "that it would be a bad mistake for Davey Johnson to go to the mound for a conference? Or for his catcher to walk out to check the signs? That would *kill* him?"

Dr. Burns shrugged. "You must remember that I know only the texts. I've never even been to Kathmandu, the old brown city. But it would be dangerous, yes."

One of the Mets coaches wanted to hear how "these lung" people trained.

"It takes years," Dr. Burns replied. "The ascetic sits cross-legged on a large and thick cushion. He breathes in very slowly, filling his body with air, and then with his legs still crossed he hops up in the air as if . . ." Dr. Burns looked up at the ceiling for inspiration.

"Someone stuck a pin in him . . ." rose a voice from the room.

"Something like that. He repeats that exercise a number of times. According to Tibetan authorities, if you discipline yourself that way for many years, you become very light. They say you can even stand on an ear of barley without bending its stalk."

The door clicked shut. Davey Johnson had left.

"Why baseball?" Frank Cashen asked. "Why didn't he go back to England and play cricket?"

Dr. Burns put his fingertips together. "Baseball

is the perfect game for the mystic mind. Cricket is unsatisfactory because it has time strictures. The clock is involved. Play is called. The players stop for tea. No! No! No!" Burns sounded quite petulant. "On the other hand, baseball is so open to infinity. No clocks. No one pressing the buttons on stopwatches. The foul lines stretch to infinity. In theory, the game of baseball can go on indefinitely."

After a moment Frank Cashen stirred and said, "Dr. Burns, something about baseball disturbs Sidd. In his note of conditions to us he wrote of certain elements of the game of baseball not *adhering* to what he called 'tantric principles.' What does this mean?"

"Ah!" said Dr. Burns. "I must conject. I suspect he's referring to such aspects of baseball as stealing second"—Dr. Burns' eyebrows rose as if to accentuate the horror of what he was saying—"or the hidden-ball trick. Or robbing someone of a base hit. Or fooling a batter with an offspeed pitch. There simply may be too much chicanery in the game to his liking.

"Mind you, there are many Buddhists who wouldn't think much of what Sidd is devoting himself to—this dabbling with baseballs—it's a sort of a silly juggling, twiddling of thumbs, showoffy, soft-shoe shuffling kind of thing. They bring up the story about the Yogin and the Buddha. Do you know it?"

We all stared dumbly at him.

"Well, the Yogin told the Buddha that he had

been practicing for twenty-five years and by arduous mind-matter exercises he had learned to cross the river by walking on the water.

"The Buddha said, 'My poor fellow . . . to think you've spent all that trouble to get to the other bank of the river when all you had to do was to get the ferryman to take you there for a few pennies.' "

Dr. Burns began to laugh in delight at his analogy . . . such a high wheezing laugh that he eventually had to produce a large red bandana-sized handkerchief from the breast pocket of his blazer to subdue it.

Nelson Doubleday then made an astute observation. "It's important in that case," he said, "that we promote baseball to Finch. We've got to convince him that baseball is worth all the mind-matter he's spent learning how to throw a ball. He must not feel ridiculed by what he's done. We've got to glorify baseball—make him think that he's involved in the National Pastime, a holy tradition. Crossing the river . . . that Buddha is *nuts* if you ask me. I mean, who wouldn't rather cross a river by walking on it with his damn bare feet than ride on a ferry boat?"

"Right!" someone called out.

"We could call in some of the great custodians of the game—Red Barber, Mel Allen. Get him to read Roger Angell's books. We could get him to see Robert Redford in *The Natural*. Maybe we could get Robert Redford down here to see *him*. Get him up to the Hall of Fame in Cooperstown

. . . impress him with Babe Ruth's bat, things like that. . . ."

"Isn't Redford a San Francisco Giant fan?" someone asked.

"We can work around that."

"Doesn't Redford get shot with a silver bullet in the film?"

"Yes, but it works out quite nicely in the end."

I walked out of Cashen's office into threatening weather. It was good to be going back to the bungalow in Pass-a-Grille. When the hard warm winter rains came to the Tampa area, thrashing the palmettos, the bungalow seemed to settle down in the sandy earth—cool and dark—and it was like those times in Vietnam in the monsoons when you knew little bothered to move.

I parked the car in its shelter and then walked out to the Gulf and stood on the seawall at Pass-a-Grille to watch the storm come in . . . a thunderstorm, violent, unseasonal, and quite terrifying, as all meteorological oddities on such a mammoth scale tend to be—a black cloud the length of the horizon that seemed to ache to drop funnels to the water. Lightning flickered out of it. I hurried back to the bungalow. When the storm reached in and went through Pass-a-Grille, it bent the palms and thrashed their fronds with such a racket that I barely heard the little bell-like front-door chimes my sister had installed.

The figure standing at the door was rain-soaked, his hair plastered down, a drop of water quivering at the tip of his nose. He bowed. "Namas-te," he said. "The Mets have given me your number and your address," he said. "I am very embarrassed. I tried to telephone."

"I'm sorry about the telephone," I said. "I very rarely pick it up."

I invited him in. The heavy rain pounded on the bungalow roof. We walked through the leafy-like gloom to the back porch. "I'm sorry about the light," I said. "The electricity goes off in any kind of storm. Even with candles, it's like living in the bottom of a well."

In the darkness I could barely make out his features. He was tall, as I suspected, small-headed, and when he sat in front of me out on the porch in a straight-backed wicker chair, his knees rose up like a basketball player's at courtside.

"My name is Sidd Finch," he said. "I believe you know that I am a tryout with the New York Mets baseball organization. I am a pitcher. My relationship with them—by my own request—is very tenuous."

"So I understand," I said.

"You know some of this?"

"The Mets people have told me a few things."

"They gave me a list. Your name was on it. They said you would be helpful. Forgive me. It's quite an emergency, I'm afraid. I would like to explain."

I nodded.

He went on to tell me that he had been staying with Mrs. Butterfield on Florida Avenue. She had

65

been a kindly lady, understanding in every way, although sometimes he could feel she was not especially keen about his musical aptitudes. "I play the French horn," he explained. He drew out the word *horn*, very nasal and British. "The fact is that Mrs. Butterfield asked me to leave."

"The French horn?"

I could tell that he was shyly heading up to some kind of admission: one knee swaying, his words halting, he began fidgeting in his chair; increasingly he looked like a gawky adolescent. For a moment he stared intently into a potted palm in the corner.

"My habit," he finally said obliquely, "after practice at Huggins Field, where I pitch in a canvas enclosure, is to be driven to one of the beaches near here. I sit on the sand dunes and meditate. I cannot drive," he said, spreading his hands woefully.

"Sometimes after meditating I set up targets and pitch at them—tin cans, and pieces of paper stuck against the sand."

He paused again.

"The other day I was doing this when a girl stepped off a Windsurfer down by the water's edge and came up toward me."

I have often thought back on that meeting between the two—the girl pulling the Windsurfer with its bright sail up beyond the reach of the water and Sidd noticing her setting out determinedly for him through the dunes, the puffs of sand kicked up by her bare feet, almost as if a rendezvous had been *prearranged*. In fact, its coincidence had always made me slightly suspicious—it was all too pat. I could not rid my mind of the notion that she had been sent by someone.

Sidd told me her name was Debbie Sue. She had been tacking back and forth that afternoon just offshore and had seen him throwing things in the dunes. She was wearing a red tank suit. She climbed up the slope of a dune and he looked up to see her staring down at him. For a while he continued pegging baseballs at his tin cans until finally, under her steady gaze, he glanced over and said, "Namas-te"—that word that means both "hello" and "good-bye." He stammered out that they had chatted rather shyly on the beach and the upshot of it was that Debbie Sue asked him to have dinner with her and that he had nodded and accepted. She sailed her Windsurfer back to a cluster of the craft where she had rented it earlier . . . Finch walking along the water's edge, watching her.

Mrs. Butterfield took immediate exception to Debbie Sue. She had been out to a movie that night. On her return she had found Debbie Sue in her parlor holding a figurine made of coquina shells in her hand and commenting on it—not disparagingly, Sidd assured me—but in wonder. "Will you look at this?"—that sort of thing, and then not long after Debbie Sue announced that what with the storm raging outside, she wished to spend the night.

Mrs. Butterfield took Sidd aside. "I do not wish

to embarrass you or her. But I will not stand for this. Your companionship with a French horn I find acceptable, if barely, but not with a young female."

Sidd tried to explain to her how they had met.

"Nice girls don't step ashore from surfboards," Mrs. Butterfield had announced.

Apparently, Debbie Sue, standing in the kitchen, had overheard this exchange and called out loudly, "Mrs. Butterfield is an old goat!" which, as Sidd described it, "Kind of cemented things."

"Where is she now?" I asked.

"Mrs. Butterfield?"

"No. Debbie . . . ah . . . Sue?"

"She's out in the rain. She's standing by the bird bath."

V

I TELEPHONED THE Mets the next morning and told them that Sidd had appeared at my bungalow. I said that his sudden presence had so surprised me that I hadn't time to get really angry at the Mets for putting him on to me. I explained that he had apparently had a small run-in with Mrs. Butterfield . . . something to do with his French horn playing. I was not going to tell them about Debbie Sue. But of course they knew.

Jay Horwitz came immediately to the point.

"We understand from Elliot Posner that Sidd Finch is involved with a *woman*."

I replied after a pause, "That could very well be so. She windsurfs."

He explained that the kid who drives Finch to Pass-a-Grille after practice had seen the pair together. In fact, he had driven them from the beach to Mrs. Butterfield's boardinghouse.

"Yes. They arrived here by taxi in the middle of the rainstorm."

"Has she moved in with you, bag and baggage?" he asked.

I said that she had, but that their "bag and baggage" wasn't much. A toothbrush. What she *and* Finch together had as worldly possessions—forgetting his French horn—could almost be put in a large purse.

"What is she like?" Jay asked.

"I haven't seen much of her. They're still asleep. She's kind of a free spirit."

"You say she stepped off a Windsurfer?" he asked.

"So I understand," I replied.

I thought of her the night before, the rain plastering a knee-length man's shirt against her body as she came in the door. She was shivering slightly. She had announced cheerfully, "This is much better than Mrs. Butterfield's. It's like being in an aquarium—cool and lovely. We're all underwater!"

"She's quite spectacular," I told Jay.

"I see," Jay said tentatively. "Well, we're sort

of worried about this development. Are you sure this meeting between the two was coincidental? You don't suppose she's a plant from the Commissioner's office. Maybe Peter Ueberroth knows about Sidd and worries about the impact he'll have on the game."

"Possibly."

"Or the Los Angeles Dodgers. She sounds sort of Californian."

I replied that I had no idea. I said I would let the Mets know if anything surprising or untoward happened.

"You're good to do this," Jay said. "We didn't know it was going to happen."

"They didn't want to go to a hotel," I said. "The girl told me Finch was pretty straight."

"The blimp pilot thought it would be great."

"So I understand," I said.

Actually, life in the bungalow seemed to go on pretty much as before. I kept to the schedule of my master chart—my little fishing expeditions, my somnambulations on the hot boards of the marina piers, my occasional visits to Amory Blake, and my trips to the public library to research "odd occurrences."

The Mets sent their car to pick Sidd up every morning at 11:30 or so for his stint in the enclosure at Huggins-Stengel. The driver blew the horn out in the street. Sidd wore his baseball uniform (it had the number 21 on the back of the jersey) out to the car; he carried an odd, decrepit black glove with him, along with a kit bag that apparently contained clothes into which he changed when he met Debbie Sue out on the beaches later—jeans, a bathing suit, a cotton shirt, whatever. She stayed around the bungalow until she left for the beaches about noon.

I was entranced by her—small-breasted, long-necked, with a delicate, pointed head, high-cheeked. Her eyes were blue, sometimes with blue liner to emphasize them; her mouth was pale and wide, but I don't remember that she ever enhanced it except with a small gleam from a chapstick. Her energy! She rushed for the phone when it rang. "Owl, it's for you." It was her practice to produce instant nicknames for people. Within minutes of meeting her I had become "Owl," not because I resembled one, but because my family's name, Temple, made her think of the university whose athletic teams are known as the Owls. "Oh, Owl, you look bushed?" she'd say.

Like so many girls brought up in the South, she ended almost all of her sentences with a question mark, as if she lived in a kind of wondrous world in which she was not sure of anything. "I went to the Bay last night? With Sidd? We swam out in the darkness and porpoises were out there? We could hear them snuffling? And breathing?" And so forth. Even her name seemed a tentative thing. When asked for it she would reply, "Debbie Sue?" as if she were charmingly addled and not quite sure.

Her hair was tawny, sun-streaked and unkempt, as if hurled into a mare's nest by the sea in which she spent so much time; however tumultuous, it always seemed to frame her face in breathtaking ways. She tossed it. She ran her hands through its folds with impatience, with no results that were discernible. Often, she flung the whole shebang forward away from the nape of her neck, her head down, the golden mass spilling for the floor, and then flung her head back as if violence could bring order to that lovely disarray.

She was tall, with legs that she folded under her on sofas, endlessly restless and shifting about, as if life itself was to be spent settling into a comfortable position. The only time I saw her motionless was when I found her asleep on the settee that hung on chains out on the back porch—sprawled across the cushions as if shot. A single-thonged sandal had fallen off and lay on the floor under a long-toed foot suspended out from the edge of the settee. It was almost impossible to sit on that particular piece of furniture without its moving; yet she was so relaxed, the settee hung like a potted plant from a rafter. A wisp of hair moved in the faint motion of her breathing.

It was rare to find her in such a state. Most of the time, in the most minimal of coverings, her bare feet slapping on the linoleum flooring, she hurried about the bungalow in haphazard perpetual motion. She seemed endlessly in search of something—looking for a cigarette, and then after a few puffs hopping up to extinguish it not close at hand but in a distant ashtray. She paid frequent inspections to the refrigerator, the creak of the door opening, and then a moan to indicate that she was not allowing herself to remove anything from its shelves. Returning, she never seemed to slide into a sofa, but rather to fling herself upon it, then flopping in utter relaxation, as if the effort to soar in among the pillows had spent her completely. I tend to exaggerate, but in truth she was exhausting to have around. In comparison, Sidd and I moved through the bungalow as if undersea—she darted across our paths like a spirited tropical fish.

Sidd was easy to be around—though I understood what Mrs. Butterfield meant by being "startled" by him. He had a tendency to appear suddenly from the shadows, often preceded by the crash of something falling over or a grunt from catching a shin on the side of a piece of furniture. For an athlete he was extraordinarily clumsy, or perhaps it was that he never could get his eyes adjusted to the gloom of the bungalow. He looked like a grown-up moppet—a long neck, narrow shoulders, and a bird-cage chest. His smile showed slightly uneven teeth, and sometimes his hand would drift up to cover his mouth, which increased his demeanor of shyness, uncertainty.

He was thin-hipped, with long legs that he set way down in front of him in a farmer's stride; the fingers of his arms grazed alongside his kneecaps.

He was hardly a prize, I thought, for someone as attractive as Debbie Sue. But she seemed obsessed by him—reaching out to touch him or tousle his hair as she perched on the side of his chair.

His reaction to this was what one might have expected from one so shy—a confused and somewhat startled, if pleased, acceptance of what was being done to him.

I had put them in separate rooms on the night of their arrival—for no other reason than it seemed the proper thing to do with a monk. Debbie Sue was under no such compunctions, and afterward I never bothered about it again.

Usually I ran into the pair in midmorning, fussing in the kitchen. Sidd would turn to me, his fingertips together: "Namas-te." He explained that the Tibetan word for greetings and farewells meant "I salute the spirit within you."

Debbie Sue loved "namas-te." Sometimes I would get up before them, and she would float into the little kitchen to find me standing in a decrepit bathrobe, staring bleakly at a coffeepot making its way toward a boil; she always surprised me with her entrance—wearing a brief T-shirt, this time with a bright-hued, perky Mickey Mouse with the sole of one shoe showing. She would give a slight bow, and with her fingertips together she would say not "namas-te" but its translation—"I salute the spirit within you"—in a theatrical, sleepy voice. I would say the same to her. We exchanged the phrase like lovers.

I found I was enjoying their company. I telephoned my sister—one of the few outgoing calls of the decade—and said I had two boarders. She was incredulous. "A Buddhist monk and his girl?"

"A very sudden but apparently solid romance," I explained.

I said nothing to her about Sidd being a pitcher with the New York Mets. If I had said so, my sister would have assumed I had gone completely around the bend—giving myself over to a strange, shadowy world of phantoms and bewildering imaginings.

"That's quite a step," she said.

"What?"

"Taking in boarders. What does the young woman do?"

"She windsurfs," I said. "They love the beaches. He meditates and she swims. She's teaching him how to catch a Frisbee. She's the daughter of a golf professional who lives up the coast. Played on the golf team. Duke."

"What?"

"Duke University. She's dropped out for some reason or other."

My sister said, "Your mother wants to know how your book is coming along." It was her oblique way of finding out for herself if I was beginning to write.

"I'm sorry," I said. "Nothing much has stirred."

"How is Amory Blake?"

"I have a vague idea I'm helping *him* with a book."

She didn't ask me to explain. Before she hung up she suggested that my new boarders might provide inspiration. "Take notes," she suggested.

Debbie Sue and Sidd came back from the beach

to the bungalow about six o'clock. Debbie Sue called from the front lawn, "Owl!" Her voice carried. When the two were late I wandered around the bungalow. Once I went to the supermarket and bought a chicken and the fixings for something quite grand—my way of showing I was pleased they were there. But no one could cook. We stared at the chicken in its plastic wrapping. So Debbie Sue and I had the beef tetrazzini from a package and Sidd had a salad. A cheese. Ice cream. Tea. After dinner we went out through the bungalow to the screen-enclosed porch in back. The frogs were beginning. The evening fell.

Sometimes we talked about baseball. Sidd would describe his stint in the enclosure. He said he wouldn't mind if I came to watch. He asked technical questions about baseball itself. A few afternoons he had watched a few intrasquad games from the little stands at Huggins, but his knowledge of the game itself was pitiful. It was practically a matter of telling him how many innings there were. He knew almost nothing about the game's history.

I told him that the Mets had prepared for him by dropping baseballs out of a blimp.

"How interesting."

"It was the only way they could think of to get the ball going fast enough. It was Nelson Doubleday's idea."

"Did anyone get hurt?" Sidd asked.

"I don't believe so," I replied. "Frank Cashen said they lost quite a few baseballs. The field was muddy. A lot of the balls went deep into the muck with a kind of a thunk. One day some farmer is going to plow up all those baseballs and he's going to spend a sleepless night or so wondering how they got there."

Debbie Sue, swinging in the darkness on the settee, fantasized how "neat" if something "real weird" had been tossed out of the gondola. "A stuffed toy animal," she suggested, "to keep the catchers from being bored. A kangaroo'd drop down out of the sky."

Debbie Sue lit a cigarette. Its tip glowed as she puffed on it awkwardly. It swung in an arc as the settee creaked on its chains. The frogs were in full chorus out in the back. The darkness enveloped us.

Debbie Sue occasionally offered to get a fourth for dinner, or to invite someone over afterward to join us ("one of my windsurfing pals?"), but I was never very enthusiastic about it, and neither was she. Perhaps she didn't want to take any chances with another girl around Sidd. Besides, we had become comfortable, the three of us, and a fourth in those first days, no matter how compatible, would have seemed an intruder. Sidd would have been less likely to talk about the Himalayas, or anything else for that matter, and he certainly would not have played the French horn or produced any of his sound effects for us.

That was the best part of hearing him talk about the mountains—that he would occasionally stop and punctuate what he was telling us with an uncanny representation of some sound—the cry of a bird, or the wind soughing through bamboo forests, or the creak of prayer wheels turning, the flap of banners, footfalls on the pebbly mountain paths, the cry of children in a distant valley, echoes, a rooster crowing far off. He could produce an infinite variety of sounds with no more than an odd flutter of his throat. Sometimes I wondered why he ever bothered with his French horn; he could have imitated its sound without carrying that black case around, but no, he allowed it was the difference between singing and playing an instrument.

The first imitation I heard him do was the sound of a rock dislodged by the hooves of a blue goat high in the mountains—his throat muscles pulsing as he produced the click of the rock ricocheting down the cliff face until its last distant reverberation in the mountain vastness.

"God, how did you do that?"

His imitations seemed to quiver the air around us, a kind of stereophonic effect that disguised where the sound was coming from.

"I have"—and he made a slight inclination of his head to indicate that it was a talent that he was by no means responsible for—"an ear that can not only memorize the intricacies of rhythms, but allows me to imitate them. That is why I can play the French horn with a certain amount of proficiency. I can hear Brahms and play it, but I can't read it off the sheet music."

Debbie Sue looked admiringly at Sidd. She

touched his face. "He can do taxi horns. London and Paris horns, and a refrigerator door slamming. He's awfully good at a bathtub emptying!"

As the evenings went on I got to know something more about Sidd's background. His father was an anthropologist who liked to say that he had traveled among people who had been forgotten by the world and who in turn had forgotten the world. He was fascinated by the hill people of the Himalayas.

"Father was well known in those parts of the world. He was once blessed by the thirteenth Dalai Lama," Sidd said. "He told me the Lama touched him with a colored ribbon attached to a stick. The most respectful of blessings is when the Lama puts two hands alongside the head, or one hand, or two fingers, or even one finger. My father was British, of course, studying tribes in the foothills, and the Dalai Lama probably did not think highly of him— some kind of meddler, I suspect he thought he was, so he was touched with the tip of a ribbon from a stick."

I asked about his mother. "I never knew her," Sidd said. "She saw my father off on his expeditions. She thought of his trips as being what she might read in novels.

"My father named a mountain after her, Mount Edwina. It was not a major mountain, but a pretty one. . . ."

Sidd told us she was older by a few years than his father. Browsing for "things" in catalogs and

Country Life, she turned up at auctions to bid for them. She had an extraordinary collection of scarab brooches that lay on velvet in glass-covered display cases in a long gallery on the third floor of the London house. She saw to her husband's social life in London. She organized the musicale evenings. Even on winter nights she used a fan, circulating a heavy musklike perfume among her guests.

Then one spring she surprised and rather dismayed her husband by saying she would like to go with him. She could shop the capitals on the way—Paris, Cairo, Istanbul—and then once there in the mountains she could sit in a camp chair in front of the canvas tent and read. Tea, of course. A "native" would be assigned to make sure nothing approached that would be disturbing—large lizards and so forth.

It was an ill-fated decision. She disliked everything from the moment the door of the London house closed behind her. She was appalled by the places they stopped by on the way. She was horrified by Bombay with its pavements plastered red with betel-nut spit and the white of bird droppings . . . and the street barbers with their customers standing in front of them with their heads bent to get their hair cut. In Kathmandu she kept to her hotel room. It was better out in the fresh air of the encampments.

Sidd's father did the best he could to make her comfortable. He pitched her tent so that when she sat in her camp chair she had the most spectacular views of the mountains. But then one evening she stood up from her camp chair and took a few steps in a heavy mountain fog. She slipped in the mud, went down, and started a long slide that took her over the edge of the abyss and into what must have been an exhilarating drop in some ways, so long that she must have wondered vaguely if that was all there was to it. . . .

Sidd, of course, never recounted it to me this way . . . it was a vision that floated into my mind after he had described it in rather flat terms . . . sadly, as if it were something he thought I should know but that he did not really want to mention. He remembered his father's discomfiture when her name came up. He told us his father rarely went up to the third floor, with its display cases of scarab brooches.

Debbie Sue loved to hear about the London house. It was enormous apparently. Some of the rooms were so large that they seemed to beg occupancy—like hotel lobbies, with heavy chairs with armrests set along the gallery walls. Sidd said that as a boy he would hide behind the weight of a damask curtain and wait for someone to come along, and usually someone would, heralded by the click of heels on the marble flooring, muted suddenly by the softness of a carpet, then the heels again, and a maid would hurry by with something on a tray for someone higher up the social echelon than she. There was inevitably the whine of a distant vacuum cleaner.

He described the library, which had a balcony reached by a small circular stair. As a child he would peer down through the railings on the heads of the guests his father had collected for elaborate dinners. The room below was so vast it never looked crowded, and from above, with their ball gowns spread out, he said the women moved like a regatta across the carpet.

"What sort of people came?" I asked.

"The fancier parties were the musicales," Sidd replied. "That was when my father met Dennis Brain, the great French horn player from the London Symphony. After dinner my father would guide everyone into the music room, which was set up with gilt and red ballroom chairs in rows. The musicians sat at one end under a very noisy portrait of a stag at bay. The painting served to give the music, even the most delicate of instrumentations, a kind of curious wild quality—as if it were being played under desperate circumstances. One of the musicians told me that they always played a little faster at my father's musicales. My father loved brass instrumentation. He was like Peter the Great, who had brass bands play for him at dinner. One Christmas my father gave me a French horn."

Debbie Sue asked how Sidd got along with his father.

"He was an austere gentleman—quite formal with me, which I suppose would be natural since in some inner corner of his mind he would remember that I was an orphan and not of his blood. He wore tweeds. About him there was always the faint scent of violets, some kind of cologne he wore. He was all I had. I can remember the sadness when he stood in the great front hall amid his suitcases, all very functional and worn, with big leather straps for reinforcement, because he was going off to the mountains, to the Kalahari, the steppes, the rain forests, wherever. His last words to me were always 'Now, young man, you are in charge,' and the front door would close behind him. He was referring to quite a large retinue—cooks, butlers, chambermaids, many of them standing in a row behind me as he left. The house was enormous. It's on Denbigh Close. Do you know Denbigh Close? A little park, Logue Park, on the corner. My friends from school would come to play for the afternoon, and for tea, and somehow it was never the same between us afterward. I never could show them through the place with any sense of confidence. 'This is the drawing room,' pulling back these tall oaken doors with latches as big as books. 'The billiard room.' They were never anxious to play hide-and-seek or sardines or any of the you're-it games we played in *their* houses. 'Oh no. Let's not.' They must have thought that I could push at a paneling and disappear into secret passages and creep around behind the walls while they wandered nervously down the corridors with the suits of armor, and the war paintings, and the occasional grandfather clock.

"The *pièce de résistance* of all this was the ballroom, which was built below the street level and during the war was reinforced with steel beams. One day, when I was ten years old or so, my father took me down on my birthday, opened the double doors that led down a flight of steps, and there, covering just about every inch of the place, was an elaborate electric train set. I would have guessed fifteen or twenty sets had gone into the making of that complex . . . just *miles* of track, dozens and dozens of switches, ten or so mountain tunnels to go through, with little Swiss chalets on the sides, lots of railroad crossings, the bars snapping up and down as the trains went by, three or four stations with platforms, water towers, cranes, lead cattle standing around in a stockyard, transformers everywhere to keep the power pouring through this vast network. My father took me over to a main control panel and showed me how it all worked.

"Whoever put the whole thing together had not populated it in any way. He had not put little lead people here and there doing things, such as standing behind the ticket window, or waiting on the platform with a little dispatch case, or out in the fields with those lead cows. The trains went by— long, lighted coaches with seats inside, everything in exact detail—and no one was sitting there. No one was driving the miniature red cars waiting at the railroad crossings where the crossbars went up and down.

"Then one day I discovered someone. He was sitting in the control cabin of a crane. He wore a bowler. His face was painted pink and he had a mustache. He had a round peg in his backside that fitted into a hole in the driver's seat. When I discovered him among all that miniature machinery it gave me quite a start, this man staring out the little window of his crane. He looked a little startled himself. I gave him a name—God of All He Surveys."

He paused, cocking his head slightly. Debbie Sue was so still I thought she had fallen asleep, but I could see the glint of her eyes in the half-light. The settee hung motionless from its chains.

"Did you go down there often?" I asked. "To the ballroom."

"Actually I got to like my father's trains," Sidd said. "Especially at night. I'd go down there and turn off all the ballroom lights and switch on the lights in the various establishments in my landscape. There weren't very many—lights at the station, at the crossings, a petrol station or two, and a couple of the farmhouses had lonely lights in them.

"I ran just one train through my system—an engine, and maybe thirty freight cars behind it, so it moved slowly and rather laboriously. Often I took the God of All He Surveys out of his crane and put him in the caboose. He was outsize and barely fit in the back platform. I had to put him in a little sideways, so that he had a quite cock-eyed view of that miniature world receding behind him as he traveled along."

When he was twelve Sidd was sent to the Stowe School, a public school near Oxford, and actually on the grounds—Sidd said—of property originally belonging to one John Temple, which amused

85

him: he wondered if perhaps the founding fathers of the place were in the lower branches of my own family tree. He told me wryly that the Temple hospitality in the Pass-a-Grille bungalow was far warmer than it had been at Stowe. He had not had a good time there.

"I felt profoundly lonely. My father sent me postcards and letters. He urged me to steam off the stamps, often very large ones, from the exotic places his explorations took him to—usually of large local birds with gaudy plumage or native dhows with brown sails on a delta. The messages that accompanied these big-stamped postcards were perfunctory. Yet I was always tremendously moved when I received these communications. He was my only . . . person. I couldn't seem to make friends at Stowe. I was a terrible athlete. Chasing a cricket ball, I stumbled into a pond. I almost drowned. I had to be pulled out.

"So I'd walk through the grounds in the evening with my horn. Sometimes I'd go down to Eleven Acre Lake and play across the water. There are various miniature arches, and also temples, like teahouses. I'd go and play in them. Their little vaulted roofs made interesting sound modulations."

Apparently Sidd did extremely well academically. In his last year he applied to Harvard. His father felt a change of culture was important. A couple of days after he received notice of his acceptance, there was a knock on the door of his room.

"The 'Head' wished to see me. It was a winter

night. A proctor went with me to the Head's rooms. Could I have done something wrong? I couldn't imagine what. I was practically a cipher in the social circles of the school. The French horn? The notes drifted a long way in the still-dark afternoons. Perhaps people in the neighboring farm cottages had complained."

" 'Sit down please, Finch.' The Head rested the palms of his hands on the table in front of him. 'In this life there are many things which are imponderable,' he said. 'We have received news, I am terribly sorry to tell you, that your father has perished in an airplane crash in the Himalayas. You may wish the use of the school chapel to pray, and that naturally is granted if it pleases you.' "

The next day Sidd left for London. The two executors of his father's estate met him at Paddington. They sat silently on either side during the cab ride to the London house. In the library, the pair stood in front of the fire, rocking back and forth, warming themselves before they hitched their trousers delicately and sat down opposite him. They were not as direct as the Head. They told the boy that his father had "disappeared" on an airplane flight in "very difficult terrain."

"Disappeared?"

"The plane has not been found."

"I wish to look for him."

The executors said that was quite impossible. He would be returned to school in a week's time, just as soon as his father's affairs were settled. Since the young man was the only heir . . .

"I wish to look for him. I wish to leave instantly for the East. . . ."

The executors stood up. One couldn't just *leave* instantly for the East. He was not of legal age to make such decisions. Quite impossible. He was now the ward of legal guardians.

"I gave them all the slip," Sidd told us. "It was really quite simple. I wrote the school saying I was not returning because of the circumstances of my father's disappearance. I drew a bank draft sufficient to cover my expenses, in particular an airplane ticket to the East. I packed a small bag, got into a cab, and with the staff standing in the street I loudly announced, 'Paddington,' and went instead to Heathrow for an airplane to Bangladesh. It took them a time to sort everything out, and by the time they had I was heading into the mountains from Kathmandu. I wrote the executors a polite letter apologizing for my subterfuge. They made quite an effort to get me out, informing consulates and so forth, but I was quite a few steps ahead of them. I had contacts.

"A number of people knew my father, of course. One of them was an elderly Tibetan named Karma Paul, who lived in Darjeeling. He was involved in the organization of a number of Everest expeditions—a charming man who spoke five languages. He thought me eccentric and foolish and too young to be looking for the wreckage of an airplane in a Himalayan ravine. He worried about eccentrics coming to this part of the world from the West. He had helped Maurice Wilson. Do you know of him? He was a Yorkshire mountaineer who tried a solo climb of Mount Everest in 1933, a man of almost no experience in the mountains whose motivating theory was that mountaineers were too *fat*. Wilson ate only uncooked grasses, like a sheep, and when he died on the mountain—astonishingly high up—Karma Paul told me, 'I should never have let him go. I shouldn't let *you* go. Your father is in the snows, and that is *that*, my dear boy.' He went on to say that Wilson had been discovered by the Eric Shipton expedition—a skeleton in an old wind-shredded tent. One of his boots was off, lying beside the bones, and the other was still on the foot. Wilson was bent forward in this queer way, the laces of the boot still entwined in the bones of his fingers, as if he were preparing to dress and rush down the mountain to escape the cold. I remember that Karma Paul suddenly stopped in the middle of telling me this— he realized, of course, he was describing a scene that could very well be paralleled in the wreckage of my father's small plane, up on some mountain ridge, and he bowed his head and apologized. He was very helpful after that.

"I went up into the foothills. There are forests of azalea up there, and junipers. The smells walking through these groves are intoxicating. There are willow plantations, and I spent some time in a monastery on a hill of willows beyond Syang. Usually from the window you can see a shrine, a chorten. Butterflies. The flowers outside the window are purple. The temple bells from the valley. You empty the washbasin on the floor and the water runs out a hole in the corner. When I first lived there I worried that a cobra or a krait would come up through the hole during the night, so I put the basin over it and I waited for it to move in the night.

"The grass is tall and shines in the sun. At higher altitudes the pines are twisted the way you see them in Chinese paintings. The prayer flags are strung across the monastery roofs. When the banners flap the prayers printed on them blow out into the wind, and it's supposed to bring good luck. The flags are called 'Horses of the Wind.' . . . The clouds and fog at that altitude seem to pulse with color. The shadows are abrupt and dark. In the winter the winds are fierce. The gusts ring the bells on the yaks—seventy miles an hour, sweeping down along their flanks, by the horns— so that downwind you can hear this sound above the roar of the winds."

"Do the bells for us," Debbie Sue asked.

Sidd smiled and said he wouldn't do the terrible winds—it was a strain on his throat—but he did a few bells for us—a dull distant clanking.

"That was the kind of country my father had gone down in—near a place called French Pass, which is a glacier between two enormous mountains—Dhaulagiri and a twin, Dhaula Himai. Another plane went down there in 1969, seven years before. It was supporting an American expedition

90

trying to climb Dhaulagiri. We went by the site, going up through the French Pass, and my heart jumped when I saw the glint of metal among the snow and rocks.

"We gave up after a while. No sign of Father's plane, or even rumors—the elevations were so high and desolate that a tribesman turning up at the campfire and telling us that he had seen a bright flash in the sky . . . that sort of thing . . . was simply out of the question."

But, as Sidd told us, he did not return home. He spent almost six months wandering through Sikkim, Nepal, Bhutan, even up toward the Tibetan border.

"Once in a ruined monastery called Chorten Nyima, I stayed in a small room with a naked monk who sat motionless in the posture of a Buddha. He was meditating. His body was dusted blue, which symbolizes space, emptiness. I laid out my mat and slept. I could not hear him breathing. It was like occupying a space with a large statue. He was in the exact same attitude when I awoke in the dawn and left the monastery."

The settee creaked on its chains. "Are Tibetan monks circumcised?" asked Debbie Sue.

"I didn't notice," Sidd said.

"It was your chance. You should have looked. Are there nuns?" Debbie Sue asked.

"Yes. *Ané la*. They live in separate quarters. At the Rongbuk monastery at the foot of Mount Everest there's an empty oxygen cylinder left there from some expedition that is used as a temple bell.

91

When it's time for the monks and the nuns to go to their separate quarters, someone comes out and bangs it with a bar."

The settee creaked on its chains. Debbie Sue murmured what a beautiful and lonely sound that must be.

He imitated it for us; the bungalow filled with the bell sound, which he made echo off in distant folds and ravines, dying away, until we could hear the frogs once again, bellowing out in the back.

Where in all of this, I asked, had Sidd learned to throw a baseball with such astonishing skill? "Can you tell us . . . ?" I felt myself leaning forward from my chair; I heard Debbie Sue stirring.

Sidd nodded and explained that most of the physical feats in that part of the world involved the practice of lung-gom. (It startled me to hear the same word we had heard from Dr. Burns in Frank Cashen's office.) He told us that some of the monks who practiced lung-gom became so light that they wore chains to keep themselves from floating away like balloons.

"Come on!" Debbie Sue exclaimed.

"I have read about it, heard of it," Sidd said. "It was not of concern to me—floating up into the snowfields—because what I did was to apply lung-gom not to the leg but to the arm. It surprised the monks. The leg is much more important to them. They must use their legs to get around that difficult terrain. In their way of life the arm is involved in the simplest of things—to ring a temple bell, to bang a little drum, to raise a cup of buttered tea to the lips. But I got very interested in the idea of causing a commotion at Point B when standing a long distance away at Point A. To throw an object that connects those two points is a very heady thing to be able to do . . . especially if you can do it time and time again with accuracy. It is something archers and hunters know all about—the trigonometric closing of lines.

"The preparatory exercises are mainly spiritual . . . mental concentration on certain elementary forces, along with the recitation of specific mantras, ngags, to activate the psychic centers. For a long time throwing hard with accuracy did not seem much of an accomplishment. The monks were befuddled. I would take a short walk from the monastery to search for a perfect stone in the *thang,* which is the word for pasture, and I would throw it across the thang at a rhododendron tree.

"One day the *khempo,* the head lama, called me in. He told me that the yaks in the pens were being disturbed by a big predator coming down out of the snowfields. Two young yaks had been taken. There was great consternation among the other yaks. They kept their heads turned toward the mountains to the north. The monks thought it was probably a snow leopard—a pair, they thought—but it was possibly—and the head lama's eyes widened—a yeti—the Abominable Snowman! No one had actually seen what had gotten into the pens. So the head lama assigned me to sit in the ravines above the yak pen and peg rocks at whatever it was that was coming down from the snowfields."

Debbie Sue asked if the people didn't have something more suitable to deal with snow leopards, or the yetis especially, than pegging rocks. A gun for instance?

"The Tibetans use slings," Sidd told us. "And they are very good with them. Some of the slings have rubber that stretches back far behind the body where they twirl them and take aim. *Dop-dops* can aim at a leaf and knock it off a tree."

"Forgive me. What is a dop-dop?" I asked.

"He is a person who works in the monastery. Sweeps. Helps in the kitchen. The dop-dop ordinarily would be the person to keep the snow leopards from bothering the yaks in their pens. But I had a contest with a dop-dop. It was seen by a monk standing in the shadow of a rhododendron forest. The dop-dop said that he was better with his sling than I was with my arm. I replied that if I wished to knock a leaf off its line of fall with a pebble I could do so. He was scornful. *'Nah!, nah!, nah!'* He snapped the rubber of his sling.

"So the dop-dop put the half-shell of a hen's egg on a rock about seventy feet away. I said it was too close. The egg was as big as a half-moon. The dop-dop hooted with scorn. He took aim and popped the egg with a pebble from his sling. He was a fine shot. He walked out to put another eggshell on the rock for me to throw at and I told him to keep walking . . . waving him on until he reached the edge of the forest. I could barely hear him. '*Nah, nah, nah.*' When he put the eggshell down, I threw. He jumped back and I could see the pieces of the eggshell flicker up into the sunlight.

"So the head lama called me in. The monk had told him about the contest. The lama said he had always been impressed by the Westerner's ability to throw objects. Once in Kathmandu he had seen a movie about baseball. What was it? He tapped his finger alongside his nose. *Pride of the Yankees*—that was it. *Most* interesting how baseball players throw the ball to each other, so accurately and with such dispatch!

"So I stayed in the rocks above the yak pens waiting to peg whatever came down. It was a good place to meditate. I was so still I became one with the rocks. I could imagine lichen growing behind my knees. I waited for a week. The moon shone on the flanks of the yaks in their pens. I could see the sheen of their horns. One afternoon the horns, dozens, turned to the north, and I knew something was coming down from the snowfield.

"It was the snow leopard—like a shadow. He moves without moving, as if he were on a moving stairway. What gives him away is the black tip of his tail. It twitches. I am told it is a genetic characteristic—so the leopard cubs can follow their parents in the glaze of a blizzard. At first I thought the slight movement up among the boulders was a pack rat, popping in and out of sight, but then the outlines of the leopard emerged. . . .

"I waited until he had taken a few steps toward

the rocks above the pen, gliding down between the tree trunks—the yaks shuffling nervously below—and then I let fly. Point A to Point B. The snow leopard gave a kind of nonleopard, quite rabbity sort of hop, and looked around as if some internal muscle in the vicinity of his shoulder blades had gone awry. He disappeared up toward the snowfields.

"The head lama was pleased. He was very pleased that it was the snow leopard and not the yeti.

"I got to be very good at it," Sidd told us. "The snow leopards appeared above the yak pens less and less. When they got pegged they looked absolutely bruised with indignation. They didn't quite know what had happened. Before they disappeared back among the rocks, they stood and looked around with those sorrowful, hurt looks that house cats get when you embarrass them in some way."

"What about the stones?" I asked.

"The dop-dops carry their stones around in a leather pouch. I, too, look for stones that feel absolutely perfect to the touch. I put them aside. I walk to where the snow leopard has been, and I look for the stone so that I can use it again. That is what I find so agreeable about baseballs—they fit so perfectly into the hand; there are seams over which to fit the fingers. The ball becomes one with the hand."

After a pause Sidd said, "I will admit to an awkward thing. I got to *like* throwing to a pinpoint target. I began to urge the leopards to come down out of the rhododendron forests to disturb the yaks. When they didn't appear, almost in pique I would fling my stone at a distant stalk, a butterfly fanning its wings on top, and crack the stalk so the butterfly would vault into the air, fluttering. It became a distinct pleasure to make a connection between myself and a distant object over an expanse of space, what in Zen is called the *ma*. The physical feat became all-important. And, of course, when you get very good at something you wonder how you can apply it to something more gainful and useful than hitting an occasional leopard with rocks. One evening, when I was so still that once again I was imagining the lichen growing behind my knees, *baseball* came to mind."

I asked him if he had seen a baseball game.

Yes, at college he had gone a few times. To Fenway Park. He went alone. He had no friends at Harvard. He did not know whom to ask to go with him. He did not understand many of the technical details of the game and was too shy to ask his neighbor in the stands—almost undoubtedly (it occurred to me) a man staring straight ahead, chewing gum very rapidly and muttering that the Sox would find some way to blow *this* one.

Sidd told us what he found especially appealing about pitching. "Do you know what a *mandala* is? It's a design, usually on silk or cotton—a banner, really, in which the purpose is to focus attention on the center. It's a familiar aid to meditation. A baseball field is something like a mandala—in which the focal point is in the middle of the diamond of the base paths—the pitcher's mound. When I see a pitcher walk across the base paths, on the way there I feel as if he were walking across the silks of a mandala to the center of consciousness."

It was after midnight. Sidd yawned and said that if he didn't get to bed, he was going to scare the Mets authorities in the enclosure the next day. His control would "wobble." Debbie Sue sighed and said the porpoises in the Bay were going to be disappointed. She tugged at his shirttail. That was one of their nightly rituals—to swim out in the Bay to where the porpoises came by the shore. Sidd hated it because he was such a poor swimmer. Debbie Sue could hardly wait. The midnight swim. The porpoises expected them. He held her head between his palms. "I do not feel like the sea tonight," he said gently. "Namas-te."

We watched him disappear down the little hallway to their room.

"What he's really going to do is meditate," Debbie Sue told me. "It makes me jealous. He's going to empty his mind. In a while I'm going in to make it difficult for him. I'm going to crouch next to him. He gets into the lotus position and he cups his left hand over the right. It's always done that way," she said. "The active hand is the right, and when you put the left over it, you are quieting it down, bringing it to rest. It always makes me shiver to see him doing it.

"Owl," she said suddenly. "Do you know what

I did on the beach today? I asked him to throw a baseball as far as he could."

"Come on!"

"That's right. Right out to where a freighter was on the horizon." She seemed rather harried when she announced this, fidgeting around on the settee, which squeaked in the dark, and more so when I went on to say that I thought she was doing Sidd a terrible disservice by asking him to do such a thing. "You'll destroy him. After all, that's an arm he's got there, not a mechanical catapult."

"I don't know what got into me," she said. "I actually wanted to see if he could do it."

Once again the nagging suspicion crossed my mind: she had been commissioned by some agency to cripple him in some way.

She said, "I stood there looking out at the Gulf, waiting to see how far out the baseball would land. I heard him wind up behind me, and this little gasp, you know, of effort? And I waited. And waited? Nothing happened. The Gulf out there in front of me? Just as flat as a pancake . . . and the first thing I thought was that he had thrown it clear out of sight: It was *awesome!* The ball must have landed in South Carolina, or someplace."

I grinned in the dark at Debbie Sue's idea of what lay over the horizon of the Gulf of Mexico.

Then she said, "I turned around and he was still holding the ball. He had this sly smile and I said, 'Oh, you've *faked* it! You're not supposed to cheat. Wait'll I tell Owl.' "

"What did he say to that?" I asked.

"He said it was another ball he was holding. He'd thrown the first one. It was probably just coming down now. *Splash,* and he made one of these great imitations of his, so that I could just *see* that ball plopping down and turning over out in the Gulf, and bobbing? So I said, 'Throw it again—this time so I can see it.' "

I asked, "Did he do it?"

"He totally refused. *Totally!* He just bowed and said that to throw the ball to the horizon once was quite enough."

"Well, don't do it again, Debbie Sue," I said. "You can damage his rotator cuff." I hadn't the slightest idea what the rotator cuff was, but I know that baseball people dreaded injuring it the way skiers despaired of a leg fracture.

"I'd rather die," said Debbie Sue.

I went to sleep that night thinking of the baseball landing far out in the Gulf, startling a fisherman sitting in his boat on the calm sea just beyond sight of the shoreline. He would assume that a mullet had jumped clear of the water, but then he would turn and see the baseball revolving and bobbing, the ripples extending from it to indicate it had just dropped down. From where? Thrown out of an airplane? He would look up in an azure sky and find it clear from horizon to horizon. Would he speculate that it had dropped from out beyond the atmosphere itself? What else was there to think?

VI

ONE AFTERNOON I went with them to the beaches. I had told them that morning that according to my cardboard schedule it was my afternoon for the marina and to go to the library to look up strange occurrences. But I made an exception. Sidd came back to the bungalow after his noon-time practice in the enclosure to go with me.

We got in the Volkswagen. Debbie Sue had been out shopping somewhere and she planned to meet us at Treasure Island Beach.

"Debbie Sue is showing me how to throw a Frisbee," Sidd said. "I am dreadful at it. It flutters like a bird. I have hit myself in the foot."

Sometimes I wondered why someone of his complexity of mind, and given his curious introspective history—years in the monastery and so forth in the Himalayas—would be devoted to someone who, to put it baldly, was so breezy, coltish, wacky. Learning to throw a Frisbee! Perhaps that was the very reason—that he realized that she was extricating him from a way of life that was stultifying, an extension of the reason he had turned up in Maine and asked to pitch.

"How was practice today?" I asked.

"As usual," Sidd said. "Mr. Reynolds has developed a new stance to catch the pitch. He stands with one leg braced behind him. He leans forward. It looks as though he wants to push down a wall. His eyes continue to indicate worry. I tell him to try not to be concerned."

We drove through the streets of St. Petersburg. It was a sun-drenched afternoon. We went by a municipal swimming pool, its surface roiled by splashing children; from the cement courts nearby the thump of basketballs carried through the car window on a warm wind off the Gulf. We passed by the grounds of a country club—tennis courts and the green of its golf course stretching off through the palms. We stopped for a light. In front of us a group of bicyclists were poised, high on their seats, long tanned legs out, toes down, to balance as they waited for the light to change.

Beside me, Sidd suddenly said, "I can do very few things. I can't play tennis. I can't golf. I hardly know anything about swimming. I can't bicycle. I have limited myself."

"Well, you can throw a baseball," I said. "And you can make extraordinary sounds. And your French horn."

"That's all very specialized," he said. "My horizons are limited. I can throw a ball but I am very feeble at catching one. Mr. Stottlemyre is in despair. He takes off his baseball cap and hits himself in the middle of the forehead with the palm of his hand. He eats sunflower seeds."

"It's never too late to learn any of these things," I said.

"Debbie Sue is throwing the baseball to me out

in your backyard," Sidd said. "She is going to teach me how to ride a bicycle. I am pleased. The monastery prepares you for the spiritual, but not for a practical life.

"Debbie Sue is a very good golfer. She took me to play yesterday. She's quite a different person when it comes to golf—very serious, quite grim really. Simply no nonsense. We went to Big Tony's golfing range. I am not innocent about golf. I know something of the terminology—sandblasters, wedge, hole in one, Arnie's Army, and all that, and at Stowe, in front of the north portico, there is a golf course. But I have never tried the game— never picked up a club. She put the ball on the tee for me. She said, 'If you can throw a baseball into the sun, you ought to be able to hit it there with a five iron.' I had no idea it was so difficult. I dug a huge chunk out of the earth. Big Tony came out of his office. I hit a seven iron that I had rented from him into the ground and snapped the shaft. Big Tony said, 'Hey!' I gave up. I sat with him and we watched Debbie Sue finish off the pail of balls. Debbie Sue is beautiful to see hitting a golf ball. She has a long, fluid swing. The club hangs down her back as she watches the flight of the ball. Big Tony said she could win on 'the tour' if her head was screwed on right—a 'beach bum' he called her. I tried to pay for the broken club."

I realized that part of my affection for Sidd was that he was a bit like myself—a cripple. Except for his astonishing skill at throwing a baseball with uncanny accuracy, and so forth, he *was*, in fact, "out of it" as we used to say. He could not drive. He couldn't cook. He had very little savoir faire. He didn't understand menus. Modern contrivances were beyond him; rather than manipulating them, they seemed to manipulate him. He had trouble replacing telephones in their cradles. In the morning I'd hear him murmuring to the faucets as he turned them on for his shower. I understood why he wished to be apart from the Mets locker room. They would have kidded him unmercifully. He could barely swim. Traffic confused him. Even walking to dinner in Pass-a-Grille, where the traffic is relatively contained, if I'd look elsewhere just for a second there'd be a scream of brakes and Sidd would run up to me, ashen-faced, as contrite as a guilty dog, from some near calamity on the street.

Debbie Sue loved all this. It made her feel—as she told me once—like a den mother: a warm, protective feeling.

She was waiting for us at Treasure Island Beach. She rose from the sand and ran for us. The Frisbee flicked out from the vicinity of her waistline and came on a swift line toward us. I heard Sidd gasp as he threw up his arms, not to catch the Frisbee but to protect himself, covering his face as if what was coming for him were the outstretched talons of a falcon. The Frisbee sailed by and off to one side and hissed into the sand behind us.

"Owls on the beach," she said, looking at me. "Neat."

We had a long conversation in the sun. Sidd

had gone for a walk, perhaps to meditate in the dunes.

"Sometimes he's up there for an hour. When he comes back we lie on the sand and feel the sun cook. He can get very distant. Sometimes he likes to talk about baseball. Yesterday he asked me why baseball was called the National Pastime. I had trouble with that one, so I told him what *I* liked about it."

Apparently these were such items as the little whisk brooms the umpires use to clean off home plate and the fact that they turn their rear ends to the field when they do so, presumably not to offend the sensibilities of those sitting behind the foul screens. She liked the big dusting mittens the ushers use to sweep off the seats when they snap them down, and she wanted a pair of them to wear around Pass-a-Grille. She liked looking into the cool of the dugout and wondering what they were talking about in there. "It's so much better than a bench, which you have in football, and all you see from the stands is a row of backs with numbers on them. In baseball it's a little house you can step into, just like a badger's."

She told me she liked the outfielders. They slowly stalked about out there . . . and suddenly they were active, scampering until they were under the ball, and once there they were so *cool*, as if it were the easiest and most boring thing in the world they were about to do. She liked the way Darryl Strawberry's body, with its tiny behind, sat way up there on those long legs. She told me she had once dated a shortstop at Duke, but she didn't tell me much about him or her times there.

"Shouldn't you be up there at school?" I asked. "It's not vacation time, is it?"

She shook her head. Apparently the social pressures were too much for her. She couldn't abide dormitory life or the regimen of class schedules. She couldn't "adjust." I had the feeling the students had made fun of her—her vitality, her mannerisms—crushed her in some way. She was terribly lonely—really the same sort of problems Sidd had at Stowe, which was surprising, of course, because she was—at least in my eyes—so unbearably beautiful. Sometimes that was the case, wasn't it—that beauty warded people off: it was too complex a quality to deal with. No matter. She left there after a while. Rather wistfully she once sang the Duke song for me:

> Dear old Duke, thy name we sing,
> To thee our voices raise . . .

The idea of going on the golf tour did not appeal to her. She hated travel, the competition, the thought of crowds. "I think a nice crowd is *three,*" she said, "you, me, and Sidd." She leaned across the sand and laid her head on my shoulder. "I've never been so happy."

She turned on her side in the sand. "He's been teaching me things. I am trying to teach him golf and how to ride a bicycle and how to catch a baseball, and he's trying to turn me into a monk.

. . . Putting me on The Path? He gives me these little exercises to try. Here's one: 'With mouth slightly open, put the mind in the middle of the tongue.' "

She did it for me—eyes closed as she concentrated. "There! How was that? Did I look vacant? Here's another. 'Look at the bowl without seeing what is in it or on the sides.' Sidd tells me if I do this for a while, I will become *aware*. He tries to get me to imagine myself as an empty room with walls of skin—*empty*. Oh, Owl, I'm very bad at it. I told him it was impossible. I had too many grouper sandwiches and I had a stomachache.

"He tells me that if I close my eyes and concentrate I can see my inner being in detail. I try. 'Spots,' I want to tell him. 'I see spots when I turn on the beach and lie faceup, like this.' " The sun glistened on her eyelashes. "So I lie to him. 'Sidd, I think I see the universe.' Sometimes I rest my head on his bare stomach and I turn my ear to his navel to listen to the tumo-heat. I can hear his stomach gurgling sometimes, but that's all."

"You're having a wonderful time with him."

"He's going to see through me," she said mournfully. "He's going to get bored. He's going to get bored teaching me."

"I think he enjoys telling people things," I said. "Especially you. He's been taught for so many years . . . all those self-disciplines. It must be a relief to find some one—"

"He teaches me numbers in Tibetan. I learn them. He likes it when we drive into McDonald's

107

and I call out the window of the car into the little speaker, 'Okay, we'll have *knee* Big Macs,' which is two in Tibet, 'and hold the pickle, and *soom* orders of French fries!' which is three . . . ." Her lip began to tremble. "We'll have *chik* salad for my friend.

"I can count to eight—*chik, knee, soom, she, nah, deb, bi, su* . . . Owl! Isn't that incredible? Six, seven, and eight spell out my name!

"I love him," she said, looking so forlorn that I thought she was going to break down completely. "I just don't have any luck with love. Do you know who I loved first? Jack Foote! I was sixteen and he was thirteen. He was the most angelic person . . . I mean he *looked* angelic. He sang in the choir of St. John's Episcopal church in Naples. I went every Sunday. My parents had no idea why I'd gone so religious. I sat in the first row and stared at him in his red choir robes. At night I dreamed of being with him in the choir stalls . . . rushing by the minister in the pulpit, and getting to him in there among those wooden benches, all those red robes fluttering . . . ?"

"Did Jack Foote know about this?"

"Oh, I think so. He would catch me staring at him. I never could pick his voice out from the others. I think he was worried. My God, he must have felt those *waves* of feeling I had for him. Poor Jack Foote. He went off to Culver Military Academy eventually. I used to dream of him in his black jack boots and how I would rush out onto the parade ground and tackle him in the ranks on some wintry day, the hardness of the ground, and all those greatcoats. . . ."

I told her she was getting carried away.

"Of course, Owl." She arched her back off the sand of the beach and yawned. "But it is funny, isn't it, that I should fall in love with a choirboy and then a monk. At this rate I'll end up with a *bishop!* I'll take over a cathedral. You know what? Sidd tells me about the eyes in the temples in Bhutan that are the size and shapes of dolphins. They don't follow you, like the eyes in portraits. They're looking at something else . . . off to one side . . . He told me there's a fresco of these eyes in the London house. His father brought it back—"

"You like to hear him talk about the house in London."

"Owl, *that's* where I want to go. I want to go with him to the lawyers and get the key to the house. It'll be a terrific scene. They'll look at his blue jeans and his big boots? They'll ask, 'Who are you?' He'll tell them. 'I am Hayden Sidney-Whyte Finch . . . long-lost heir . . . also known as Sidd Finch." She gave this a highly dramatic reading, her attempt at an English accent tempered by her Southern roots. "But they won't want to give up the key," she continued. "They'd finally have to, wouldn't they? We'd run down the stairs and hop in a hansom cab."

"A hansom cab?"

"Oh, Owl. I don't even know what a hansom cab *looks* like? But in the movies people are always jumping into them when they're going to reclaim their inheritances. You can't do it any other way. We'll open these huge doors when we get there. It'll be musty inside—great halls, and the suits of armor with dust sheets over them. Sidd will hold my hand. We'll take a tour. 'This is Mum's room. She died in a fall before I came to Denbigh Close. I'll show you her scarab brooches up on the top floor. This is Dad's dressing room, with his military boots in the corner. He died in an airplane crash. This is Nanny's room. She whipped me once with a riding crop, one of Dad's, when I wouldn't finish my supper. She shouted at me, "You're nothing but an ungrateful orphan waif!' " Oh, Owl, it'll be so romantic! We'll go down to the ballroom in the basement where the railroad trains are. Sidd'll pull a sheet off this huge control panel." Her eyes shone. "He'll turn on the system. Click!"

She sat up and shaded her eyes. She looked down the beach for Sidd. "I hope he's sitting up in the dunes trying to think of The Void and all that—and not succeeding."

She giggled. "I like to think he can't quite get rid of me. I'm waiting just outside his consciousness? He gives up and I march in with a big brass band. Pom-poms." She looked out at the Gulf. "No porpoises out there today," she said. "Will you come and swim with us tonight—the porpoise romp? It's awfully exciting."

I said I'd think about it.

"You have plans?"

"No," I said truthfully.

"Did you write today, Owl?" She hoisted herself around and sat up; she rested her chin on her kneecap.

"I'm afraid not."

Both Debbie Sue and Sidd were concerned by my writer's-block problems. Back in the bungalow she would peer at the blank paper in the portable typewriter out on the side porch, curled from the humidity, and suggest that I type out the word "The" to see if anything happened. I grinned and said that Robert Benchley, *The New Yorker* humorist, had tried it. He stared at his "The" for a while and then went off to a poker game where he spent a pleasant hour or so hoping that in the process his creative impulses would get a jolt of some sort. Back in his office, he took another look at the "The." Nothing stirred, so he left for an hour or so with his Round Table acquaintances in the Algonquin Bar. Finally, telling them that he had some work to do, he went back to his office. There was the "The." This time an idea came. He sat down and finished the sentence. It read "The hell with it," and having done this, he locked up his office and went out into the evening.

"At least he wrote a sentence," Debbie Sue said.

I told her that my writer's block was a truly monumental one. "It's so large I really don't worry about it," I said. "It's like having a huge debt—so large that you can't panic yourself about it anymore. It's simple. I am an ex-writer."

After an awkward silence, Debbie Sue asked, "Well, what happens when you sit down at the typewriter and start . . . just pecking away?"

It was possible to do so, I said, but what came out was worthless—sort of like a chimpanzee fingerpainting.

"What words do you type?" she wanted to know.

I shrugged. "Mostly they're the same. I seem obsessed with 'Along the driveway the lilacs were in bloom.' I type that one a lot."

"Oh, but that's beautiful, Owl," Debbie Sue said. "It's so romantic."

"That's as far as it goes," I said. "There's nothing at the end of the driveway."

I told her about Amory Blake. "He's trying to make me a *cartoonist*. He has me drawing characters with balloons over their heads, which I am supposed to fill in with dialogue."

Debbie Sue was intrigued. "What are they saying? Have you got your characters talking?"

"The balloons are empty."

"Oh, Owl, how sad. At least you could put some *sounds* in the balloons."

"Oh, there are awful stories about writers' blocks," I told her. "When William Faulkner left Warner Bros. they found an empty bottle of bourbon in his office and a sheet of paper on which he had written, five hundred times, 'Boy meets girl.' "

Sidd appeared down the beach. As he came toward us I wondered if anyone (about four or five desultory folk were lolling there in the wan early spring sun) could have guessed they were looking at possibly the most devastating force in the game of baseball. The bones of his rib cage showed as he strode toward us, a shy smile working at his features. Debbie Sue had bought him a pair of colorful jams with parrots down the side, somewhat oversized, so that it looked as if at any instant he could step out of them and leave them behind on the sand.

He flopped down next to us. "Did you write today?"

I told him I was sorry, I hadn't.

"I've been thinking about it," he said. "The answer is first to go through a kind of basic Catholic repentance. Lie down and review in your mind. Don't blame yourself. Demean the hate. Think of beings as detached absolutes."

"Come on, Owl," Debbie Sue said; she smiled at me companionably. "Let's see you be a detached absolute!"

"I'll give you a mantra," Sidd said. "It might help. It's from a lama who tutored Milarepa, Manjushri, who is the archangel of the Word. It goes 'Om Ara Ba Tsa Na Dhi.' Like all mantras, it has to be repeated over and over again. It's important to draw out the *Dhi* . . . like a soft cry."

"What does it mean?" Debbie Sue asked.

"It means, in so many words, 'Living ripens verbal intelligence.' Repeat it after me—'Om Ara Ba Tsa Na Dhi.' "

We did, sitting solemnly there in the sand. Sidd

said he would write it down for me on a notepad when we got back to the bungalow.

"They work, Owl," Debbie Sue said. "Guess what? Sidd stopped me from smoking. He told me that Tibetans believe cigarette smoke kills these delicate little things . . . what are they called, Sidd?"

"*Gandharvas.* And also *dakinis.* They are winged spirits, quite helpful ones. You can find them plucking harp-like instruments and carrying flowers at great religious events."

"That was enough for me," Debbie Sue said. "I stubbed my cigarette out in a plate. He taught me a little mantra, just in case. It goes: *Om Bhaishajya* (which you say twice), *Maha Raja Samudgate Svana.*"

"In so many words, it means: 'Oh doctor, doctor, great doctor, get with it!' " Sidd told us. "I gave it to Davey Johnson who is trying to stop chewing tobacco."

"What's the theory?" I asked. "Do you say them very fast or slowly?"

"There are some who say that if you recite a mantra slowly and perfectly it's better than rushing through it a million times . . ."

We practiced the writing-block mantra—drawing out the *Dhi* at the end.

Debbie Sue sighed. "I'm hungry. I feel like writing a cook book," she said.

It was almost dark when we left the beach. We stayed to watch the sunset, vast brush strokes of purple from the rain squalls far out in the Gulf.

Debbie Sue told us she had seen a waterspout out there once—"a thin, squiggly line reaching down to the sea," so harmless-looking that she wished she had her Windsurfer with her on the beach so that she could have sailed out to "take a bath" in it.

Sometimes after supper Sidd brought the French horn out to the back porch and played it. He hitched one melody or horn call to another in effortless succession. I don't recall any bumbles or errors—astonishing, I would suppose, from such a difficult instrument. Sometimes I recognized a refrain—Siegfried's horn. Always, at the first notes, the frogs in the lily pond out back would stop their chorus for a minute or so before erupting once more.

We asked how Sidd had come to choose the horn. He told us that it was his father's favorite instrument. The great horn players of the day were invited to the musicales in the London house. His father's good friend was Dennis Brain, probably the greatest horn player who ever lived. Sidd had never known him (he was killed in a car crash in 1957) but his father often talked about him.

"He actually had Dennis Brain's horn in the house," Sidd said. "The car had gone into an elm tree in a rainstorm. The horn was discovered in the grass, a little way from the car. It was badly smashed. My father had it reconstructed by Paxman Bros. of London. He let me play it sometimes. There's a photograph of father wearing a

115

little rose in his lapel sitting next to Dennis Brain in a sports car. Brain was very fond of cars and drove them at high speeds. My father would drive to concerts with him. He'd arrive at the concert hall scared. He'd calm down during the concert, but then halfway through he'd begin to get scared again because he knew Brain was going to drive him back home."

Sidd went on to say that Brain came from a famous family of horn players. His father was well known for the length of time he could hold a note. He once bet a brilliant violin player that he could sustain a note on a horn longer than the violinist could hold a note on a string with one slide of the bow. He did, too, holding a note for seventy-five seconds while the violin player drew the bow imperceptibly slowly until the tip of the bow fell off the string.

In the darkness of the porch Sidd gave us an imitation of what that had sounded like, the violin note like a sigh, wavering finally, and then abruptly chopped off by silence.

"The frogs love it," Debbie Sue announced. "Listen to them."

She wanted to know if Sidd had taken the French horn with him to the Himalayas.

Sidd replied that he had not, but he had become accomplished on Tibetan instruments. "Once I picked up a *tungchen,* which is the Tibetan long horn. Actually you don't pick it up, because the end lies on the ground when you play it. The tungchen has a terribly long sound box and you have to work up quite a column of air through it in order to get anything to come out the far end. People say it sounds more like a diesel horn than a musical instrument. I learned it fairly easily. The monks looked at me in surprise. The first piece I played on the tungchen was 'London Bridge Is Falling Down'—I haven't the slightest idea why—and then I played the Beatles' 'Strawberry Fields.' Terrific echoing effect. In fact, the last phrases of 'London Bridge' were drifting back from the mountains when I was quite a bit into 'Strawberry Fields.' The monks asked me to play the tungchen at the ceremonials. They said *they* would be responsible for the selections."

"They didn't want to hear 'Strawberry Fields'?" Debbie Sue asked.

"No. They preferred pieces with only one note—long, very persistent wails. It's a fine melancholy background for the chanting that the monks do. . . ."

"You couldn't really carry the tungchen around," I commented.

"You'd need a whole row of yaks," Debbie Sue suggested.

Always around midnight Debbie Sue announced that it was time to go out and romp with the porpoises in the Bay. Sidd invariably groaned. They would borrow my Volkswagen and go off for a couple of hours.

I went with them once. We undressed on a narrow pebbly beach and waded out. Just offshore

117

the bottom took on the consistency of a kind of muck; the ooze worked its way pleasantly up between the toes. The shelf dropped away very gradually, so that we waded a long distance before the water was at our waists. Debbie Sue led the way, the outline of her naked behind barely visible to guide us, slowly setting, truly like a pale moon, as the water reached slowly up her body.

Sidd did not like being out there. As he waded, little exclamations escaped him, as if a bare foot had fetched up against a shell or the back of a crab. It *was* rather eerie. The night I went it was so dark and foggy that the Bay, flat and absolutely still, seemed to meld into the night sky. There was no horizon. The temperature of both air and water was about the same, so that when we got out to where the shelf dropped off into deeper water, we seemed to float within a vast, dark sphere.

I have no scientific explanation why the porpoises turned up—possibly they happened to pass there on a regular sweep along the shore. Nor do I know how many there were—two, perhaps three. Suddenly we heard their backs break the surface, the distinct puff of their expirations, and then the faint suck of water and the Bay closed in behind them. Debbie Sue let out a yelp of excitement. They were invisible in the dark—a faint fish smell hung around us. Once or twice, close by my legs, I felt the soft pressure of a displacement of water, which meant that a large body had gone by within feet of mine.

The porpoises spent almost fifteen minutes

around us. Debbie Sue wouldn't leave until they had moved on. She called to us from farther out in the darkness, "They might come back!" I waited, treading water, while Sidd, next to me, was tall enough so that his long toes gave him a precarious anchorage on the bottom. His head was tilted back to keep his chin clear of the water.

Back on the beach, we carried our clothes in bundles to the car rather than endure the discomfiture of putting them on our damp bodies. We drove home naked, the warm wind coming in the windows drying us off.

I was worried about the police, especially when we got to the streetlights of Pass-a-Grille. I said, "Even here they tend to look upon naked threesomes with suspicion."

Debbie Sue said, "We'll tell them we have a monk in the car and they'll understand."

VII

THE METS KEPT in touch. Jay Horwitz called up on occasion in the evening. Debbie Sue, who could not bear to let a phone go for more than a ring or so without pouncing on it, would call out, "Owl, it's for you?"

On the other end Jay would mourn that he didn't want to press me in any way, but was there news?

I told him there wasn't anything concrete, but at least Sidd seemed happy. He was continuing to meditate in the dunes and practice back in there—there'd be the distant crash of cans and sometimes one would sparkle briefly in the sky, kicked up by the power of the pitch. He seemed in harmony with himself.

"Any hint?"

"Well, he gave me one of those sayings the other day."

"Yes . . . ?"

" 'When the chickens are cold they roost in the trees; when ducks are cold they dive in the water.' "

Jay paused for a few seconds. "Not exactly . . . scrutable," he said.

"I'll keep you informed," I told him.

"Toronto comes in here April 2. Davey wants to put the kid in against the Blue Jays 'B' squad to see what happens."

"I'll mention it."

"What about the girl who answered the phone?"

"Yes, Debbie Sue . . ."

"What's he doing with a girl anyway?" Jay asked. "Aren't monks supposed to be celibate?"

I looked around to see if Sidd was within earshot. "Sidd's more of a student than a monk," I said, ". . . a kind of 'wine taster' . . . *sips* of culture rather than a fulltime imbiber."

"A wine taster? That's a new one. What about the girl, though?"

I did not tell Jay what had happened earlier that morning—that my own suspicions had gotten the best of me. It was Jay himself who had suggested that Debbie Sue represented some interested party: an infiltrator—sent either to spy on Sidd or somehow disrupt things . . . perhaps by the Commissioner himself. So, padding down the bungalow corridor after her, I suddenly—very much on impulse—cupped my hands to my mouth and bellowed, "Ueberroth!" She jumped, quite frightened, and turned around.

"Owl, don't ever holler that awful word at me."

I apologized. I told her that something had caught in my throat.

"I don't know what it means, but it's *gross!*"

"Well, *we* have no read on her," Jay was saying on the phone.

"I'm not doing much better," I said. "She's apparently a good golfer. A student, or was, at Duke."

Jay asked if I had followed through on Nelson Doubleday's suggestion that we get Sidd to see some baseball movie classics. *The Natural,* of course, with Robert Redford had been mentioned, and also a film I had never heard of called *It Happens Every Spring,* starring Ray Milland as a chemist who, by chance, discovers a compound that avoids wood. When Milland applied the compound to baseballs, he made as effective a pitcher as Sidd Finch apparently was in real life.

"I can send over the cassettes," Jay said.

"We don't have the appropriate machines," I admitted.

"No VCRs? My God, what goes on there at night?" he asked.

121

I told him that we talked. We did a certain amount of reading, and Sidd did his meditating, telling us about the Himalayas, and so forth. Sometimes we turned on my sister's television set. I didn't say that late at night Debbie Sue and Sidd very often went down to the Bay—Sidd murmuring and complaining—to swim with the porpoises.

Jay thanked me for the report. He urged me to reach him if there was a hint of a decision.

I promised and hung up.

The next morning I stopped by Huggins-Stengel to watch Sidd pitch in the enclosure. I arrived late. He had already taken his practice throws and gone off to the beach.

I hung around for a while. The batting-cage had been wheeled onto the field. Davey Johnson was standing behind it looking through the thick mesh at his hitters taking their turns. Recognizing me from the Dr. Burns seminar in Cashen's office, he waved me over. I found it exhilarating to be so close to things—the faint hiss of the pitches as they came in, the pop and the long flight of the baseballs going out, and seeing the batters check their stance and adjust and work on their swings. The balls the hitters let go whacked up against the canvas at the base of the cage. Johnson had his foot up on the support-bar behind the mesh.

"How's your boy?"

"Sidd? He seems content enough," I said. His usage of "your boy" made me think once again how the manager seemed to distance himself from Sidd.

"I understand he's going to make up his mind by April first."

"I didn't know."

"That's what I hear." He shifted his weight slightly. His manner was low and unruffled.

I asked if Sidd was making life hard for him.

"Well, that's an interesting point," he replied. "It may well be disruptive, frankly. It's hard to explain to the rest of the guys. I never liked the idea of the guy coming out here for ten minutes and then going off to the beach or wherever. He only throws a half-dozen pitches—just like he wants to keep his hand in, you know."

I nodded and said that I had come out to watch but had missed him.

"It's a sight," Johnson said, shaking his head. "What he does doesn't really belong in baseball, at least nothing I ever imagined." He looked over. "Do you realize he throws full-bore right from the start?"

"I didn't know," I said.

"Yep. Hell, warming up is practically an art in itself. Almost all pitching coaches try to get their people to take a short run around the field to loosen the muscles and get the adrenalin flowing. Then some light exercises—touching the toes, stretching the leg muscles. The first toss to the catcher is from about twenty-five feet . . . then he slowly backs up to the rubber. Finch does none of these things. He steps into the enclosure and takes

123

off his boot! That's his warm-up. Then he steps up and lets fly." He chuckled. "Ronn Reynolds tells me *he's* the guy who should be warmed up. He jokes they should wheel up a field gun about forty feet out and fire a couple of artillery shells into his catcher's mitt!"

A foul ball shot back: I flinched as it spun against the cords with a faint whine just in front of us, and dropped.

"Have you had this kind of trouble with a player before—I mean the disruptive element?"

Johnson smiled and said Oh yes, he'd had such problems. "When I managed the Miami Amigos we had an outfielder named Danny 'Sundown' Thomas. He was called Sundown because his religion kept him from doing any athletic stuff from sundown Friday to sundown Saturday. So on Saturday he wouldn't even show up at the ballpark. But then suddenly, at 7:30, just as the sun went below the horizon, Sundown'd rush in, dressed in his uniform, pounding his fist into his glove, all eager to play. Yep. Very disconcerting. Then we had a pitcher, Oscar Zamora, who had a shoe business in Miami. He only agreed to pitch on weekends when he wasn't out selling. It was not the most stable of conditions. It makes it hard on the other guys."

The progression of players continued into the batting-cage. I realized how removed I was from things when I could not recognize any of them. Keith Hernandez was the only one I was fairly sure about: the dark moustache.

"Do you think anyone's caught on to Finch?" I asked.

"There're some guys poking around, I hear. *Sports Illustrated*. Guy came up to me a couple of days ago and asked if we had a cricket bowler in camp . . . from Pakistan. He was embarrassed. He said his home office had wanted him to ask."

"What about the players?"

"They've got to know something's going on," Johnson said. "One or two of them must have heard the pops out there in the enclosure. Steve Garland, who's our trainer, must wonder about Ronn Reynolds' left hand. He keeps treating it for trauma. Then at noontime when we load up the bus to go on over to Lang Field for a game, the guys must wonder why Ronn Reynolds is left behind. He stares after the bus like we're leaving him on a desert island."

Johnson turned from the cage and faced me.

"You haven't got any idea if he's going to sign?"

"No."

"If we sign him, Cashen wants to send him down—no matter what—to Triple-A. It's the procedure. How do you think he'll take that?"

On a hunch I said that baseball was a very personal exercise for Sidd, and that I didn't think it would make any difference.

Batting practice was finished. The grounds-crew came out and hauled the cage away. One of its wheels squeaked sharply. Johnson and I started walking for the clubhouse.

"Have you told Sidd that his ways could be . . . well, disruptive?" I asked.

"Yep, I've been straight with him."

"Do you recall what he said?"

"Recall? How the hell can I forget. What he said was: 'When I see smoke beyond the mountain I know there's a fire. When I see horns beyond a fence I know there's an ox.' "

"Hmmmm."

"Exactly my own words. What was that anyway?" he asked.

"A koan. It all has to do with paradox. The mind is stretched with contemplation. Mental elasticity."

"Well, mine sure got stretched. Don't get me wrong. I like the kid. Maybe he's not easy. He doesn't exactly *mingle*. He's like one of those things in cuckoo clocks—appears and then he's gone. But he seems to *worry* about people. He gave me—what do you call those things—a *mantra* to quit chewing tobacco. It's a bad habit of mine. He wrote the mantra down on a piece of paper and told me its god was the color of sapphire. He gave it to me. He put his hands together like he was praying. A little bow. Class."

"Have you tried it?" I said.

"I'm going to save it up until the season starts," he said with a grin.

Often at night we went to Hurricane's, a restaurant on the beach where a jazz combo played. Debbie Sue tried to get Sidd to take his horn. She

126

had an idea that he could sit in with the group—his horn in his lap until finally he would raise it to his lips, the first mellow tones stilling the commotion in the place, the crowd looking up from their blackened snapper and their shrimp baskets; even the other musicians, eventually, would put down their instruments and listen, the horn music welling out into the street beyond the people crowded at the door. Sidd smiled and said he liked to play just for us. Or perhaps for the porpoises out in the Bay. That would mean sitting on the beach so he wouldn't have to swim out there among them.

That night Debbie Sue wanted to go to a disco. We went to one named Dent's on Gulf Boulevard. Sidd and I sat together and watched Debbie Sue when she said she was bored with us and needed to "stretch her bones"—as she put it—on the dance floor. She danced alone, but almost immediately a circle of men materialized, so that at any time she could have taken a couple of steps forward and collected herself a partner. As it was, she never committed herself, but revolved slowly in a solitary orbit, her limbs moving at double the beat, her eyes vacant, often shielded by the tumble of her hair, jaws agape, and after a number of minutes of this she would drop back down into her seat as if pole-axed and ask for a glass of ginger ale.

Neither Sidd nor I danced with her. He seemed absolutely immune to the beat of the disco music submerging us with its volume—never a tap of the feet on the floor or a fingertip on the tabletop.

Once, in the din, he leaned across the table and asked me, his voice popping in my eardrums, if, when I had a chance, would I explain the little white bag he had noticed on the pitcher's mound during an intrasquad game he had spied on at Huggins.

I shouted at him that the bag was full of rosin, which filtered through when a pitcher picked it up; it made the fingers feel supple on the ball.

I leaned back to take a breath and then I cupped my hands and yelled through the storm of noise that Jay Horwitz had asked me to tell him—that the Mets hoped Sidd would play in the Toronto Blue Jay "B" squad. It was coming up in a week.

Sidd's eyes widened slightly.

We got home at one in the morning. The dancing had not robbed Debbie Sue of any of her energy; the porpoise romp out in the Bay was what she wanted to do now. I declined firmly, and Sidd murmured and wondered if it couldn't be postponed.

"Namas-te," he said over his shoulder as the two left. They came back very late. For the first time I felt a strong wrench of jealousy—knowing that Sidd would be holding the length of Debbie Sue's body, still damp from the sea, against his own. From my bedroom I could hear their bare feet on the cool floors of the bungalow, the opening of the refrigerator door and the scrape of dishes as Debbie Sue scrabbled around to make them a late-night sandwich. Their voices murmured. I

128

heard them discussing whether to come in and wake me up ("Owls don't sleep at night, Sidd") so they could tell me about their adventures out in the Bay.

I tried to get myself to sleep before they went into the bedroom. The bellowing of the frogs out in back helped, but occasionally their chorus would stop as if a conductor's baton had been drawn across the surface of the pond . . . and the murmuring and the intermittent sounds from their room drifted through the bungalow. I got up to turn on the ceiling fan. It was cool in the winter and unnecessary, but the little electric motor made a soft whining sound, and when I lay back down the draft from it stirred around the pillow and made me think of being on a yacht somewhere at sea.

That night Sidd played the French horn for her. I always imagined he did so lying down on the bed, but Debbie Sue assured me that it wasn't as romantic as that—it was troublesome playing the French horn upside down.

"So he sits on the edge of the bed?" I had asked.

Debbie Sue nodded. "He plays these lovely classical things—very softly. He hunches over his horn. I look at the curve of his back. Out in the garden what he plays gets the frogs excited, doesn't it, Owl?"

"Of course."

"Does anyone complain?" she asked.

"Not yet."

That night he played "Strawberry Fields"—the tune he told us he had played when he first picked up a Tibetan horn. At least that was what he was playing when I drifted off.

VIII

SIDD WAS ESPECIALLY fascinated by what I could tell him about the famous Japanese home-run hitter, Sadaharu Oh. I had written two pieces about him. The first was an article for *Sports Illustrated* about athletes' autographs. During the course of researching the article, I happened to spot Arnold Schwartzenegger, the body builder, sign a napkin in a New York restaurant. Considering the length of his name (and the porous nature of what he was writing on), it took him quite a while; I thought what a ponderous and awkward name for someone of such fame to sign . . . pushing a pen through so many letters to get the thing done. I decided to write a paragraph or so in the article mentioning long-named athletes who had such problems (Billy Grabarkewitz, who was an infielder for the Dodgers, or the football coach Marty Schottenheimer, or Slobodan Zivojinovic, the Yugoslavian tennis player), balancing this with athletes with short, snappy names (Mel Ott, Ron Cey, et al.) and for whom an autograph was a simple, short scribble of the pen. I assumed the champion of this latter group would be Mr. Oh, the aforementioned Japanese, whose signature would presumably be a little calligraphic slash, or whatever.

It turned out that Oh by itself did not mean anything. It signifies "King" but it has to be qualified by the Sadaharu. So when my self-addressed envelope came back from Japan, the signature of the great batter ran down the entire length of the page, just about as long a vertical drop of letters as Arnold Schwartzenegger's was across the page horizontally. His name suddenly became a contender in the wrong category!

The shortest autograph in my research, incidentally, turned out to be the basketball player Oscar Robertson's, "The Big O," who signs an "O." The loveliest was a football player's—Lynn Swann of the Pittsburgh Steelers, who draws his name with an "S" as the outline of a swan floating on the water, with the other letters filling out the bird's feathers and so forth.

"Did you ever meet Sadaharu Oh?" Sidd asked.

I told him I'd had two opportunities. Once Oh had come to Hawaii on a Japanese All-Star team. I was in the islands on assignment. I went to a press luncheon where I thought I was going to hear the great slugger speak. I was too late. His seat at the dais was empty. A pitcher from his team was speaking to the guests through an interpreter. He was talking about the contest between the pitcher and the hitter—the duel. I could still remember the word the translator used—*shabu*.

"Yes," Sidd said. "I know of the *shabu*."

I went on to say that the pitcher himself was a

pleasant-faced gentleman. His baseball cap—which he had apparently worn through lunch—was cocked back on his head, which gave him a kind of perky look. But beside him the translator was trying to indicate the near-savage confidence the pitcher felt he had to have to win the *shabu*. His face was twisted with mock fury. "The effrontery!" he sneered his translation at us. "This guy who dares to step up to the plate to face my pitching!" He relaxed and looked over at the pitcher to get his next lines. The pitcher spoke briefly. He nodded and smiled. The translator turned and snarled at us, "I throw strike. He swings. He misses. To imagine he can touch the Master!" The translator turned to be prompted. His lip curled. The pitcher's teeth shone. "What! He is still at the plate? In Tai Chi we call this stupidity! So I throw him another strike. He cannot hit it. But what's this? Still at the plate?" The translator looked as though he were going to faint from the shock. The pitcher's voice rose slightly but pleasantly, as if a child were being praised. The translator picked up a spoon and banged it on the table. "Stupid, presumptuous, pompous, silly!" he shouted. "Why should I be carrying this wimp! Three strikes! About time!" The translator let out a long-drawn breath . . . as if he, too, was relieved that this infernal nuisance had been removed from the batter's box. At the pitcher's next comments the translator's eyes popped and he threw up his hands. "But what's *this?* Another jerk coming out of the dugout. What a bore!"

Sidd laughed. "It is true, isn't it? There is always someone waiting in the shadows of the dugout."

The second time I told Sidd I had actually met Oh. I had been commissioned to do a piece on him. It was published in a magazine, now defunct, called *Quest*. I saw him play in Aumamoto, Kyushu, in a game against the Hanshin Tigers. I was on self-imposed leave from Vietnam. It was the beginning of what my sister used to call "the time of the shakes." I went to Japan in an effort to settle myself down and get my nerves under control. I thought a baseball game would help. With its pace, the nonmilitary nature of its procedures, the predictability of its rituals, it had none of the metaphors of where I had been. It was, indeed, the last helpful remedy before I went back into Southeast Asia and the time of the shakes began in earnest.

Actually, I remember very little of the circumstances of the baseball game itself (who won and so forth) and not much of the short meeting with Oh afterward. I do not recall even writing the article or where I did so—the vaguest recollections of a Japanese country inn come to mind, with paper walls and tatami mats, and that my back ached from sitting on the floor to write without a backrest. I do recall something of the nature of baseball itself in Japan—that amplified music seemed to play throughout the game, and that the fans returned the foul balls back onto the field from the stands. I remember the managers in the dugouts communicating through little megaphones, the kind used by coxswains to shout at their oarsmen. And then, of course, I have a vivid memory of Oh at the plate. I remember the sun shining on the enormous number 1, which was the numeral he wore on the back of his jersey.

In fact, they called him "the Big One." And no wonder! He was the home-run champion for fifteen years. He would turn the number to the pitcher just before stepping into the batter's box so that he was preceded by the visual notice of his presence. He said of this procedure, "I feel like a rough Japanese sea. My number rises toward the pitcher like a dark wave before I strike."

His statistics were awesome. He hit over a hundred more home runs than Henry Aaron (868 to 755) while playing a year less (the same as Babe Ruth—twenty-two seasons) and over seasons shorter than those here in the United States. The apologists for the American home run hitters point out that the Japanese pitching is not as fine-tuned as ours, and that their fences tend to be closer to the plate. No matter. Oh eventually received the batter's ultimate recognition: a pitcher on the Hanshin Tigers named Kakimoto told everyone he had a secret way of keeping Oh from hitting a home run. His comments were circulated in the papers and a large crowd was on hand to see what he was going to do when the Tigers and the Giants next met. In the second inning Oh came up with the bases empty. Kakimoto walked him intentionally.

To hit the ball Oh had perhaps the most unique style in the history of batting—picking up his forward foot, balancing then on the other leg for an instant like a stork (indeed, the style was called "flamingo batting"), and then striding into the ball as it came into the strike zone. His coach called it "the dog-lifting-his-leg-at-the-hydrant batting style."

"Oh said his ability to hit came from his 'spirit center,' " I mentioned to Sidd. "This was located two fingers below the navel. Just like tumo-heat," I said.

Sidd nodded and smiled.

Oh's batting coach persuaded Oh to learn *aikido*, the practice of weaponless defense, and the concept of *ma*—the space or time "in between." In baseball, ma would be the distance between the pitcher's hand and the batter's box. Whoever can control the ma prevails. "You must master ma," Oh was told. "You must bring your opponent into your own space. His energy then belongs to you."

One of the tricks in baseball, Oh learned, was to pretend that the opponent was a distant mountain—what his tutors called "a distant view of close things." Imagining the pitcher as a "distant mountain" would make the ball appear to be slower as it traveled that enormous distance to the batter. When I got back to Vietnam I tried this in a softball game. I looked out from the plate and pretended the correspondent from the Baltimore *Sun* on the mound was a "distant mountain." I swung early and skied the ball to the third baseman.

Sidd asked if I had actually met Oh.

I said that after the game I had gone to keep an appointment with him. My interpreter took me to the wrong dressing room. I looked for a player wearing a big 1 on his jersey. It was too late. Players were coming out of the shower. The interpreter finally got things straight. He took me to the visiting-team locker room. The star was looking out the window at a parking lot. He had already dressed. I looked at my notes. An indication of my troubles to come, I could not phrase a question from them. I said I wished to talk to him about baseball.

He was very polite. "The truth is, outside baseball, I am a fairly boring fellow."

We barely exchanged more than a sentence or two. I asked him about autographs—my mind reverting to that first piece I had written about him. Didn't he feel suffocated by the large number of people asking him to sign something?

He had a practical answer. He said his procedure was to look out the locker-room window—just as he was doing now—to estimate how many fans were waiting for him. Multiplying this number by 6.5, which was the number of seconds he spent scribbling in each autograph book or on a scrap of paper, he then divided that figure by sixty to give him the number of minutes it would take him to work himself through the crowd to slide into the front seat of his car and slip away. That

136

was how he answered the only question I asked him.

Perhaps because we had been chatting about Sadaharu Oh, the next morning at breakfast I told Sidd about a dream, a very vivid one, I'd had the night before. I very rarely remember my dreams, which is fortunate since I suspect most of them are nightmares best left to quake far beneath the surface. The dream was about a baseball game in India. Sidd was on the mound. I had a brief glimpse of an elephant, waiting, complete with mahout, out in the bull pen, ready to bring in a relief pitcher.

Sidd was evidently in trouble. A couple of men were on base, dancing down the base paths, joshing at him, and invoking Hindi epithets. Up to the plate came the batter—a small, balding Gandhi-like figure with bow legs. I was told he was from Burma. As he came I remember thinking that being bow-legged was such a distinctive feature of great athletes—Pele, Willie Mays, Pancho Segura. He was wearing a diaperlike dhoti and carrying a silver baseball bat with which, as he stepped into the batter's box, he whacked his uplifted bare foot on the heel, dislodging a shower of sand and small stones from between his toes.

Finch wound up, *his* bare foot hanging in the air, poised there with the dirt streaming from it . . . like the water from the uplifted bow of a yacht pitching in a heavy sea. The ball sped in that terrifying streak toward the plate, and the little Gandhi-like figure uncorked a swing. It all seemed instantaneous—the pitch and swing occuring at the same time, except that the action *continued:* the silver bat gave off a musical, terrifying *bong,* and the ball rose in a majestic trajectory out toward the elephant in the bull pen. I could see the mahout's face shine in the sun as he turned to watch the ball go overhead. The Gandhi-like figure trotted bow-legged around the bases accompanied by a man who hurried out from the dugout to shield him from the sun with a little silk parasol. When the pair reached the plate the slugger delivered a series of high-fives to the upstretched hands of his teammates clustered there to meet him. The parasol bobbed above them.

Sidd wanted to know what happened then.

I said that the dream, like all dreams, was somewhat fuzzy, but I had the impression that the Burmese slugger had hit two more mammoth home runs, and a Baltimore-chop single—a term I had to explain to him. On the base paths after his single he was accompanied by the parasol carrier. He moved on to second on a sacrifice bunt, hurrying down with the parasol held beautifully in place above him by his companion, but he was stranded there.

Sidd seemed fascinated by what I was telling him. Subsequently he would bring up the Burmese batter in conversation and ask me to tell him about him again. It was as if for him the dream figure had taken on corporeal qualities.

He wanted me to tell him about the real-life

titans of baseball—Ruth, DiMaggio, Mantle, Mays—I did the best I could. He also began asking me about fastball pitchers—trying to pin me down on how fast they could throw. I remembered what Frank Cashen had told me. "Nolan Ryan. Goose Gossage. About a hundred and three miles per hour. Pretty small potatoes compared to you."

He looked embarrassed. "There is nobody faster?"

Something stirred in my mind. "I've heard of one who was supposed to be much faster than either Ryan or Gossage. Or Feller or Koufax, any of those fellows. Unbelievably fast. He had a Polish name."

Sidd brought his palms together. "Please . . ."

"A friend of mine, Pat Jordan, in my *Sports Illustrated* days, wrote about him. Pat's a former pitcher. He wrote a fine book about baseball called *The False Spring*. This Polish guy never made it to the big leagues because he was wild. But he was a legend. . . ."

Sidd said, "I would be most grateful if you could find out about the Polish pitcher. . . ."

His name came to me. Steve Dalkowski. I told Sidd what I remembered. He was in the Baltimore Orioles organization in the 1960s. He had a chunky physique, well under six feet (one expected terrific speed to come out of a tall, rangy frame), and I remember Jordan telling me that his teammates called him "Moon Man" for the thick round glasses he wore. It did not help a batter's confidence to

139

step in at the plate and see the rims of those things glint in the afternoon sun.

There were all sorts of stories about him. One was that Ted Williams in spring training had picked up a bat and stepped in to take a look at Dalkowski's stuff. After one fast ball, Williams put his bat down on the plate. He stated that the only time he'd ever get in a batter's box against this guy again would be in a game situation where he *had* to.

Sidd seemed eager to find out more about Dalkowski (very much as he kept pressing me about the Burmese slugger with the silver bat) . . . indeed to such a degree that, coupled with my own curiosity, I reached for the phone one afternoon and called up *Sports Illustrated* to ask after Jordan.

They were astonished to hear from me. Was I coming back to write for them? No, I told them. I was looking for a fellow staff member, Pat Jordan. I was told he was freelancing for them. He was working out of Fort Lauderdale. They gave me his phone number.

That week I had a chance to drop in on him. It coincided with a short trip to Miami. I had to postpone a visit to Amory Blake. He urged me to go. "A trip will be good for you." He suggested a leisurely swing back up the coast, perhaps a look at Disney World in Orlando on the way back.

I flew to Miami, and rented a car. I finished my business and on the way north I stopped off and saw Pat Jordan in Fort Lauderdale. We sat on the little patio overlooking a canal. Both Pat and his wife, Susan, were body-building enthusiasts—in such superb shape and so oiled-brown from the sun that I felt pasty sitting with them. Susan had the muscles of a runner, quite unlike the smooth sheen of Debbie Sue's young legs. "Two truths," Pat said. "One is that every woman has to make peace with the realization she is not beautiful. The other is that every man has it come to him that he's not going to make it as a great athlete." He leaned forward out of his deck chair. "But you can always do something with your body. That's why Susan and I work out. We go to the gym every morning at seven o'clock." I said that was terrific. I was going to do the same at some point. I took a sip of the vodka and soda Susan had made for me.

Opposite, across the canal, moored along the seawall, was the forward half of the fuselage of a DC-4 airliner. Its owner was fashioning it into a houseboat. Halfway down its length was an ovaloid patch where the wing had been. "Terrible eyesore, isn't it," Pat said. "The guy who owns it took it out, down the canal, a couple of big outboard motors propelling it, not long ago, and all the neighbors stood along the seawall and shouted at him."

"Quite a neighborhood," I said.

Jordan gestured. "The guy down the line is an insurance collector—a guy who makes his entire living initiating lawsuits. He hangs around supermarkets waiting to hear somebody drop a jar of mustard or something so he can run around, slide in the stuff, fall down, and sue. He's the kind of guy who jams on the brakes and hopes somebody smacks into him from behind. He makes quite a nice living at it."

"You're surrounded by the stuff of novels," I said.

We reminisced for a time about the old days at *Sports Illustrated*. Susan went to jog for an hour. I told Pat a little about Sidd Finch, really no more than that he was up in St. Petersburg trying out with the Mets, that he had some theories about pitching, speed pitching in particular, and that he was curious about Steve Dalkowski.

"Another crazy who wants to pitch in the big leagues," Pat said mockingly.

"He's got great control," I said. "Learned it pegging stones at snow leopards in the Himalayas."

"Ho. Ho. Ho."

Pat was engaging and wry about his own pitching days. He was funny about catchers. "A pitcher'll walk three guys. So the catcher lifts his mask up on top of his head and he walks halfway out to the mound, the tops of his knee pads clacking, and fires the ball back. He shouts out, 'Throw *strikes!*' What the hell! So *they* know so much. Joe Torre did that to me once and I shouted back at him, 'Waddya think I'm doing out here? Trying to throw *balls?*' "

"Tell me about Dalkowski."

Jordan said, "We practically grew up together. We pitched in Connecticut high schools just down the line from each other. Dalkowski really cost me my career. He made you think that the strikeout was the only thing. I'd get two and two on a guy, and rather than trying to get him to pop up a slow curve, I'd try to steam a fastball by to strike him out. Gotta match Dalkowski! I'd lose that batter. I lost too many, trying to copy a living legend who never even made it to Triple-A. Dalkowski ruined more pitchers than he did hitters. He did everything wrong. He short-armed the ball, like a girl. He was blind—wore thick glasses. He started drinking when he was fourteen—hanging around those New Britain bars with pickled pigs feet on the counter and the bartenders don't know what a mixed drink is."

"What did he pitch like?"

"He had a small compact delivery. His arm flicked out from the side of his body. The Orioles, who had signed him, felt that the secret of his speed lay in a curiously thin and elongated wrist. Dalkowski himself had no idea. It was a gift.

"All of this started in high school. He got faster and faster. He struck out seventeen and eighteen batters a game, and usually walked about the same number. Sometimes he was able to control his delivery. In one game, with a lot of scouts in the stands, he struck out twenty-four batters and walked only four.

"He got signed into the Oriole organization in 1957. They shipped him to Kingsport, Tennessee, where he learned to chew tobacco. The reason he didn't go directly into the majors was, of course, his control. His coaches tried all sorts of things.

They'd put a batter on either side of the plate—very nervous guys they must have been—to get Dalkowski to throw down the alley between them. Then they thought maybe his control would improve if he didn't throw so fast. So they made the poor guy warm up *hard* for half an hour before a game to wear him down."

An ambulance went by, its siren wailing. Jordan said, "In this part of Florida, when you hear a siren it's either old people dropping or young people running into each other."

I asked if Dalkowski worried about hitting a batter.

"They used to say that Walter Johnson, 'The Big Train,' was scared of killing someone with his fastball. He thought of himself as a potential murderer. It got to him. It got to Dalkowski too. Finally he threw a fastball that sailed in and took a kid's ear off . . . sent him to the hospital with a concussion. The kid, who was in the Dodger organization, was never quite right after that. Had trouble remembering his name. That must have affected Dalkowski. There were any number of legends. Dalkowski threw a ball through the home-plate screen. In one game he threw a ball so fast that the batter had to go back into the clubhouse to change his pants. Dalkowski told me about it—'I threw so hard that night that I scared the whole *town.*'

"People swung in self-defense just to get out of there. Fans'd come up after a game and ask to touch his arm . . . so they could tell their grand-

144

children. I saw this. The guy came up and asked. Steve stood there blinking behind these round spectacles and he held his arm out like the man wanted. The guy looked at the arm as if it weren't really attached to anything—just dangling there like a piece of modern sculpture hanging from a wire. And he touched it, real light, with the tip of his finger.

"He was a kid, really. At Stockton, when he was there, he got fooling around with a tractor in center field and drove the thing through the clubhouse and almost got the manager, Billy DeMars, who was sitting in his office out back. On the spot DeMars bawled him out and fined him $175. Couldn't have been much of a clubhouse! But the bawling-out must have been allright, because Dalkowski went out that night and struck out seventeen and walked only two. He was obviously in need of a father figure like DeMars to keep him on the tracks."

"How fast do you reckon he was?" I asked.

"No one knows for sure. The Orioles tried to measure him at the Aberdeen Proving Grounds. But there were a number of mitigating circumstances. He threw not from a mound but on level ground. A mound was fifteen inches up, or was then, and you generate maybe ten miles per hour more speed from there. It took him forty minutes of throwing just to get the ball into the parameters of the radar measuring equipment—that'll give you some idea of his control problems—and by the time he got the ball where he wanted it, he must

145

have been exhausted. So take off eight miles or more per hour. Then he'd also pitched the night before, which usually was followed by a binge in the bars, so he couldn't have been feeling so hot. Take off five for that. As it was, the mechanism clocked him at 93.5. The consensus was that if he'd been in top pitching form and thrown from a mound, his fastball would have clocked out well over a hundred and ten miles per hour. Maybe a lot more. It left Steve's hand the size of a white dot, the proverbial aspirin, then disappeared . . . and then all of a sudden it appeared at the plate the size of a moon! It exploded! Batters went white! The odd thing was—so catchers told me who had caught him—that the fastball was as light as a feather. It was like catching one of those perforated plastic jobs—a whiffle ball. Cal Ripken caught him once in Pensacola. He was the one who told me a pitched ball from him was as light as a feather. He said that his pitch took off two feet. It went up. His control problems—thank God for the batters—were vertical rather than horizontal. If he didn't throw it at your shoe tops, you couldn't catch it. You had to keep your glove high. Once Ripken signaled for a curveball and he crouched down for it. Dalkowski never caught the sign and he threw a fastball, which sailed up and hit the umpire on the mask, broke it, and put him in the hospital for three days with a concussion. The ball hopped up to eye level."

I asked Pat if Dalkowski had any idea how he was able to throw the ball with such velocity.

He shook his head. "He wasn't much on theory, you know. He once told me, 'Sometimes the plate looked real close, like I could hand the ball to the catcher. Then the next time the thing'd be a country mile away and I couldn't find it worth a damn.' "

On a motorboat just down the way a girl turned on an electric polisher and began sanding the planking of the foredeck.

"It's almost a shipyard you've got here."

"Does your guy Finch have any idea about his pitching?" Jordan asked.

"He's a Buddhist. The technique is called lunggom"

Pat grinned and said it took all kinds. "Dalkowski once told me that a higher power took it away from him just when he had it all together. In a preseason game against the Yankees in the mid-sixties he hurt himself. In the first inning he'd struck out Roger Maris on three pitches. His arm went fielding a bunt. He flipped the ball to first and heard something go in his arm. Even after that he was throwing well over ninety. He was truly a living legend, though he never even got into Triple-A ball. He played in every Class C league in America."

"Where is he now?" I asked.

"He works the fields out in California, picking whatever crop they need hands for . . . out in Stockton, Fresno, Grapevine. He's just about the only white man out there in the groves. They say he's a hell of a picker . . . especially with oranges.

Those great baseball hands nip them off the branches like it was nothing. Down at each end of the row he keeps a bottle of cheap wine—white port—so that he's got something to work toward. Maybe that's what makes him faster than just about any of the other pickers. He's a legend in those fields."

IX

ON THE WAY back from Miami I drove up the east coast to Vero Beach, where the Dodgers have their spring training camp. The Mets were scheduled to play an afternoon game there; I bought a ticket. I thought vaguely that the management might have talked to Sidd and persuaded him to come down from St. Petersburg with the team.

The Dodger complex is much fancier than the Mets'. It has its own golf course; the streets, neatly groomed, are named after past Dodger heroes (Koufax Avenue). The hometown uniforms are such a brilliant, laundered white that it is an ease on the eyes to wear sunglasses. Tom Lasorda, their manager and famous for his consumption of pasta, moves among his players like a spinnaker. A kind of carnival atmosphere imbued the game itself. When a foul ball arched back over the stands and landed in an artificial lake, the announcer played a recording of a splash on the public address system and then the alarmed quacking of ducks.

I saw no sign of Finch. But Nelson Doubleday was sitting in a front box with Frank Cashen. After a while they spotted me up behind them in the stands and motioned me down to join them.

Doubleday introduced me to his wife, Sandra, a willowy blonde who said she knew my sister. "This guy and I met in a blimp," her husband said. She smiled politely.

"That's true," I said.

"What's the word?" Doubleday asked, coming right to the point.

"Sidd? Well, I think he likes the game," I said. "Sometimes at Huggins he watches the intrasquad games from out behind the bleachers."

"Does he talk with you about baseball?" Doubleday wanted to know.

"He's always asking . . . well . . . questions any foreigner would ask. He wanted to know what the rosin bag is for. He's struggling with the rules. He didn't understand you could tag up and take a base after a caught fly ball. We still have the infield fly rule to come."

Doubleday stirred in his seat and said in exasperation, "To think we have the best pitcher in baseball and he doesn't know what the goddamn *rosin* bag is for!"

After the game I drove north along the coast and spent the night in a motel in Melbourne. I thought about following Amory Blake's suggestion and stopping off for a day at Disney World on my way across the peninsula to the Tampa area.

I called the bungalow. Debbie Sue answered.

"Owl! Owl!" She said they missed me. They were climbing the walls. When was I coming back?

When she stopped for a breath I suggested that she and Sidd take the Volkswagen and we'd meet at Disney World the next day. They could drive down after Sidd's stint in the canvas enclosure at Huggins. We'd have the afternoon and part of the evening.

I don't know how Debbie Sue got Sidd to agree, but the two of them turned up on schedule. I waited for them at the entrance to the Magic Kingdom. I saw them coming down the midway, Debbie Sue in her Mickey Mouse shirt, Sidd in a striped jersey, Levi's, and heavy boots. Debbie Sue immediately bought him a Goofy hat with two teeth hanging off the brim, and two black ears that hung down alongside his head.

We stood in line for the rides, Debbie Sue impatient, craning, standing on tiptoe, to see why things weren't moving. She insisted on going through the Haunted House three times; we waited over an hour to take a second trip through Space Mountain. In the lines Sidd and I had a chance to talk about Dalkowski.

"My friend said he scared whole towns when he pitched," I told him. "Control. That was the ingredient that was missing."

Sidd asked if Dalkowski knew what the secret of his speed was. I replied that occasionally he talked about a Higher Power. What he'd repeat over and over to Pat Jordan was "I had it and then I lost it."

I told Sidd that he had never made it. He worked now in the fields out West as a crop-picker.

Sidd looked so melancholy in his Goofy hat that I had to smile at him.

"If he had control," I said, "he would have turned the league upside down."

"Was he a freak?"

"Maybe."

We left Disney World after dinner. We turned the rented car in and drove back together in the Volkswagen. Debbie Sue was still exhilarated by the Disney World rides. An hour out of Orlando she saw the spoked lights of the Ferris wheel at a county fair against the night sky. She shouted with pleasure. "Please! Please!" We gave in to her enthusiasm. We paid a dollar to park in a grass field.

The carnival was attached to a small circus. The performance under the tent had just ended. Outside, an elephant reached up with his trunk and helped the trainer remove a tasseled ceremonial blanket from his back. We watched jugglers perform in a sideshow booth. Insects fizzed against the lights; there was a constant throb of electric generators. Calliope music accompanied the slow revolutions of the Ferris wheel. Debbie Sue and Sidd rode together. I stood below and watched their chair sway at the apex of the ride. Debbie Sue's face appeared over the side, small and pale from that height, and she shouted down where was I?—that Owls belonged up there with them in the sky!

We wandered down the red-dirt midway. We stopped by a booth where for a dollar the customer could buy three baseballs and try to knock over a pyramid of heavy wooden bottles. We watched a few people try it unsuccessfully. A couple of bottles always seemed to be standing after a customer was done. The prizes—stuffed animals with small button eyes—squatted in rows, squashed together, up on the shelves.

"Come on, Sidd, try it."

He shook his head.

She nagged him but he refused. Finally she said she'd show him how. She put a dollar on the counter. With a little hop, she threw the first ball into the booth. The bottle at the top of the pyramid fell off.

"Do I get something?"

"They *all* gotta go, lady," the counterman said. He gazed out at the midway, his jaw working slightly on gum. He took almost no interest in the fate of his bottles behind him. Debbie Sue knocked two more over with her last throws. Hardly looking, he set the bottles back upright in their pyramid before plumping himself back down on a little stool behind the counter to resume his contemplation of the midway goings-on.

Perhaps his laconic attitude finally induced Sidd to try. He pulled out his wallet and extracted a dollar. I realized it was the first time I was going to see him throw. First he took off his boot and set it carefully by the foot of the counter. He backed off four or five steps to give the motion of his delivery plenty of room. He looked at the pyramid of bottles briefly, working his fingers around the seam of the baseball, and then, swaying back, he shot his leg, bare-footed, up into the air, stiff as a spear, and whipped the ball into the booth.

It was as if he had tossed in a grenade. The ball, whacking into the center of the triangle of bottles with sledgehammer force, produced a kind of chain reaction. The pyramid disintegrated; various splinters and bottle parts spun about like shrapnel. A bottle twirled up among the stuffed animals, clearing two or three off the shelves and setting the button eyes of three or four others bobbing. The counterman yelled, "Hey!" He half crouched as he looked back.

The baseball continued on through a baseboard into the booth *behind*. We heard the tinkle of falling pieces—china figurines, apparently, and mugs. Voices from back there called out, "Hey! Hey!"

Sidd looked a little startled at what he had done—his face drawn with apology under his Goofy hat. He spread his hands apart. He sat down in the midway, his back to the counter, dusting the dirt from his toes, and started pulling his boot back on.

"I'll have that one," Debbie Sue was saying, pointing to a large wool bear with a red ribbon around its neck.

The news of what Sidd had done swept down the midway. The countermen stood up and stared at us as we walked by. Debbie Sue stopped and played a few games. The countermen seemed very deferential, advising, helping, sliding the rings over the poles, or whatever—anything to keep the tall gawky gentleman standing behind her wearing the Goofy hat from stepping in. He carried the stuffed animals she won.

We put the animals in the front seat of the Volkswagen. Debbie Sue cuddled in the back with Sidd. "He was like a gunfighter, wasn't he, Owl—stalking down the midway and all those people jittery behind their counters?"

From the back seat Sidd cleared his throat. "Dalkowski could have done that," he suddenly said to me.

"If his control was on," I replied. "Oh, absolutely."

The next day I arrived back from Amory Blake in midafternoon. I did not expect to find either of them in; the sun was bright and a warm salt-scented wind was blowing in off the Gulf. To my surprise, Debbie Sue met me at the door. She looked worried. "The Mets have been calling all morning. The story's out."

"What story?" For a moment I thought she was referring to the destroyed booths at the carnival.

"Someone found out about Sidd and the Mets. It's in *Sports Illustrated.*"

"Where's Sidd?"

154

She told me he was out meditating by the frog pond. She had a copy of the magazine in her hand. We went out to the back porch and I took a look at it. The article was called "The Curious Case of Sidd Finch"—a fourteen-page spread accompanied by photographs of various Mets personnel—Nelson Doubleday, Frank Cashen, Mel Stottlemyre, and others, even one of Finch himself pitching on the beach, three soda-pop cans set up in the far distance as targets. Finch was in the foreground, with his hiking boot anchoring that strange delivery, a long bare foot aloft, his baseball cap on backward—unmistakably Finch, though the photograph was snapped from such a great distance that he seemed to float between the gray sky and the beach in a kind of ethereal mist.

The article was written by George Plimpton, the darkside-of-the-moon-of-Walter-Mitty fellow who, as a participatory journalist, had played briefly with the Detroit Lions, the Boston Celtics, the Boston Bruins, and so forth, in order to write about his experiences. I occasionally ran into him in my *Sports Illustrated* days—a solemn, tall figure who always seemed to hang around the premises of the editorial floor of the Time-Life Building long after everyone else had left. He walked wearily down the long corridors, as if taking a constitutional in a prison. He was trying to meet his deadlines. He did not have an office. They shunted him around to cubicles that were temporarily unoccupied because the reporters—or "writers" as they called us—were off on assignment. When I went by the open door of his cubicle he would look up instantly, as if desperate for interruption. He told me what it was like to work late in that midtown skyscraper—the place empty and quiet except for the distant moan of a floor polisher; occasionally a cleaning lady would peer in and point at the big wastebaskets by his desk and ask, "Okay?" The memorable sound, he told me, was the creak of the skyscraper itself—the girders contracting—could it be?—from the cool after the summer heat—pronounced enough at times to make him imagine he was at sea. "It's like an aircraft carrier in here—abandoned," he said mournfully.

For his article about Sidd Finch he must have had a lot of cooperation from various sources in St. Petersburg, and from the Mets themselves. Apparently the story had begun to unravel when Mel Stottlemyre, the pitching coach, felt he had to know how Finch would react with batters actually standing in at the plate. On the morning of March 14 he had gone over to the pre-practice calisthenics and walked in among the pulsation of push-ups and jumping jacks. He had pulled out three players—John Christensen, a young outfielder, Dave Cochrane, a switch-hitting third baseman, and Lenny Dykstra, a swift center fielder who at the time was thought to be the Mets lead-off man of the future and indeed has turned out to be so. Asking them to collect their bats and batting helmets, Stottlemyre led the players to the canvas enclosure.

He was reported as having said, "We'll do this alphabetically. John, go on in there, stand at the plate, and give the pitcher a target. That's all you have to do."

"Do you want me to take a cut?" Christensen asked.

Stottlemyre apparently laughed at this. He said, "You can do anything you want."

Christensen bats right-handed. As he stepped around the plate inside the enclosure he nodded to Ronn Reynolds. Reynolds whispered to him from his crouch, "Kid, you won't believe what you're about to see."

A second flap down by the pitcher's end was drawn open, and a tall, gawky player walked in and stepped up onto the pitcher's mound. He was wearing a small black fielder's glove on his left hand and was holding a baseball in his right. Christensen had never seen him before. He had gray eyes, Christensen remembers, and a pale, youthful face, with facial muscles that were motionless, like a mask. "You notice it," Christensen explained later, "when a pitcher's jaw wasn't working on a chaw of tobacco or a piece of gum."

Then, to Christensen's astonishment, he saw that the pitcher, pawing at the mound to get it smoothed out properly and to his liking, was doing so with a left foot that was bare; on the other was a heavy hiking boot.

Christensen's description of that first confrontation read as follows:

"I'm standing in there to give this guy a target,

157

just waving the bat once or twice out over the plate. He starts his windup. He sways way back, like Juan Marichal. The hiking boot is anchored on the pitching rubber. The left foot, the bare one, goes up in the air, the dirt spilling out from between the toes. The ball comes in from an arm completely straight up, and before you can blink, the ball is in the catcher's mitt. You hear it crack in the mitt and there's this little bleat from Reynolds.

"I never dreamed a baseball could be thrown that fast. The wrist must have a lot to do with it, and all that leverage. You can hardly see the blur of it as it goes by. As for hitting the thing, frankly, I just don't think it's possible. You could send a blind man up there, and maybe he'd do better hitting at the *sound* of the thing."

Christensen's opinion was echoed by both Cochrane and Dykstra, who followed him into the enclosure. When each had done his stunt, he emerged startled and awestruck.

The magazine had interviewed Ronn Reynolds. He described being called into Cashen's office one day in early March. "I was nervous because I thought I was being traded. He was wearing a blue bow tie. He leaned across the desk and whispered to me that it was very likely that I was going to be a part of baseball history. Big doings! The Mets had this rookie coming to camp and I was going to be his special catcher. All very hush-hush.

"Well, I hope nothing like that guy ever comes

down the pike again. The first time I see him is inside the canvas coop, out there on the pitcher's mound, and I'm thinking he'll want to toss a couple of warm-up pitches. So I'm standing behind the plate without a mask, chest protector, pads, or anything. I'm holding my glove up, sort of half-assed, to give him a target to throw at . . . and suddenly I see the windup, like a pretzel gone loony, and the next thing, I've been blown two or three feet back, and I'm sitting on the ground with the ball in my glove. My catching hand feels like it's been hit with a sledgehammer."

The article disclosed very little about Sidd Finch himself. The Mets front office, it reported, was "reluctant" to talk about him. The article did mention his early childhood in an orphanage, his adoption by a famous anthropologist, the supposed death of the latter in a plane crash in the Himalayas; there was a short mention of Stowe, and Finch's acceptance at Harvard.

The editors *had* tracked down his assigned roommate at the time, Henry W. Peterson, Class of 1979, now a stockbroker in New York City with Dean Witter. What Peterson remembered about being his roommate was illuminating: "He was almost never there," he told *Sports Illustrated*. "I'd wake up morning after morning and look across at his bed, which had a woven native rug of some sort on it—I have an idea he told me it was made of yak fur—and I never had the sense it had been slept in. Maybe he slept on the floor. Actually, my assumption was that he had a girl in

Somerville or something, and stayed out there. He had almost no belongings. A knapsack. A bowl he kept in the corner on the floor. A couple of wool shirts, always very clean, and maybe a pair or so of blue jeans. One pair of hiking boots. I always had the feeling that he was very bright. He had a French horn in an old case. I don't know much about French horn music but he played beautifully. Sometimes he'd play it in the bath.

"He knew any number of languages. He was so adept at them that he'd be talking in English, which he spoke in this distinctive singsong way, quite oriental, and he'd use a phrase like *'pied-à-terre'* and without knowing it he'd sail along in French for a while until he'd drop in a German word like *'angst'* and then he'd shift gears into *that* language. For any kind of sustained conversation you had to hope he wasn't going to use a foreign buzz word—especially out of the Eastern languages he knew, like Sanskrit—because that was the end of it as far as I was concerned."

When *Sports Illustrated* asked Peterson why he felt Finch had left Harvard, he shrugged his shoulders. "I came back one afternoon and everything was gone—the little rug, the horn, the staff. Actually, there was so little to begin with that it was hard to tell he wasn't there anymore. He left a curious note on the floor. It turned out to be a Zen koan, which is one of those puzzles that cannot be solved by the intellect. It was the famous one about the live goose in the bottle. 'How do you get the goose out of the bottle without hurting it or breaking the glass?' The reply is, 'There, it's out!' "

I looked up from *Sports Illustrated*.

"Has Sidd seen all this?" I asked Debbie Sue.

She nodded.

"The Mets must be having a fit. They'll assume Sidd thinks that someone on the staff leaked all this stuff."

"He didn't seem very bothered," Debbie Sue said.

She reported that he had gone down to the little pond to improve on his frog imitations, and afterward he was going to meditate on the far side of the palmetto grove.

I went back to the article.

There were some notable omissions . . . nothing in it about dropping baseballs out of a blimp to get the catchers prepared for the Finch fastball; nor had they uncovered the astonishing fact that Finch had developed his skills by throwing rocks at snow leopards creeping down on yak pens.

What was surprising was that no mention was made of Debbie Sue. She would have been a paparazzo's dream there on the dunes. The photographer (Lane Stewart) had taken some graphic pictures on the beach, quite heavily grained from the considerable distance he had clicked the shutter, but they were of Sidd alone, a foot, the bare one, with its hideously long, crooked toe discernible, arched high against the misty-looking dunes in the background. But no Debbie Sue. Obviously the photographs had been taken before the two had met.

There was a photo portrait of Mrs. Butterfield, a rather imperious lady, sitting on her porch wearing a double-stranded necklace of small shells. She verified what Cashen had told me about her vague discomfiture with Sidd Finch's horn playing, but no mention was made of his incredible ability to imitate and throw sounds. Nor did Mrs. Butterfield say anything about Debbie Sue. Apparently she had been interviewed before she had come home from the movies to find the long-legged girl from the Windsurfer lalapaloozing around her boardinghouse.

I noted some mild errors. It was reported that Finch had been offered a number of inducements—"huge contracts, advertising tie-ins, large speaking fees on the banquet circuit, having his picture on a Topps bubble-gum card, the chance to endorse sneakers and baseball mitts, chats on *Kiner's Korner* (the Mets postgame show with Ralph Kiner) and so forth." I knew for a fact that the Mets, while obviously aching to dangle such offers, had not actually spoken to Finch about any of them.

The article reported that the Mets had made inquiries among lamaseries in the United States (it turned out there are more than a hundred Buddhist societies) in the hope of finding monks or priests who were serious baseball fans. The idea (I wondered if it was Nelson Doubleday's) was that such a monk might be persuaded to show up in

Pass-a-Grille and waylay Finch . . . stop him in the street ("Namas-te") and invite him to tea, over which he would push the charms of baseball and persuade Sidd that the two religions (baseball and Buddhism) were compatible.

The Mets management had also taken notice of Finch's French horn playing. According to the article, the notion had occurred to someone that his dilemma was that he could not decide whether he wanted to play professional baseball or a French horn. In early March the club contacted Bob Johnson, who plays the horn and is the artistic director of the distinguished New York Philomusica ensemble. He was asked to come to St. Petersburg and make a clandestine appraisal of Finch's ability as a horn player, and, even more important, to make contact with him. The idea was that, while praising him for the quality of his horn playing, Johnson should try to persuade him that the lot of a French-horn player (even a very fine one) was not especially gainful. Perhaps *that* would tip the scales in favor of baseball.

So Johnson came down to St. Petersburg and hung around Florida Avenue outside Mrs. Butterfield's rooming house for a week. Johnson reported later to *Sports Illustrated*, "I was being paid for it, so it wasn't so bad. A sort of vacation for me. I spent a lot of time sitting opposite the boardinghouse on a municipal bench looking up, so I'd get a nice suntan. I held a metallic sun reflector under my chin. Every once in a while I saw Finch coming in and out of the rooming house dressed to play baseball and carrying a funny-looking black glove. He was picked up and driven away.

"One night I heard the French horn. He was playing it in his room. I have heard many great French horn players in my career—Bruno Jaenicke, who played for Toscanini; Dennis Brain, the great British virtuoso; Anton Horner of the Philadelphia Orchestra—and frankly I would say Finch was on a par with them. Very hard to believe. I was staggered. He was playing Benjamin Britten's 'Serenade,' for tenor horn and strings—a haunting tender piece that provides great space for the player—when suddenly he produced a big evocative *bwong* sound that seemed to shiver the leaves of the palms. Then he shifted to the rondo theme from the trio for violin, piano, and horn by Brahms—just sensational.

"The shift from one to the other was quite odd, it occurred to me later, almost as if one had shifted from one classical music station to another. But never mind, it was sensational. It may have had something to do with the Florida evening and a mild wind coming in over Big Bayou, and the sound of the tree-frog chorus in the background; it was remarkable. I told this to the Mets and they immediately got nervous. They sent me home— presuming, I guess, that *I* was going to hire the guy. That's not so farfetched. He can play for Philomusica anytime."

According to the piece, Davey Johnson, the Mets manager, seemed to have the most controlled and phlegmatic attitude about all of this. In the canvas enclosure, he had apparently seen Finch throw about half a dozen pitches. "They talk about a guy who can throw a strawberry through a locomotive," he said. "I thought of that when I saw Finch throw. He's dangerous. Hell, if that fastball's off target on the inside, it'd carry a batter's knee-cap back into the catcher's mitt."

But as far as talking to Finch about becoming a baseball player, he was leaving that to the front office. "I can handle the pitching rotation. Let them handle the monk. There's only one thing I can offer him, and that's a fair shake."

The *Sports Illustrated* article ended with a series of hypotheses. Suppose Finch could resolve his mental reservations about playing baseball. Suppose he was signed to a contract. Suppose he came to Shea Stadium on April 9 for opening day against the Cardinals. Presumably he would mow down the opposition in a perfect game. Twenty-seven K's. They'll put the K's up on the front of the tier in left field. Perhaps Willie McGee of the Cards might get a foul tip. Suppose Davey Johnson, realizing that in Finch's case the symbiotic relationship between mind and matter were indefatigable, pitched Sidd every three or four days at that blinding, unhittable speed. What would happen to Dwight Gooden's ego? Would Gary Carter, Ronn Reynolds, and the backup catchers last the season subjected to the steady concussion of fastballs coming in 160-odd mph? What, in fact, would it do to major league baseball as it is known today?

Sports Illustrated had gone to Peter Ueberroth, the newly elected Commissioner of Baseball, about this. The Commissioner was asked if he had heard anything about the Mets' new phenomenon.

No, he had not. He had heard some rumors about goings-on in Mets spring camp, but nothing specific.

Did the name Sidd Finch mean anything to him?

Nope.

The magazine told the Commissioner that the Mets had a kid who could throw the ball over 150 mph. Unhittable.

Ueberroth had taken a minute before asking, "Roll that one by me again?"

He was told in as much detail as could be provided about what was going on within the canvas enclosure of the compound—that a super-pitcher was coming into baseball—so proficient at his skills, so unbelievably fast, hurling the ball with such absolute accuracy, that the delicate balance between pitcher and batter could well be thrown into disarray. What was baseball going to do about it?

"Well, before any decisions, I'll tell you something," the Commissioner finally said, echoing what the magazine suggested could very well be a nationwide sentiment for the coming season, "I'll have to see it to believe it."

"Whew!" I exclaimed when I had finished the piece. I looked across at Debbie Sue.

166

"It's going to be different now," she said.

I shrugged. "Perhaps."

Sidd appeared across the little lawn. He was carrying a weedish-looking flower, which he gave Debbie Sue.

"I've read the piece in *Sports Illustrated*," I said. "You've seen it?"

"Yes."

Sidd did not seem disturbed. Perhaps he was relieved that the private sanctuary of his days in the canvas enclosure and the bungalow were over. We settled ourselves on the porch. Debbie Sue went to make us some iced tea. The phone rang on occasion. No one bothered to answer it.

"I understand from the article that Davey Johnson offered you 'a fair shake.' "

"Yes," Sidd said. "It was very nice of him, though at the time I was not sure what a 'fair shake' was. A milk shake? Debbie Sue has corrected this misapprehension."

"It means that he hopes always to be on the level with you."

"Yes, I understand," Sidd said. "I like Mr. Johnson. He chews tobacco. He wishes to stop, but his concerns make him reach for the round tin. You can see the outlines of the round tin in the back pockets of many of the players' pants. I have given him a mantra that will help him stop. When I join the team there are two or three other mantras that may be of use—"

"You're joining the team?" I said carefully.

"Oh, I think so," Sidd said. "I have worked it

out in my mind. I do not think I will play into the twilight of a career, but I will do it for a while."

"Have you told Debbie Sue?"

We could hear her stirring ice cubes in a pitcher out in the kitchen.

"She is very emotional about it."

"Have you told the Mets?"

"Not yet," Sidd said. "I thought you'd like to do that yourself. I suspect they've been calling all day."

I wondered if he suspected my links with the Mets were stronger than they had suggested.

"If you wish me to," I said vaguely.

I called them up a half hour or so later. Jay Horwitz was ecstatic. They had been worried about the effect of the *Sports Illustrated* article.

"He didn't seem to be bothered by it," I said. "He seems rather relieved that it's all out in the open."

"How about the girl?"

"She seems edgy. It's going to be quite a change for her."

"It's all a publicity director's dream," Jay said happily. "Wait'll I tell the press about lung-gom."

I asked Jay if he knew that Sidd had perfected his skills by throwing rocks at snow leopards . . . to keep them from getting into the yak pens.

"Good God!" he said. "Snow leopards! Yaks!"

He called a few minutes later to say the Mets had decided to call a conference the next day, April 1, at noon in the clubhouse. He would tell the reporters about the snow leopards and the yaks and so forth. He could hardly wait to see the expression on the face of Dick Young of the *New York Post*. After warming up in the enclosure Sidd would then go out and throw a few from the mound on the Huggins field so the press could watch his stuff.

"This seems reasonable, doesn't it? He'll answer questions?"

"I don't know," I replied. "I'll ask him tonight."

We went out that evening to celebrate. Debbie Sue spun between the two of us as if we were her ballet partners. We went to Jack's with the fishnets hanging from the ceiling and the tables outside on the dock. The Venetian lanterns lit the water. The yachts came down the canal to tie up. The men, wearing white ducks and blazers, and the women, with sweaters draped over their shoulders, stepped off on the dock to have dinner.

One of the pleasures of going out—at least for me—was the attention Debbie Sue attracted. I have no idea how it affected Sidd. I never saw him look out into the perimeters of the place. But I could see the people stirring at their tables, gossiping about the girl with us. I behaved as if Debbie Sue was with me rather than Sidd—solicitous, leaning toward her perhaps more than usual, rearranging the napkin in her lap, laughing sharply at odd moments, behaving, in sum, like a dolt.

I was contained enough to remember to say to Sidd, "They want you to put in an appearance at the press conference tomorrow." It was difficult to imagine Sidd standing before the microphone banks, his little bow, his palms together, and his soft "namas-te."

"What happens at a press conference?"

"They will ask you how your arm feels. They always do."

"And then?"

I shrugged. "You can tell them how your arm feels and then you can say 'namas-te' and go to the beaches."

"Owl, that's not the way it's going to be," Debbie Sue said. "They are going to hound him."

"Very likely."

"I will speak to them if I have something to say," Sidd said.

"That is not how it works," I said. "It's if *they* have anything to ask."

Debbie Sue thought he should play the French horn for them. " 'Strawberry Fields.' And then," she said, "you can do some of your better sounds. What would they like to hear? You could do an old-fashioned typewriter. A goose honking."

She dipped angrily into her dessert. I had no idea why she was upset. Sidd felt her mood as well. To amuse her he did a goose call right there in the restaurant, absolutely perfectly, and as heads turned Debbie Sue looked down at her plate, her hair tumbling forward, and I had the woeful feeling that for some reason she was crying inside that golden tent.

We got back from Jack's around eleven. To my relief, and I'm sure Sidd's, Debbie Sue didn't mention going down to the Bay for the usual porpoise romp. She'd said she'd had a long day.

I heard the tap on the door—soft, somewhat tentative. I was awake—as usual, trying with an unsuccessful series of mental exercises to calm my mind's busy meanderings sufficiently to drift off.

Debbie Sue came in and sat on the end of the bed. In the vague light I could see she was wearing one of my button-down shirts

"Do you mind talking?"

I made a move to get up. "No, don't budge." Her hand drifted out and she grabbed at the mound where my feet pushed up the blanket.

"I'm thinking of leaving Sidd." Her voice was throaty; I could tell she was close to tears. "It's no use. It's not going to work."

I asked her what the problem was.

"It was all right when things were simple. But now it's different. He's going to pitch. Crowds. He's going to become a celebrity. And besides, I don't see much point in being in love with a man who's interested more in The Void. Right? He's tried to help *me* reach The Void. Empty the mind, he tells me, and he says to think of the wake of a submarine disappearing into the deep. Count to a hundred. I sit in the lotus position and I try. My mind just doesn't work that way . . . . His skin smells a little bit like pepper? Have I told you that? I'm hopeless."

Absentmindedly she began massaging my toes through the thickness of the blanket.

"Do you know what he said to me once? He said, 'Debbie Sue, you are a very unlikely candidate for achieving *bodhicitta*'—that's what everyone strives for."

"What did you say?"

"I said, 'Well, fry my ass.' It just came out. He didn't seem to mind. I don't think it makes much difference to him."

I asked, "Do you have arguments with him?"

"Oh, no. But Owl, being in love with a Buddhist monk isn't easy. But what am I doing this for? I don't see him settling down, do you? Monks don't. They're in love with something else. They're in love with the idea of being monks, at least that's what I think. I wish it were all different. I love to hear him talk about the trains in the ballroom of that house in London. I love to hear him play his horn. I love it when we swim naked in the Bay at night. But it's all going to change."

"Maybe baseball will change him," I suggested. "Baseball will be his expression of bodhicitta."

"I'm too selfish," she said. "I don't want anything else to have him."

She sat for a while in the darkness. "Tell me something, Debbie Sue," I said. "How did it start? What happened there in the dunes when you came ashore that day on your Windsurfer?"

"Why?"

"Well, Sidd's . . . ah," I said awkwardly, "not exactly a prize catch—at least not on the beaches around here."

"What about love at first sight?"

172

I shrugged. I could sense her smiling in the darkness at the foot of the bed.

"I know what you think, Owl. You think I was *sent* by someone. That's why you yelled that awful word at me a couple of days ago in the hall—'Ueberroth!' You thought I was going to break down and fess up to everything. 'Yes, yes, I *am* from the CIA.' "

"Something like that," I admitted.

"Oh, Owl, you're too paranoid. Sometime I'll tell you what happened in the dunes. But not tonight."

I asked if Sidd was aware of her dilemma.

"I think so," she said, "I think he reads my mind. Yesterday he told me a sutra of Buddha's to help me out. It's about a tiger who chases a man to the edge of a cliff. The man grasps a vine and swings out over the edge. The tiger comes to the edge and looks down at him. And then from down below, another tiger appears and looks up at him. And then guess what? Two *mice*, one black, and the other white, begin to chew on the vine. The man sees this. So he lets go of the vine with one hand and he grabs a *strawberry* from a bush growing in the cliff face. He pops the strawberry in his mouth? He thinks, '*How sweet it tastes.*' "

"He's telling you to look on the bright side of things?" I asked.

"Oh, I guess so," she said. "But it doesn't help much."

I asked her what she thought she was going to do.

"I might go and see my father. But I'm not going to tell him what's happened—that I've fallen in love with an English-Buddhist-monk-*pitcher*. I don't know if he could take all that. I can't tell him I've gone crazy over a guy who can *throw* a ball farther than he can hit it with a golf club. Besides, I don't know how Dad feels about Buddhist monks. He'd get it into his head that I was going with a white-bearded guru, snuggling up against his shoulder in the back seat of a Rolls-Royce?"

We shifted on the bed.

"Do you know what I keep thinking about?" she asked.

"What?"

"Do you remember the oxygen tank he told us about near Mount Everest . . . the one they ring to separate the monks from the nuns in the monastery when it's night? I think a lot about what an awful sound it must be."

"I remember you said how beautiful it must be."

"Yes. But I was thinking of the bell and not what it meant."

"Well, I hope you think it over before you decide."

She promised she would. "It may be just a phase," she said. "I like to have phases."

I told her that I thought a good night's sleep might help. "I'd stick it out for a while. See what happens," I said. "You can't do yourself any harm. It might help matters."

At the door she turned and I heard the whisper of her shirt as she bowed and announced, "I salute the spirit within you."

X

THE NEXT MORNING Debbie Sue seemed in fine spirits. She begged off going to Huggins for either the press conference or Sidd's appearance on the mound. "I'll watch it on television," she said. She suggested I wear a Mickey Mouse shirt she had bought at Disney World in case I wandered into the view of the television cameras. In deference to her good mood and not wishing to jostle it in any way, I agreed to wear Mickey Mouse. She also wanted me to wear Sidd's Goofy hat with two teeth hanging from the brim of the cap and two long black ears on the side, but here I resisted.

I left before Elliot Posner arrived to drive Sidd off to Huggins. I had two appointments on my master chart that morning. One was with Amory Blake and the second, of course, at the Mets noon conference with reporters and television people at which Finch was to be presented.

I had a strange occurrence for Blake I had read in the newspaper in Miami the time I saw Pat Jordan and talked to him about Steve Dalkowski. It was an Associated Press story about a man named Paul Tavilla who specialized in catching grapes in his mouth dropped from tall buildings.

It caught my attention because it reminded me of the day we had dropped baseballs out of the blimp.

This guy had caught a grape in his mouth dropped from a fifty-two-story building in Tokyo. He was trying to do the same thing on the sidewalk in front of the seventy-two-story InterFirst Bank Building in Dallas, Texas. According to the AP story, thirty pounds of grapes had pelted the sidewalk around Tavilla. None of them had landed in his mouth. He kept at it for almost an hour, staring up with his mouth ajar. He complained that the reflection off the glass building made it hard for him to see the falling grapes, and that the wind was a problem as well. "This is the worst wind I have had to encounter," he said to the reporter.

"Very interesting," Blake said when I described Mr. Tavilla's problems in Dallas. "Verifiable?"

I said the article was an AP dispatch and I gave him the date it was filed. "I have it at home."

"How's your writing?" Blake asked. "It would please me if this item of yours was written down on a yellow legal pad."

I lied and said I had almost done it that way. "It's slow," I said.

"Do you have any cartoon captions for me?" he asked.

"I'm having difficulties with the drawings," I said.

When I left him he was writing down in a looseleaf notebook what I had told him about the man who caught grapes in his mouth.

I had trouble parking the Volkswagen at Huggins. More cars were parked along Fifth Street, which borders the field, than usual, and I noticed a couple of big television vans. Too many reporters were on hand to cram into Frank Cashen's minuscule office, so the conference was held in the larger confines of the clubhouse locker room. There was no sign of Sidd. I stood in the back of the room. A lot of the reporters had copies of the *Sports Illustrated* article with the story about Finch.

Jay Horwitz had given everybody a fact sheet about Sidd. It mentioned his education, his trips to the Himalayas, and that his skills could be attributed to the "Tibetan practice of lung-gom." Jay stood in front of a bank of microphones. His pale face looked out over the crowded club house. The lamps accompanying the television crews snapped on, the light so strong that, even in the sun streaming through the clubhouse windows, our shadows flickered in and out of the cubicles.

Jay said, "Sidd Finch's here at Huggins, but he's very shy about appearing before the press at this time. He's throwing in the canvas enclosure some of you may have noticed at the north end of the complex. He'll be coming out to the playing field to throw a few pitches for you. Then tomorrow night, at Al Lang Field, Davey Johnson plans to pitch Finch for three innings in the 'B' squad Blue Jays game."

Jay stepped aside and Davey Johnson took his place at the microphones. His voice seemed to have a slight edge to it; it occurred to me once again that the manager was disturbed that an element existed among his responsibilities that he could not quite fathom. "This guy's for real," he started off.

A babble of questions rose.

Johnson said, "You'll see for yourself out on the field. I don't know what more I can add. . . ."

Someone's persistence got him through with a question about fielding drills. "Does he go to sessions for the pitchers?"

"He hasn't been required to do that," Johnson replied. "No. First of all, as you know, the guy didn't decide until yesterday whether to play baseball. He's only just signed a contract."

"But aren't those drills important?" the reporter persisted.

Johnson made an abrupt, impatient motion. "We do have sessions that deal with a pitcher's responsibilities on fielding plays, what to do in bunt situations, where he should go after a basehit. We review balk situations, cut-off assignments, things like that. To tell you the truth, I don't think—from what I've seen there in the canvas enclosure—that any of these things are applicable in Sidd Finch's case. Baseball people talk about taking a thrower and turning him into a pitcher. No need here. Finch doesn't need to know anything about pitching. It's a good idea to rub up the ball so it isn't too slippery. We might teach him that, but nothing much more."

"Davey, we hear the guy's here in camp for only a few minutes every day."

"That's right. Doesn't even take a shower. He leaves the canvas enclosure and gets right in the training-camp car and is taken away to where he's been staying in Pass-a-Grille. The kid who drives the car—Finch can't drive—tells us he doesn't sweat in there. Cool as a cucumber. He has never seen him mop his brow. He doesn't even stick to the seats."

"He doesn't what?"

"Stick to the seats . . ."

After a few more questions Davey Johnson was followed to the microphones by Mel Stottlemyre. He seemed much more at ease with the questions . . . as if Finch was just another cipher in a long line of people he was training to maximum efficiency.

"How fast is he, Mel?"

"Quickest I ever saw . . . ever dreamed of."

"Is that figure in *Sports Illustrated* right? A hundred and sixty-eight?"

"Damn close."

Someone asked if anyone had figured out the key to Finch's ability.

"We can tell what part of it is," the Mets coach said. "We've looked at films and slowed everything down. There are a number of things to notice . . . an incredible cocked-wrist snap, for one. It's just a blur, even in the slo-mo footage. He has very long, supple wrists and fingers, but I'd guess the strength is terrific. Snap a chopstick between his fingers! Did you know that the crack of a whip is caused by the tip flicking so fast that it breaks the sound barrier . . . what you hear is a little sonic boom? Well, that's what I've read anyway, and it's what I'm reminded of with that flick of Finch's wrist. It actually makes a sound, a kind of *craack*. You'll hear it."

"What about the arm motion?" someone asked.

"The wrist snap comes off the arm snap with the elbow leading exactly as it should, parallel to the ground; it's another blur in the tapes. It's a perfect motion. The body balance looks a little crazy, the foot way up there like the guy was trying to kick something over his head, but it makes a perfect fulcrum for his delivery. You're not going to find me fiddling too much with it," he added with a laugh. "You're not going to find me telling him he's rocking too far back on his hind foot, or anything like that."

Mel Stottlemyre cleared his throat. "We're rather proud of what we've done with this kid. We taught Sidd how to throw the slider. Apparently they don't know how to throw the slider in Tibet or Nepal. The interesting thing about Sidd's slider is that it's going so fast you can't tell whether or not it *is* a slider. The thing just—*bam*—arrives in Ronn Reynolds' glove. For all I know the pitch could have gone out over the alligator pond and back." He laughed and slipped a sunflower seed between his lips.

"How about the change-up?" someone else asked.

Stottlemyre shrugged and said that the normal change-up takes about fifteen percent off the pace

180

of the ball. "That would put Sidd's change-up down in the hundred-and-thirty-miles-per-hour range where a fastball hitter might be able to put his bat on it. We didn't reckon there was much sense in that, though Ronn Reynolds"—a wry smile crossed the coach's face—"put up a strong case for nothing *but* change-ups. If you're going to ask me if we taught him how to throw a knuckleball, the answer is no. Since pitchers have no idea where a knuckleball is going, there wouldn't be a catcher in camp who wouldn't head for the hills."

Ronn Reynolds stepped up. In uniform, he was carrying his mask and catcher's mitt. He had just a few minutes before heading for the enclosure.

He was asked, "Do you have a special stance, Ronn?"

"I have to keep my arm crooked a bit," he said, "so that when the ball smacks in there, it'll give. If I kept my arm straight and stiff, I could lose a damn shoulder."

"It's that violent a blow, Ronn?"

He nodded. "It's a concussion."

"Where do you pick up the ball after it's left that guy's fingertips?"

Reynolds thought for a second or so. "Maybe ten feet from the plate. There's no time to do anything. A good fastball you can pick up pretty quick—maybe thirty, forty feet out. But not this thing."

Someone asked, "Ronn, does his fastball rise?"

Reynolds smirked. "I can't tell you. It's going too fast."

"Does it make a sound?"

Ronn Reynolds thought about it. "Well, it doesn't. Maybe a little *pft*. A real good fastball will make a sound like ripping silk. But not Finch's. It just arrives. Or to put it another way, suddenly it's *there. Pft-boom!*"

"What's that again?"

"Pft-boom!"

When Reynolds was done Jay Horwitz once again stepped to the microphones and from the back of the room I suddenly heard my name mentioned.

"We're glad to have Robert Temple here," Jay was saying. "Sidd Finch is staying in his house in Pass-a-Grille. Bob is perhaps his best friend. We've asked him—since Sidd himself is apparently somewhat reticent about press conferences—to try to answer a few questions about Sidd's background. Afterwards, we'll go out to the field and see the guy himself."

Heads turned as I walked up toward the microphones. I must have made a somewhat odd impression. It could hardly have added to the portentousness of the occasion that I was wearing Debbie Sue's Mickey Mouse T-shirt. When I got to the podium I could see that a few of the press sitting down there in front recognized me—if not by sight, by name. I could see my name being mouthed as one of them would lean over to another: "Isn't that the guy . . . ?"

Some floodlights went on. First they wanted to know why Sidd would not speak for himself.

"He's shy."

The pencils worked busily.

"What's his problem?"

I had thought about it myself long enough to answer, "I think it's a problem of collision of cultures. He is, after all, an Englishman. He's also studying to be a Buddhist monk. And now he's a pitcher. It's a strain to be any one of these three."

I said all this haltingly, and without humor. "Bob," someone called out, looking down at the press release, "what is this lung-gom?"

I was immediately seized by a violent coughing fit. I am inexperienced in standing before microphones, in particular an amplifying system, so the sound of my temporary misery, before I turned my head away, was magnified to a verifiable typhoon in the clubhouse.

"Essentially," I was finally able to say, "it's a kind of mind-over-matter state that controls the physical. I am not an expert in these matters."

"Where'd he learn this stuff?"

"He told me he studied lung-gom at a place whose name means 'The Happy Cave' in the Upper Nyang Valley."

"Hold it! Hold it!" I was asked to spell the name of the place and "lung-gom" for someone who didn't have Jay's press sheet.

"There are all sorts of rituals about this place," I said. "One of them is that the monks wishing to attain lung-gom enter a meditation cubicle, and when they emerge a long time later it is almost as if they have shed a personality and have been born again. Sidd told me he spent a long time in one of these cells. It sounds like a place of torture or punishment. Actually it's simply a rather practical place to *think,* freed from life . . . with a view of the sky through a hole in the roof. I believe he had some things in there with him connected with daily rituals—a book, a bell, butter lamps, a couple of pans. Sidd told me he was sealed up in there for about a year."

"Sealed up?"

"The length of time really depends on the will of the monk himself. The shortest periods range from one to three months. The middle-range monks stay in there three or four years, and when Sidd Finch was there a hermit was in his fourth year and intended to stay in there for six!"

Some of the pencils had stopped working. A number of the reporters were staring at me. They looked like students being given an exam in a course they had not signed up for. I went on, "The only entrance to the meditation cell is closed up. No one is allowed to speak to the lung-gom-pa. In fact, they can't even see him. When Sidd reached through this little opening for his supplies, he covered his hands with a sock or a cloth bag.

"You might be interested to know that Sidd told me that he wasn't allowed to heat up his tea pot with yak dung, which is the most commonly used fuel in those mountain areas. Why? Because yak dung might contain beetles and a worm or two—animals that would be consumed in the fire under the kettle. That's not something anyone wants to do who is trying to generate love and compassion for all living things. So the stuff Sidd used is a kind of giant, hardened moss that apparently doesn't have any animal life hidden in it."

Suddenly I noticed Jay motioning to me from the side of the room—frantically, as if the urgency of what he had to say preempted everything else. Jay hurried me outside.

"Christ, that was awful," I said. "I've never been so embarrassed. They must think I'm crazy . . . yak dung!"

"That's nothing compared to what's happened out here." Jay looked ashen.

"What's wrong?"

"A terrible thing's happened out there in the enclosure," Jay whispered to me. "Sidd's lost his control. He threw a ball through the backstop. Ronn Reynolds! Poor guy's been damn near traumatized."

"Where's Sidd?"

Jay said that he had disappeared. "Right after this he ran out of the enclosure for the car, jumped in, and Elliot Posner drove him away."

"God Almighty." I asked Jay how many pitches Sidd had thrown.

"I hear just two. The first one hit an iron pipe of the structure that holds up the canvas. High behind Reynolds. Terrible sound. Went out the top of the enclosure and landed in the pond. The second one was the one that went through the backstop. When Reynolds heard the rip of the ball going through, he hustled out of the enclosure. No more for him!"

"One can hardly blame him," I said.

The reporters were beginning to complain. I could hear their voices drifting out through the clubhouse windows. One or two came out on the field. They held their notebooks folded back. They wanted to know what the hell was going on. Where was this guy they'd been hearing so much about? The Kathmandu Fireballer? Was this all some kind of a joke?

Jay went in to see if he could restore order. He asked me to go with him. I stood off to one side. Most of the people in the clubhouse were standing up and yelling at him. "Come on, Jay. Give us a break. Where is this guy?"

Jay stood in front of the microphones. In the sudden glare of portable sunguns clicked on by the television people, his huge shadow wavered on the wall behind him.

"Finch has gone home," he said simply. "There's nothing more that I can say at this time."

The mood in the clubhouse became rather unpleasant. "Whaddya mean? You gotta be kidding! April Fool's joke," I heard one of the reporters mutter. Another came by and said pointedly at me, "Lung-gom, my ass." I think it was Dick Young of the *New York Post*. The television crews made a point of slamming down the lids of their

186

equipment trunks. There was no sign of either Davey Johnson or Mel Stottlemyre.

"What do you think happened?" Jay asked me.

"I don't know," I said. "Sidd once told me the whole process was quite fragile. Something must have snapped."

I drove to the bungalow. I expected to find Sidd. He had left Huggins Field only a half hour or so before. I called out his name. Hers. The place was deserted. Both had packed and gone. I looked around their room. I remembered Sidd had left a koan on the floor for his Harvard roommate when he left there. I peered around for one. The place was spotless. Some of the stuffed animals from Disney World were set in a row along the wall. Their bed was made. Just the faintest summery tang of Debbie Sue's suntan oil. A straw waste-paper basket was overturned, but when I set it upright I looked in it to find it empty.

The phone rang off in the depths of the bunga-low. It was Jay Horwitz.

"I have a letter here from Sidd," he said. "He wrote it out in your house. It was delivered here by the driver."

"Sidd wasn't with him?"

"No."

"Nor the girl?"

"No sign of her. Elliot dropped Sidd off at a taxi stand. He had his belongings with him. His French horn case. Elliot has no idea where he ordered the taxi driver to go."

He read me the letter. As he did so I could almost imagine the curlicues and flourishes of Sidd's curiously antique penmanship:

Dear Mr. Doubleday:

First, I wish to express my gratitude to the management of the New York Mets. The office in the front has treated my requests for solitude and secrecy with respect. I am especially thankful to the coaches, above all Mr. Stottlemyre, who showed me the art of the slider, a phenomenon unknown in my former place of habitation in the foothills of the Himalayas. Next, my appreciation to Ronn Reynolds, who was usually designated to receive The Perfect Pitch during my month of tryout. His swollen left hand attests to his fortitude, and I apologise if this has caused him to be less valuable to your ball club.

Now to the matter at hand. The concentration which is a major part of my ability to throw a ball with great velocity and to a specific point, namely the pocket of Ronn Reynolds' catcher's mitt wherever he places it as a target, is not as intense as it was when I first arrived. Today, April 1, I threw two balls which went wide of Mr. Reynolds. One hit a pipe. The other tore a hole in the backstop. I have come to realise that The Perfect Pitch, once a thing of Harmony, is now potentially an instrument of Chaos and Cruelty. As we might say in the foothills of the Himalayas, "The horsehide has developed cloven hooves."

There are other reasons as well, which are

personal and thus cannot be resolved by the management of the Mets. Alas, I had looked forward to a summer in New York (that is if I had been fortunate enough to make the team) and to travel to such places as Pittsburgh.

There might be conditions which would change the situation, but these would be personal considerations. There is a Zen koan which is applicable. It is, "What do you say to one who has nothing to carry about?" The response is, "Carry it along." My good friend, Robert Temple, will be cognisant of any further developments.

I see no point in suggesting what these might be, since I have no idea myself.

Very best wishes,
Sidd Finch

Jay asked, "What is all that? What does it mean—'nothing to carry about'?"

"I really don't know," I said truthfully. "It's one of those koans. It's got a bit of that Finch flavor, doesn't it?"

"Did you know he was quitting?"

"No," I said. "Last night I thought he was solid with the idea of being a baseball pitcher."

Jay asked if I thought the article in *Sports Illustrated* had anything to do with it.

"I don't think so," I said. "He knew that the news about him was bound to break out. I believe he was rather amused."

"Do you think they left together?"

I told Jay that I suspected so.

"Everyone around here thinks the girl is responsible," Jay said. "You don't suppose she's from the Minnesota Twins . . . psyching him out just enough to get him off the premises so they can sign him?"

"I doubt it. He was very appreciative of the way the Mets have behaved toward him."

"You think he'll come back?"

"I don't know. I'm sorry I couldn't do better for you."

"Damn shame," Jay said. "What was it we were all saying . . . that he could . . ."

" 'Change the face of the future,' " I prompted him. "Maybe it's better this way," I went on. "I think it worried him."

"Well, maybe we'll never know," Jay said. "It's almost as if it had never happened."

Almost as soon as I finished talking to Jay, the phone rang again. Debbie Sue's voice, troubled, obviously, was on the other end.

"Where are you?" I asked.

"I'm looking for Sidd."

"I thought you were *with* Sidd somewhere."

"No," she said mournfully. "I've made a bad mistake."

"He's not here, Debbie Sue," I said. "Huggins is in an uproar. I had a bad time this morning. I got talking to the reporters about yak dung."

"Poor Owl. With your Mickey Mouse shirt. Did he say where he was going?"

"Not a word."

She told me what had happened. That morning, just before Sidd left for Huggins, almost on impulse, she had said she was leaving him and going home. It wasn't going to work out.

"I told Sidd a taxi was coming for me."

"What did he do?" I asked.

"Sidd? Oh, Owl, his lip trembled. He said, 'Even a good thing isn't as good as nothing.' I thought about that, and I said, 'Sidd, what in God's name does *that* mean, tell me?' He said to me, 'No more, no less than the others,' and I ran out the door."

"Where'd you go?"

"I went to my family's. I cried all the way there—all the way down the causeway. Just as I walked in the door I realized I'd made a mistake, a bad one. So I said, 'Hi, Dad'—he was standing there with his arms outstretched—and I turned around and got into the same taxi I had come in. I called out to my dad. He was standing there staring at me with this funny look as I ran down the path—that I'd call later and explain."

"I think that's advisable," I said. "He must be quite confused—your dad."

"Poor Dad never had a chance to say a word? I'll call him as soon as I find Sidd."

"Do you know where he is?"

"No," she said. "I drove to Huggins. They told me about the catastrophe. He's disappeared."

After a pause I asked, "Do you have any ideas . . . where he's gone?"

"No," she said. "I was hoping *you'd* know. I

was hoping he'd come back to the bungalow and leave a message."

"He came back to get his things. But there's nothing left."

"No note?"

"I'm sorry. But that last thing he told you—that nothing is better than a good thing—doesn't that mean that he's going off looking for The Void again? A monastery perhaps?"

"Oh God," Debbie Sue said. "What's Dad going to say when I phone him from *Tibet?*"

I said I hoped that she would keep in touch. I tried to be jocular. If she ever wanted a partner to go out and visit her porpoises, I was available . . . preferably when there was a moon.

The Mets were on the phone for a few days wondering if I had heard from Sidd. I said I had no news. I told them I suspected he had gone to some kind of retreat. I called the Chung Te Buddhist Association in New York and got a list of places he might have gone—the Shasta Abbey in Northern California, the Golden Mountain Dhyana Monastery in San Francisco, and the Tail of the Tiger Center near Barnet, Vermont. I called two or three and asked if a man with a French horn had passed by. Whoever was at the other end put down the phone. I waited a long time for the person to come back and say that no, no such man had passed through the gates. I wrote him a letter c/o Chung Te Buddhist Assoc. of New York saying that I hoped he would stay in touch, that I valued his friendship. It was quite a long letter.

As I mailed it I realized it was the first lengthy communication I had written in a decade, short of a laundry note or two, to be read by another's eyes.

Alas, it never was. After a few weeks the letter came back from the Chung Te Buddhist Association stamped *Addressee Unknown*.

Part
II

XI

I MISSED THEM. For the first time the bungalow seemed not a sanctuary, shadowy, like a warm burrow—as Debbie Sue once referred to it—but gloomy and quiet. I went outside and sheared away some of the shrubbery to let the sun come in. I put up the volume on the phone and sometimes I found myself hurrying down the little hallway to answer it—hoping to find either of their distinctive voices at the other end . . . almost hearing in my head as I reached for the receiver Debbie Sue's "Owl, it's the owl-lover," or the modulum of Sidd's soft "namas-te."

Never. Wrong number. I had a listing very close to that of the local Baptist church. The few friends I made in Pass-a-Grille telephoned on occasion—one of them a girl to whom I confided too much and who thought the concussion and communality of a local disco would solve my problems. She wore a black, tight skirt with portholes up the thighs. I watched her through the cigarette smoke. Sometimes a young man materialized in front of her, drawn to her, and she would acknowledge his presence by adapting the strange, stiff movements of the dance to his, a pair of puppets. I watched her, thinking of Debbie Sue and how she ignored the people around her on a dance floor. My date invariably said, "Whew!" when she sat down at our table, so small that our knees knocked.

I told Amory Blake about her. He nodded and was, as usual, "pleased." He said I was "coming along very nicely."

I felt I *was* improving. I actually wrote down a strange occurrence for him. He took the three-by-five card on which I'd written it down in curiously tiny lettering—quite novel—and read it aloud to me. It was interesting to hear my words. They concerned a Los Angeles man who had attached a number of big helium-filled weather balloons to the kind of summer-lawn deck chair that reclines and has holes in each armrest for a glass of gin and tonic. His intent was to go up above Long Beach for a short flight. He planned to control his altitude by popping the balloons with an air pistol. Just off the ground, he dropped the pistol by mistake, and, wearing Bermuda shorts, he rose in his deck chair out of the backyard to a terrifying ten thousand feet or so, indeed spotted by commercial pilots bringing their planes into the Los Angeles airport. Incredibly, he came down safely . . . about twenty miles or so from his starting point. Quite a saga! I thought it would fit very nicely into Blake's files. But after he had inspected my three-by-five card, and turned it over to see if anything was written on the back side, he made a slight moue of disappointment. Perhaps my co-researchers—the chauffeur or the advertising executive—had already discovered the item. No matter.

Smitty called a few times. He was getting ready to take the *Enterprise* north—a leisurely trip up the East Coast to New Jersey. He told me that when he flew over the Florida inlets he could see a fan of sharks at the entrance, holding in the water just offshore, swimmers not a dozen feet from them. "They're harmless—thresher sharks most of them—but if those people down there only knew what was right next door to them!"

He asked me if I'd like to take part of the trip with him. It was about as nice a way to go as there was—in a big gasbag harbinger of the spring meandering north up the coast.

I demurred. I told him I was planning to come up later in the summer—perhaps July to spend a month with the family in Marblehead. I'd try to look in on him on the way.

"Hey, you remember that crazy morning in the blimp?" he asked. "Dropping those baseballs?"

"Hard to forget."

"A practical joke, I hear," Smitty said. "I'll tell you something. Those guys on the Mets sure went to a lot of trouble to pull that one off. That's the wildest I ever heard of. . . ."

The afternoon he left he flew the blimp over Pass-a-Grille. I heard the clatter of the engines. Its shadow passed over my bungalow. I wondered if Smitty had done this on purpose—a gesture. I went out into the street and waved up at the gray bulk, as big as an apartment house, going overhead.

Life went pretty much back to normal. I referred to my cardboard master chart every morning. Opening day for the Mets came and went. Gooden pitched at Shea. The Mets beat the St. Louis Cardinals 6-5 in the tenth on a Gary Carter solo-shot home run. I read about it in the papers.

I wondered about Sidd and Debbie Sue. I supposed that he had gone back to his studies somewhere, perhaps even to the Himalayas. I had no idea where Debbie Sue had disappeared. Perhaps she had caught up to him. Perhaps she had gone back to Duke to finish out her spring term. Sometimes I went down to the beaches and looked beyond the incoming lines of surf to see if she was out there on her board . . . convinced that I could recognize her slim body and the arch of it against the wind. I would wave her in with a towel. In the darkness of the bungalow I imagined this, and the glint of the sea water on her skin. I thought of writing down *Debbie Sue* on my master chart so I would be formally scheduled to go down to the beaches to look. But it was melancholy to leave the beaches without a glimpse of her, so I kept pretty much to my regular appointments. I was surprised, and a bit hurt, that they did not telephone. Of course perhaps the thing was ringing in the shadows when I was out.

As for the public, the idea got around fairly quickly that the whole Sidd Finch thing was a hoax—a grandiose practical joke. After all, the article in *Sports Illustrated* had appeared in their April 1 issue—April Fool's Day. That should have been a tip-off enough. Someone pointed out in the local newspaper that one of the meanings of the word *finch* in the Oxford English Dictionary is "a fib, a lie." And what about all those crazy excesses—the fact that he could throw a ball 168 miles per hour! And what about all those weird mannerisms—playing the French horn, for Chrissakes, and pitching with one foot bare and the other foot anchored by a woodsman's boot for balance! A Buddhist monk? Come on! How did *Sports Illustrated* and the Mets—who apparently went along with this lunacy—have the gall to try to put this sort of thing over on the public!

The following issue of *Sports Illustrated* ran a short piece on Sidd Finch's disappearance that suggested, rather unconvincingly, that he had given up baseball for the French horn. The story was buried in the magazine . . . as if the editors were trying to forget the whole business. The letters column was lively. One subscriber, incensed that what he considered his "sports bible" had bamboozled him, canceled his subscription not only to *Sports Illustrated* but to all his other Time-Life publications: *People, Fortune, Discovery, Time, Money, Life,* and so forth, just clearing the decks of them. He added a postscript: "How you like *them* berries?"

The articles about Sidd tailed off in other papers and magazines and then disappeared.

One, however, I read with considerable interest.

It appeared in the Sunday edition of the St. Petersburg *Times*—the June 15 issue—written by Mike Marshall, the Cy Young Award winner in 1974 (the first relief pitcher to win the honor) and the present-day coach at St. Leo's College, not far from Tampa. He holds a doctorate in physiological psychology from Michigan State University. I had always admired him for promoting the concept that whatever a person's physique, the muscles could be trained and developed . . . to the degree that hope existed for the fat kid who thought he was forever doomed to be picked last and sent out to stand forlornly in the deepest oak-shadowed recesses of right field.

His article—which was very technical—hypothesized about what had to be going on within the frame of Finch's body to be able to throw a ball 168 miles per hour. He started off with an arresting lead line: "We're talking death here."

Never having seen Finch, Marshall had to do a lot of guesswork. He felt there had to be a freakish difference in how Sidd's muscles were shaped—that rather than fan-shaped muscles, he had an abnormal abundance of bipinnate and multipinnate muscles, which can transfer contractions with much more velocity and efficiency. Marshall hypothesized that the force generated by this oddity could be as much as three to four times normal.

He was particularly speculative about the pronator teres muscle, "a very important muscle in baseball throwing which rises from the medial epicondyle and attaches to the medial surface of the radial bone. The greater the distance from the fulcrum of the elbow joint to the attachment of the pronator teres, the greater the leverage, and thereby the force the pronator teres generates. Mr. Finch's"—Marshall referred to Sidd throughout as "Mr. Finch"—"pronator teres attachment must exceed the norm of professional baseball players considerably, indeed by almost fifty percent—a mechanical advantage giving Mr. Finch an overdrive gear in his throwing motion."

He paid special attention to the latissimus dorsi muscle, "the horizontal extension muscle of the shoulder joint that decelerates the throwing arm after it releases the baseball. It is the multipinnate muscle type that permits Mr. Finch to do this over a very short distance and time period." I took this to mean that if it weren't for that particular musculature, Sidd's arm, moving forward at that wondrous speed, would tend to tear away from his body before he could stop it.

Here's what Marshall had to write about the pitching motion itself:

"Even with all these anatomical advantages Mr. Finch would not necessarily throw faster than other pitchers. However, I am sure that high-speed triangulated cinematography with telemetry electromyography analysis would disclose that Mr. Finch's mechanics for accelerating his throwing arm maximally are flawless. Because of the extension of his arm due to the multipinnate nature of his pectoralis major muscle we estimate that Mr. Finch can begin to apply force during the propulsion phase of a pitch when the baseball is 28.63 inches behind the ear—the previous best posterior force application being 19.18 inches. However, the most remarkable parameters must occur at the *end* of the delivery—during the anterior force application. The throwing-arm elbow stops forward of the pitcher's ear much as the handle of a bullwhip snaps to a stop and the tip of the whip accelerates to the speed of sound." I remembered what Mel Stottlemyre had said about the curious flicking sound of Sidd's motion. "Because Mr. Finch has a multipinnate latissimus dorsi and bipinnate supraspinatus and teres minor muscles, he can snap his throwing arm to a stop a dramatic 13.14 inches in front of his ear—twice any recording known, thus being able to accelerate the baseball over an incredible 41.77 inches, propelling it on an almost perfect linear forward path instead of the elliptical path other pitchers follow!

"We are able to determine the initial velocity of the released ball. Mr. Finch releases the ball at 255.25 ft. per sec., or 174 mph. The friction of the air molecules would decelerate the baseball 17.6 ft. per sec. or to the reported 168 mph Mr. Finch can throw. Mr. Finch releases the ball 66 inches in front of the pitching rubber. At an average velocity of 246.45 ft. per sec. or 168 mph, Mr. Finch's fastball crosses the rear tip of the plate .218 after he releases the baseball."

Well, there it was—a fifth of a second . . . the time span of a wink! As I sat with the newspaper in my hand I blinked a few times, pretending the ball was in the air over that time span, and trying to imagine what it would be like to stand in against such a zoom of speed. No wonder Marshall had commented, "We're talking death here."

In conclusion Marshall described two medical tests that he thought might turn up interesting facts about Mr. Finch. He felt that if Sidd's muscles were biopsied they would show over "eighty percent fast-twitch phosphogenic muscle fibers . . . which, since these fibers contract faster than either slow-twitch exaline or fast-twitch glycolytic, Mr. Finch would generate a remarkably high muscle contraction velocity."

He also wrote that since Mr. Finch was studying to be a monk, and in the Buddhist tradition as well, that it was unlikely he was using any drugs. He suspected, though, that a blood test after a pitching performance would show a very high level of adrenaline, which is produced by the adrenal glands in response to stress. Having noted the references to lung-gom in one or two of the releases about Sidd, Marshall wrote, "Apparently Mr. Finch controls his adrenaline production voluntarily." Marshall added a rather chilling fact to the latter assessment . . . which was that "continued elevated adrenaline levels increase the basal metabolic rate and over the long term ages the body rapidly."

I put down the paper. In my mind I could see Sidd leaving the mound after a particularly difficult inning under a blazing sun at Shea, stooping slightly as he crossed the foul line, a hitch developing in his stride as he moved for the dugout. How ironic that the adrenaline rush that gave the machinery of the body that extra boost (however Sidd produced it—mantras, mind over matter, lung-gom, whatever) was *aging* him . . . like the man who leaves Shangri-La in *Lost Horizon* and turns into a skeletal ancient within minutes! Could it be that Sidd would have withered away during the season and ended up on a couple of canes? It made me feel better that he had left the game.

One evening the chimes of the front door rang faintly and out on the back porch I heard the front door, which I never lock anyway, swing ajar; the sound of sandals slapped against the tiles of the hallway. Debbie Sue appeared in the door. I stood up and embraced her, feeling the bones of her rib cage and the soft tumult of her hair against my cheek.

"I knew you'd be here," she said. "Safe in your burrow."

"I'm surprised."

"I tried to telephone a few times and then I remembered you never pick the thing up. We miss you."

"You've been with Sidd?"

She cocked her head and smiled.

"I left him just the day before yesterday. He's at a monastery in Colorado. Dad's been sick, so I came back East to see him."

"It's nice to see you."

We embraced again.

"I'm glad you found Sidd," I said.

"I think he is too."

"Are things all right between you and your father?" I remembered their last meeting—Debbie Sue turning from his outstretched arms and running back for the taxi that had just deposited her.

"He's okay now," she said. "I told him I'm going back to Duke in the fall. I still haven't told him about Sidd. I try. I look in his face and I say, 'Dad . . . ?' but then I stop. I just can't get those words *Buddhist monk* out."

"You're staying in a monastery?"

"In the Red Roof Inn just down the way. I can see the monastery roofs from my window."

It turned out that tracking Sidd down had been quite simple. She had gone to the airport in Tampa and asked at the ticket counter if a funny-looking guy in blue jeans and woodsman's boots, carrying a long stick, possibly a begging bowl (though he might have packed that), and a French horn case had bought an airplane ticket . . . a guy with a faintly crooked smile, an English accent, a habit of sliding into different languages, and perhaps—Debbie Sue hoped this—the somewhat lost expression of someone whose heart is broken. The third ticket agent she had spoken to had indeed sold a ticket to such a person. His final destination was Boulder, Colorado. The Denver plane had left about a half hour earlier.

Once she herself got to Boulder, Debbie Sue had gone through pretty much the same procedure—walking around town to find out where a young Buddhist aspirant monk might go. She was directed to a monastery, or, more technically, an ashram about ten miles outside of town.

Once settled in the Red Roof Inn, Debbie Sue told me she walked out to a fortresslike structure in the hills. The grounds seemed deserted. The monks were undoubtedly inside somewhere, meditating, chanting, or whatever. After waiting for an hour, half hidden in a plot of scrub pines, Debbie Sue said she lost patience and walked through a swinging wire gate up to the monastery itself, picking the biggest building in the complex, a kind of chapel-like structure, to look for Sidd.

The windows were tall and narrow. Debbie Sue was able to chin herself up to the sill of one to peer in. The monks were in their lotus positions in long rows on their prayer mats. A temple bell chimed softly. A low "Om!" erupted from one of the monks. A drone of summer flies.

It must have been a traumatic moment for those meditating monks . . . to have a young woman's face appear at a window—fragmenting the sunlight on the flagstone floor—and a voice ring out, tumultuously in the contours of the chapel, "Sidd, are you down there?"

Debbie Sue reported that afterwards she only had time to shout, "Sidd, I made an awful mistake. I want you. I'm staying at the Red Roof Inn. Room 209!"—before she dropped out of sight.

The reaction among the people below must have been galvanic. Debbie Sue couldn't describe it because she had hauled herself up to the sill by her fingertips (the window was about six feet up) just long enough to see the lined-up prayer mats, the brown-robed rows, and to shout her vibrant message before her arm muscles gave way ("I never could have done it if I didn't have the wrists of a golfer") and she dropped back down to the grass outside the chapel walls.

"He was down there," she said. "I had a glimpse of his face. He certainly got the message!"

"I'm glad you two got together again," I said.

"It's not as nice as it was here, Owl," she said, looking fondly around the bungalow. "Sneaking into a monastery . . . the monks get spooked."

"Can't Sidd get to you? Can't he get out on leave?"

"Sometimes he sneaks out and comes to the Red Roof Inn," Debbie Sue said. "He throws a stone through my window. It's very romantic. I come to the window and see him standing on the far side of the parking lot. Like *Romeo and Juliet.* We go out and have picnics in the pines."

"Is he happy?" I asked.

"How can he be in that place!" Debbie Sue said hotly. "They chant a lot. They all shout 'Moo!' Sidd tells me that's the symbol of Absolute Eternity. He sits on a mat, not counting lunch, for fourteen hours. I told him that was silly and unhealthy, and he said that in Japan the monks sit on their mats for ten *days!* They're allowed to doze off only between one o'clock in the morning and three. Where Sidd is there's this awful man called a *sensei* who walks up and down the rows of

209

mats with a wooden paddle called a 'warning stick.' If a guy even *twitches*, the sensei steps up and whacks him across the shoulders. He shouts 'Sit still!' But sitting still isn't enough. The student has to *work* at it. The sensei tells him any old stone Buddha can sit still. No, it has to be *live* stillness. *Whack!* Sit still! Sit still! Can you bear it? I keep telling Sidd that if he ever gets whacked that way, he should get off the mat and knock the guy flat! The creep!"

"Is he in good spirits?" I asked.

"He worries about your writing. He wonders if you've tried the mantra he gave to you to help you write."

"No," I said. "I'm saving it up. What's his state of mind, Debbie Sue?" I asked.

She looked out over the back lawn, bright in the summer evening. "He's still not sure what he wants to do," she said. "One afternoon on the picnic blanket he said he felt like a man on a blind donkey pursuing a fierce tiger. I'm no help. My coming around just means trouble. I'm sure the head monk speaks to him about me quite firmly. Maybe the sensei beats him. I don't know. He doesn't tell me everything. But there are rules. They are called *vinaya*. Sidd told me there are two hundred and twenty-seven strict rules of priestly discipline. Most 'mundane' pleasures aren't allowed. That's why you don't see Buddhist monks at football games. Or standing in line at the movies. I don't dare ask, but I'm afraid *I'm* a 'mundane' pleasure."

"Do you ever talk about baseball with him?"

"More and more," Debbie Sue said. "He brings it up at our picnics in the woods. I bring him the paper, he reads the sports pages to see how the Mets are doing. He asked me to explain to him how to read a box score. I don't know myself, so we did a lot of guessing.

"He says the monks have a softball team. He doesn't play on it, but he watches carefully and he's learning lots about the game."

"That sounds as though he . . . was toying with the idea of coming back."

"Well, he is thinking about it."

"Why would he want to?"

"Come back? Well, he never really left because he *wanted* to," Debbie Sue said. "Remember the morning he threw those wild pitches at Huggins?"

"How can I forget?" I said. "I had just finished telling the reporters in the clubhouse about yak dung."

"I was on my way home," she said. "I always thought that in Sidd's mind I was number three—third after Buddha and baseball. That was his big problem—which one was the most important. Halfway home, I decided I didn't mind being third. So when I got to Huggins to tell him I'd changed my mind, I heard he'd lost it and hit an iron pipe. Owl, I had the order all screwed up. I wasn't as far down as I thought."

"So he was glad to see you when you found him in Colorado."

Debbie Sue smiled and nodded. "When he

sneaked out of the monastery, and he saw me waiting for him in the parking lot of the motel, he shouted something that is very important in his culture. Guess what it is."

"I have no idea."

" 'Ha!' "

" 'Ha'?"

She looked embarrassed. "Don't tell a soul, Owl. Promise? Well, it's the exclamation monks make when they achieve bodhicitta."

" 'Ha'?"

"That's all it is," she said. " 'Ha!' and sometimes quite a lot of weeping and laughing."

"Is that the first time you've heard it?"

She looked at me slyly. "You always wanted to know about when I came ashore from the Windsurfer in Pass-a-Grille? You thought Ueberroth sent me?"

"That's right."

"When I came over the dunes Sidd looked at me and the baseball fell out of his hand. He cried out, 'Ha!' I've heard whistles and cute remarks, you know . . . but not 'ha!' It just sort of explodes 'ha!'—nothing like a laugh at all, and it scared me a little.

"Then he made one of those incredible imitations of his—a bell . . . it was the cylinder bell of the monastery at the foot of Mount Everest, the one that separates the monks and the nuns at the end of the day? I could see his throat muscles quiver.

"I said, 'How the hell did you do that?'

"He looked miserable. But he was interesting . . . shy and kind of cute, with his English accent and everything . . . throwing baseballs at his tin cans in the dunes . . . . I mean, it was something you just couldn't walk away from. So I sat down in the sand with him."

We went out that night and had dinner in Pass-a-Grille. Debbie Sue was going back to Colorado the next day. We talked a little more about my writing. I told her that I had written a short essay about a man who flew over Long Beach in a deck chair—getting all of it down on a three-by-five card.

She interrupted, "Would you come to New York if Sidd decided to play for the Mets?"

I shrugged. "I don't know what good I could do."

"He depends on you," she said. "I don't think he'd come without you." She looked out across the restaurant dock at the dark glimmer of the canal. "I'd love to come to New York. My aunt lives in Trenton, New Jersey, but that's as close as I've ever been. Wouldn't it be like old times?"

"I don't know," I said. "Perhaps not."

She ordered three shrimp cocktails to be served separately, as if each were a full course. I ordered something more predictable and a bottle of white wine. We toasted each other.

"What did you do to amuse yourself when you weren't storming the monastery?" I asked.

"Oh, I hung around," Debbie Sue replied. "I

went to the town library one day in Boulder and looked up stuff about Nepal and Tibet. I learned little things to surprise Sidd and please him. I found a book that had charts of tantric sexual positions—almost thirty of them. They had wonderful names—A Singing Monkey Holding a Tree. I tried to take the book out of the library so Sidd and I could practice after our picnics in the pines, but I had to have a library card and be a resident. The library people got suspicious after that; I'd see a face peeking around the corner of the bookshelves."

I remarked—somewhat emboldened having had a glass or two of wine—that I was surprised that someone training to be a Buddhist monk ever had any sexual interest at all. Wasn't it part of Buddhist religions, at least among the monks, that one had to suppress all desires—much less the pleasures of carnal love?

Debbie Sue did not know what carnal love was. She had been told once but had forgotten.

I explained and she said, "Oh that!" She went on to say that Sidd had been bothered by the restrictions of the monkhood—the vinaya—oh yes, and since he probably wasn't going to be a monk *all the way* (as she put it) he could pick and choose among the various cults. "Thank God for that!" she said. "He's learned more than to throw a ball very fast—I mean of all things to pick! He's got me into lovemaking and Taoism."

I said I was a little rusty on Taoism. Maybe I

214

knew it once, but like Debbie Sue with carnal love, I had forgotten.

She gave a long sigh. "Well," she said, drawing it out, "the Taoists have lots of gods. In fact, they have a god for just about everything. They have gods for parts of the body . . . the foot! . . . They take a lot of baths. The priests eat only vegetables. They leave home. Like Milarepa, they can do these fabulous physical things, like float, and everything. They believe in alchemy—turning things into gold? When they're not making love, they're doing that. They are very into sex. . . .

"It's all in a very short book called the *Tao Te Ching*, about five thousand words in all, which makes it, Sidd told me, one of the most important short books in the world. It says wise things like 'A journey of a thousand miles begins with a single step.' Sidd thought that was a good thing for you to know about your writing. A book starts with one word."

She leaned across the little table to tell me about a kind of Taoist sex practice called *imsák*. "It says you can *see* better if you don't have an orgasm. So it tells you *not* to have one."

"Did the book tell you how to do this?"

"Well, they tell the person not to get excited or too passionate?"

"Well, I mean, how do you do that?"

"You think of something else. They have a list to choose from. Weird oriental things. A soup bowl with one kernel of rice in it. I told Sidd if he felt out of control, he should think about birds, or swimming with the porpoises, or doing the dishes. . . ."

"What did he say?"

"Oh, Owl, he gave me that sweet Himalayan smile of his. It's crazy for me to suggest anything like that to him, because he's been practicing that sort of mental control for years. . . . But then one night—now don't you tell this to anyone, Owl, or I'll shoot you—we were lying, making love, just on the edge of this little shallow lake, and suddenly Sidd made the sound of a bird in my ear—a blue jay, so clear I thought I was in the North Carolina woods. . . ."

In mid-July I got a call from Sidd. It came late in the evening. It was swelteringly hot in Pass-a-Grille. It had rained; that afternoon the mists rose off the pavement like steam. The frogs had taken over the weed-choked pond with such force that the chorus could well have come from up-country Vietnam, where the frogs are as big as small dogs—so pervading that I had begun to think about moving away. "The frogs are driving me batty," I told my sister. "When they stop they all do it at once, as if collectively garroted."

"Come to Marblehead. It's lovely up here."

"Perhaps."

I told her that the effort to move seemed so massive. It was easier to close the porch door and turn on the television.

The night Sidd called the door was open because of the heat. A fan moved the air above me.

216

"Wait a minute, Sidd," I said.

I slid the door easily along its runners and it clicked shut.

"Namas-te."

It was a pleasure to hear the soft, slightly inflected accent once again. He came right to the point. "I am coming back to the Mets."

"Have you told them?" I asked.

"I called up Mr. Cashen. It took a long time getting through. They thought it was a joke. I said I wanted to come back."

"What did he say?"

"He said, 'Oh my God.' "

Rather haltingly, Sidd asked me if I would come to New York and see him through August and September . . . perhaps share an apartment. He didn't feel he was going to feel at ease in the city. Over the phone he made one of his brilliant vocal imitations—the sound of a taxi horn, a police siren, and the sigh of a bus pulling away from its passenger stop.

"There are no mantras," he said, "to take care of this sort of thing."

He asked how the Mets were doing.

"According to the papers, they're having their troubles," I said. "A lot of injuries. But they're neck-and-neck with the Cardinals."

"They were always very good to me," Sidd said. "They kept to their word."

"Where's Debbie Sue?"

"She's right here—at the Red Roof Inn. Sometimes she comes to the monastery. At the evening meal we sit at long wooden tables in the dining hall. There is a prayer and then the meal is consumed in silence. The clacking of spoons against wooden bowls. One night Debbie Sue put in an appearance at the door. On either side were two diminutive monks, struggling with her in a most tentative way because, of course, handling a determined young woman is not something in their line of work at all. She spotted me, looking up, startled, from my wooden bowl. She called out, 'Sidd, the ice machine in the motel has conked out. Totally!'"

Sidd giggled, and I could hear Debbie Sue laughing in the background.

"I hear you peg stones through her windows."

He told me the first night he crept out of the monastery and threw a lemon through her motel window. He wasn't sure if it was the right window. So he stood off a long distance, pegging the lemon from the edge of the motel parking lot—a couple of hundred yards away.

It turned out to be the right room. Debbie Sue's silhouette appeared briefly at the window. She leaned out. Her voice soared out over the parking lot. "Sidd Finch. You crazy beautiful *monk!*"

Once again I could imagine Finch's ambivalent feelings about Debbie Sue—cringing with embarrassment at her Klaxon-like voice bellowing over the parking lot, and yet knowing that within seconds she would be flying on her bare feet toward him across the macadam, her white T-shirt like a huge moth among the parked cars, and when she reached him she would envelop him with her slender arms, the smell of soap in her hair as she would whisper in his ear some little affection she had thought up, "My bird, my love."

Once again Sidd would know that The Path to The Way was extremely difficult.

Debbie Sue came on the telephone. Her voice, as usual, was much too loud, as if at some point in younger days she had been told to "Speak up!" It made me move the receiver back from my ear. She could hardly wait to get to New York. "The monastery life isn't for me!" she announced gaily. "But, Owl, the bells are so beautiful the way they echo, and the mountains! I can't wait to see you. I can't wait for New York. It'll be like old times."

I said I would think about it. Almost as soon as I said good-bye the phone rang again and it was Jay Horwitz.

"Have you heard?"

I said I just finished talking to Sidd.

"Can you believe it?" he said dolefully. "Here we go again."

XII

A CAT CAME with the apartment. That was the one stipulation with the signing of the lease—the tenants had to take care of the cat, whose name (I was told in a long note about him) was Mister Puss.

219

I had closed the bungalow and flown up from Florida. My own New York apartment, boxlike, musty and hot, sheets over the furniture, was too small even for the spartan needs of Debbie Sue and Sidd. So I searched around. The Mets were helpful. They said most of the players rented homes in the Port Washington area, which is about thirty minutes out on Long Island from Shea Stadium, but Sidd and Debbie Sue were set on finding a place in New York City.

"You'll be staying with them?" Jay asked over the telephone.

"They seem to want that," I said. "Debbie Sue has an aunt in Trenton. She went to see her once. That's as close as she's been to New York. Sidd seems to be confused by the idea of urban life. So maybe I can be of some help."

"That's great," Jay said.

"Besides, I have a good time with them."

"Davey Johnson's thinking of using Sidd against St. Louis next week. They've come in for a four-game set. Starts with an afternoon game and then they leave Thursday night," Jay said. "It depends on his control."

"Debbie Sue tells me that out in Colorado Sidd threw a lemon through an open motel window from a couple of hundred yards out . . . across a parking lot."

"Is that so?"

"How's the team going to accept him?" I asked.

That had always bothered me—how the players would take this curious specimen into their midst.

A monk? A mystic? Would they mimic his English accent? Would they crowd around him in the locker room and challenge him to perform the Hindu rope trick?

"It'll be all right," Jay said. "They'll take anybody. We're hurting. Gary Carter has pulled a hamstring trying to keep his garage door from slamming down on the hood of his car. Keith Hernandez's got a sprain. Darryl Strawberry's got a hurting thumb from opening a jar of apple cider. It's in the nature of the game."

As I hung up I wondered why these domestic mishaps so often happened to the great athletes, freak things besetting them, very often in the kitchen. I remember Phil Rizzuto saying in a radio broadcast in the late seventies—I was driving somewhere in a convertible in the height of summer because I remember the thick texture of the leaves along a country road—that Yogi Berra had pulled a muscle in his back while reading a newspaper!

The people who owned the apartment (and the cat) were named Mullins. They were off on an extended safari in Africa. The husband enjoyed big-game hunting; he was taking his wife and two teenage sons with him to Botswana. Their apartment was in a building as far east as you can go on Manhattan's Seventy-second Street—in the last of a row of four walk-up flats . . . squat, adjoining buildings of black-brick walls and bright red doors that lead in off the street to the stairwells. The apartment was one flight up—a duplex with a spiral staircase connecting with the floor above. The windows of the front rooms looked out on the East River; the tugboats throbbed by at night. One of the front rooms had a pool table; stuffed animal heads looked down from green-tinted walls.

My sister was delighted at the news that I had moved to New York. "You're coming home," she said. "Puget Sound. The Seychelles. Lamu. Pass-a-Grille. The Big Apple." She offered me the use of her station wagon, which she kept in New York—her one extravagance, she said of the expense, since she liked the idea of being able to escape into New England at a moment's notice.

"That's on the condition you introduce me to the Buddhist and the girl who windsurfs."

Sidd and Debbie Sue turned up three days after I had signed the lease and moved in. It was odd seeing them in the environment of a New York apartment rather than the subterranean shadows of the Pass-a-Grille bungalow. Both arrived at the door carrying their belongings in bundles; Sidd had his French horn case and his long stick. We embraced. They wandered slowly through the apartment. Debbie Sue was not sure about the stuffed animal heads.

"What's the owner's name?"

"Mullins. He's off shooting in Botswana."

She suggested taking the heads down and storing them in a spare room during our occupancy, but the thought of opening the door onto such a dishevelment of glass eyes and antlers was even more disturbing. So she limited her discontent to talking and sympathizing with the heads on occasion as she walked by them.

She loved standing by the windows and looking out on the East River. She wondered if anyone windsurfed out there. It was a crime if they didn't. Books were everywhere in the apartment—spilling out of shelves that rose to the ceiling. Debbie Sue wondered if they were all read.

"Mullins is in the publishing business so he gets sent lots of books," I told her. I told her that Disraeli had once written to a friend who was always sending him books, "Thank you very much for sending me the book. I shall lose no time in reading it."

Debbie Sue said, "Christ! Look at that cat!"

The animal in question had ambled in from the neighboring rooms.

"That's Mister Puss," I said. "We have a long letter about him. Part of the deal is that we're supposed to see that he's fed and entertained."

"He's huge and wonderful. He's a trophy cat. I'm surprised they haven't shot him on sight!" She picked him up and gazed into his face. He lay in her arms like a sack.

The morning after their arrival Sidd was asked to report to Shea Stadium. The Mets were not scheduled to play that day.

He was picked up by car. The driver was not Elliot Posner, but it *was* like old times. The guy honked his horn under the windows that looked out on the street. Sidd spent four or five hours at Shea and the car brought him back after practice.

I met him at the door. Debbie Sue was out shopping. We sat down in the living room, overlooking the river.

"I pitch on Monday afternoon," he said. "The Cardinals from St. Louis are arriving in town."

"How was your first day?"

"They gave me a locker. They suggested I wear a shoe on my bare foot."

I asked what that would do to his pitching.

"Part of lung-gom is to know the body within," he said. "I discovered in the mountains that the perfect balance was better effected by not wearing anything on my left foot. I will continue to do so. I informed Mr. Johnson that I will pitch with my foot bare. I will be embarrassed. I have toes like a lobster claw."

I assured him that a bare foot was nothing new in American sports. In football both the colleges and pros had a number of kickers who padded out to kick barefooted, even outdoors in sub-zero weather.

I said, "But I wouldn't advise batting without wearing something on that foot. It's very easy to foul a ball straight down. Even with a shoe, it'll make you jump and yelp. When that happens the tradition in the dugout is for everyone in there to bark like dogs."

"Yes," Sidd said. "The trainer has given me a shoe for batting. Also a helmet. I was shown how to kneel in the circle they call 'the on-deck.' They have shown me the heavy ring that one slides on the bat to make it seem lighter. I had thought originally that the heavy ring was a talisman to bless the wood. No! One has only oneself to rely on within the confines of the batting box. They took me there. I have been shown how to knock the dirt from my spikes with the end of the bat and in what direction to face and so forth."

"Was Ronn Reynolds pleased to see you?"

"He seemed . . . subdued. I know why. He is going to be the catcher against the Cardinals. I assured him that he has not a thing to be concerned about—that wherever he sets his glove as a target I will put the ball exactly into its pocket."

"What did he say?"

"He said, 'What the hell happened at Huggins?' I apologized. I said it was a great exception. It was as rare as if a meteor had struck."

"Did he calm down?"

"Perhaps. He stared into the back of his locker."

Debbie Sue arrived. We could hear her clattering up on the stairs and then the sound of her key turning in the lock. She was carrying a package.

"I've bought something to wear to the game," she said brightly. "I went to Bonwit Teller. Guess what I said to the salesgirl? I said, 'I'm going to a baseball game to see my lover pitch. What should I wear?' The salesgirl was French. She thought a cocktail dress would be nice."

We had supper that night in the apartment. Sidd and Debbie Sue were curious about my writing. How was it coming along? Had I brought my typewriter up from Florida? I admitted that it was still sitting in the little side porch in Pass-a-Grille with the paper in it, shriveling in the humidity, no doubt. But I told them I had heard just the day before from Amory Blake, the therapist. He had written me a letter, which had been forwarded by the post office in Pass-a-Grille. He reported that he had sent his collection of strange facts to a New York publisher and it had been accepted! He had underlined "accepted" and put an exclamation point after it. A number of my suggestions had made their way into the final selection. These would be acknowledged in his introduction.

I admitted to Sidd and Debbie Sue that it wasn't quite the same as producing the stuff myself, but it was a start. Didn't they think so? Debbie Sue nodded, but she said she was going to look around the apartment for a typewriter. Mullins was a publisher, after all; there had to be one somewhere. She would set it up and roll a fresh piece of paper into it.

After dinner we fed Mister Puss, who had been described by Mr. Mullins in his note as a "digesting mechanism," and we pulled up chairs, Mister Puss supine in Debbie Sue's lap, to watch the evening come and the boats go by on the river.

I was surprised how at ease Sidd seemed, considering his assignment coming up. Finally he asked, "Robert, I need your advice. It has been my observation," he said, "that a vast amount of *chewing* among baseball players goes on—tobacco, gum, especially a brand called Bazooka, sunflower seeds, and perhaps other substances. I have spotted a player who sports a toothpick at a cocky angle. Is it your opinion that I should cultivate one of these habits so I will not stand out among my fellows for *not* doing so?"

When I asked if he had tried any of these things, he said that no, he was partial to an occasional peppermint—a Life Saver, the white variety, with the hole.

I said that I had not heard of anyone in baseball who used peppermints, but since the whole idea was to keep the mouth from going dry from tension and stress, a peppermint seemed a logical choice—it was a matter of preference.

I asked Sidd if the crowds expected at Shea the next afternoon would bother him. His preparation had been so isolated—the enclosures at Huggins-Stengel with three, or at the most, four people standing around to watch.

Sidd replied that he wouldn't really know until he stood out there on the pitcher's mound. He would remind himself, if he had to, of a famous Zen story about a wrestler named O-nami, which means "Great Wave," who was having that kind of trouble with his career—he couldn't wrestle in public. Crowds bothered him. In private he could throw his own teachers to the mat. But in public his own pupils humiliated and tossed him about. So he went to see a Zen master in a little temple set in a pleasant grove of trees that gave way to the beach and then to the sea.

The Zen master said, "Pray in this temple and

imagine that you are the waves in the sea, huge waves sweeping everything before them. . . ."

So, O-nami sat in meditation. By the time it began to get dark he could hear the water sifting through the tree trunks in the temple garden and the surf beginning to break against the temple steps. Then the water foamed in through the door, spreading out across the temple floor, sweeping away the flowers in their vases. The water rose. Even the Buddha in the shrine was inundated, and by dawn in O-nami's mind the temple had gone and there was nothing but the ebb and flow of an immense sea.

After a while the master appeared. He knew that O-nami had succeeded in his meditation. He patted him on the shoulder and told him that now he was going to be unbeatable.

Debbie Sue sighed. She said when she heard stories like this she always hoped for another ending . . . that the wrestler would step into the ring and immediately get flattened. "Waves!" she said in disgust.

Sidd smiled at her. I could see his throat muscles flutter and suddenly throughout the apartment we heard the sift and suck of water as if a huge tidal surge had risen out of the East River. Debbie Sue paled, and almost involuntarily she drew up her legs to keep her bare feet clear.

XIII

JUST ABOUT EVERYONE in the country remembers what they were doing when the word got out about Finch's afternoon in Shea Stadium. About fifteen thousand people were in the stands—an average summer afternoon crowd—and of course the number of people afterward who *said* they were there was up in the hundreds of thousands. Toward the end of the game, when it was evident what Finch was going to do, one of the major networks broke away to show the last innings at Shea. Viewers wrote angry letters, claiming that *nothing* should preempt *Hollywood Squares* or *Jeopardy*—whatever program they were accustomed to watching at that time.

Debbie Sue and I sat together in a pair of lower box seats on the first-base side behind the Mets dugout. The seats were provided by Jay Horwitz. Debbie Sue was not wearing the cocktail dress, thank goodness, but a pair of blue jeans and a T-shirt that read "BOOM BOOM" where the diminutive mounds of her small breasts pushed against the material. She pointed at Darryl Strawberry's behind—he was shagging flies in the outfield—and said that she was going to invite him to the Duke spring prom.

I had expected a larger crowd, but the Mets—

remembering the confusion and skepticism following the April 1 press conference at Huggins-
Stengel—had decided to announce Finch's
assignment to pitch only just before the game.
When Debbie Sue and I arrived twenty minutes
before the teams took to the field, there was no
sign of Sidd. We could see the Cardinal pitcher
John Tudor warming up, but the Mets bull pen
was deserted. Sidd had told me the night before
that he saw no need to take any warm-up pitches.
He had told me why . . . that in his snow-leopard
days in the Himalayas, there was not much point
in "warming up" since he never could tell when
the leopards would sneak down and put in an
appearance above the yak pens. It was a question
of spotting them and quickly letting fly.

Did I think it mattered? he wanted to know.
Was "warming up" an important ritual in baseball
that he had better adhere to?

I had told him that it was of small consequence.
I had once written a story about a top-flight English tennis player—a regular at Wimbledon in the
fifties—who didn't see any point in warming up
either (or "knocking up" as they say in England).
"I don't knock up," she would say firmly to her
opponent; she would sit and wait in her courtside
chair while the officials hustled around for someone to go out and get the other person ready.

We finally saw Sidd. He came out of the dugout
after the national anthem. As he moved in his long
farmer's gait to the pitcher's mound, his bare foot
seemed luminous against the green grass. Debbie

Sue pointed at an electric scoreboard. His name was up there as the starting pitcher for the Mets, predictably with one of the two *d*'s of Sidd missing. An increasing murmur rose from around us—most likely at the realization on the crowd's part that Finch—whoever the hell *he* was—was shoeless on one foot.

Sidd reached the pitcher's mound and looked down toward the plate. We waited. It was as if a great mechanism had stopped. Finally the umpire walked to the mound. Out there, Sidd must have told him he didn't *bother* with warm-up pitches, upon which, after staring at him for a second or so, and at his bare foot for just an instant, the umpire walked back to the plate, reaching for his little whisk broom in his rear pocket, and as he did so he waved the lead-off man into the batter's box.

Sometimes in a stadium, if it is tense, and the place has a good crowd, enough people identify with the actual flight of the pitched ball to react audibly—an exhalation of breath—so that the pitch is accompanied by a slight *whoomph*. With the first ball Finch threw there was no time for any kind of reaction: we heard the slam of the ball driving the air out of the catcher's mitt with a high *pop!*—audible, I suspect, out in the parking lot beyond the center-field fence. This was followed by a high exclamation from Reynolds, a kind of squeak, as he stood up from his stance, reached into his glove, and began pulling the ball free. A gasp and then a prolonged murmur went up from the stands. The batter, Vince Coleman, had no idea how to react. His jaw dropped slightly. He looked down at the plate. The umpire raised his right hand slowly to indicate a strike—so slowly that he gave the impression of someone wondering exactly what evidence he himself was working on.

As pitch followed pitch the astonishment at what we were seeing never seemed to diminish. Perhaps it was because it was such an unfathomable extension of the most common act in sports: all of us had seen pitchers wind up and throw a ball thousands of times. But here, the flight of the ball was barely discernible—a quick, white flash, almost a trick, a refraction of light; but the proof of what we had barely seen was emphasized by the *sound* of the ball exploding into Ronn Reynolds' glove. He was visibly tossed back by its impact. The umpire's hand came out to steady him. We saw the ball when he extricated it from his glove. When he threw it back to Finch it seemed as large as a moon.

It was odd to watch someone so remarkably adept at hurling a baseball behave so awkwardly in other departments of the game. Sidd had a troublesome time catching the ball when Reynolds threw it back to him; indeed, the catcher finally resorted to a high-trajectory lob to get it safely into Sidd's possession. Sometimes Reynolds would forget and peg the ball back hard to Sidd, perhaps to give him just the slightest taste of what he himself was suffering behind the plate. Sidd, his eyes widening as if he had glimpsed something quite horrid, would duck to let the ball sail out over second base into center field.

It didn't seem to bother him in the slightest—these displays of gawky clumsiness. Once the ball got back to the mound and he had control of it, he would set himself and stare kindly down at Reynolds, who would slowly raise his big catcher's mitt for a target, setting one leg behind the other, knowing that as soon as he was motionless, Sidd's bare foot would start for the heavens and the terrifying convulsion on the mound would begin.

Debbie Sue was surprisingly quiet in the seat beside me. I had not been quite sure what to expect—most probably an overabundance of enthusiasm ("Come on, you *Sidd!*"), which would have attracted attention and embarrassed me. But there was none of this. She tended to fidget when Sidd walked out to the mound, and especially when his time came to go up to bat. She watched his every move, often through a pair of binoculars we had brought with us. Darryl Strawberry's behind got only a cursory glance. Midway through the game she said, "He's tired. I can see his lips moving."

"He's repeating the ngags," I said.

The Cardinals, one by one, came up for the time it took Sidd to throw three pitches. Some of them started to swing their bats when Sidd's bare foot reached its apex and the delivery, from far behind his head, was on its way. Some got into a stance to bunt—standing far back in the batter's box and poking their bats out into the air space

233

above the plate in the hope that percentages would finally put the wood on the ball. I do not remember a foul. I began feeling sorry for the Cardinals. They had always been a favorite team—a passion that went back to a childhood appreciation of the design on their uniforms—the two birds, paint-red, standing on the slant of a bat. My sister used to say that it was the most "bovine" reason for liking a team, but there it was.

In the seventh inning Whitey Herzog, the Cardinals manager (whose team was behind 3-0 on a Mookie Wilson home run in the sixth), came out and complained about Sidd's toes. He pointed out that high in the air, the toes were distracting the hitters—just as illegal (Herzog insisted) as a tattered sleeve on a pitcher's jersey; he would protest the game unless something was done about it. Herzog flailed his arms and fanned his fingers to illustrate Sidd's leg action and what the toes looked like, and the dirt streaming out of them, and so forth, and it must have been convincing because the umpire concurred and called Davey Johnson out of the dugout. Sidd disappeared into the club-house and came out wearing a white sock on his bare foot. To me, sitting in the stands, the sock, often flopping at the end of his foot, seemed a more disconcerting sight pointed high in the sky than the bare toes, but then I wasn't speaking from firsthand experience.

What many in the crowd remembered that afternoon were the four times Sidd Finch came to bat. It was evident enough that he had never done such a thing—at least in a game. He had skipped pregame batting practice. Indeed, Davey Johnson reported afterward that Finch had sat down next to him at the bottom of the third inning, with his first time-at-bat coming up, and asked, "Is it absolutely mandatory that I go up to bat? I would as soon eschew it."

Davey Johnson shifted the tobacco in his jaw and said, "Well, you can't *eschew* it. You got no choice," and he showed Sidd how to hold the bat, the trademark up, and so forth. They had a little session right there in the dugout.

Tudor's first pitch was a big curve that broke in the dirt two feet from the plate and skipped to the backstop. I turned to Debbie Sue and said, "My God, Sidd's going to intimidate the pitcher into walking him."

Alas, Tudor grooved the next few pitches to see what would happen; it was immediately apparent that Sidd was hardly a threat.

What was odd was that the crowd accepted Sidd's troubles without catcalls or outward signs of derision. It was as if, however clumsy or out of place he was at the plate, or fielding Ronn Reynolds' pegs from the plate, they knew at the start of every inning that he would stalk slowly out to the pitcher's mound, gaze curiously at the rosin bag as if tempted to pick it up, turn, and, murmuring what Debbie Sue and I knew were private ngags, begin to mow the Cardinals down.

In the late innings Sidd began tiring. The will expended in sailing the ball in at such velocity had its consequences: I could see his knees tremble and his body sag after the follow-through, as if his effort had drained him of even the strength to stand. His knees would float toward the ground. It must have been frustrating for the Cardinals, standing along the length of their dugout steps, to realize all they had to do was get the bat on the ball and push it out toward the mound to be sure to get on base. But the condition was momentary. After a few seconds on the mound we could almost see the strength flow back into him.

Out in the upper-left-field deck, almost from the first, the fans began to hang out the red K's, which are usually reserved to represent each of Dwight Gooden's strikeouts. At the end of the first inning, three red K's appeared. By the end of the seventh, twenty-one hung in a long row along the length of the upper-deck facade. That was apparently the entire allotment available—the K hangers never assuming they would need to put out more than twenty-one.

Yet here they were on this hot August afternoon with this new guy Finch, with every K banner they possessed in a smart neat row along the facade . . . and two more innings to go! They began improvising. A sheet banner I had noticed in the vicinity that had read "SYOSSET LOVES THE METS" suddenly disappeared and was torn up and sacrificed to make additional K squares. They were sloppy, tattered on the sides, the K's clumsy and in scratchy black lines.

For the top half of the ninth inning—the Mets

were ahead 5-0 at this point—the entire stadium stood. A great roar went up at the last strikeout of the game. Sidd had thrown the ball eighty-two times. The umpire had called a ball in the seventh inning, the inning Sidd had to wear his white sock—very likely just to give the impression he was on top of things. Debbie Sue looked out at the left-field tier through her binoculars and announced that the twenty-seventh K was the back of a man's shirt. Someone out there had ripped it off his back so that astonishing line of K's could be completed.

The Mets streamed out of the dugout at the last pitch, but it was not the pell-mell rush that one might have expected, nothing at all like the cap-throwing euphoria typical with the usual no-hitter. Ronn Reynolds did not launch himself into Sidd's arms, as Yogi Berra did into Don Larsen's after his perfect game in the 1956 World Series. The Mets marched out like people who are a little late for a football game, not quite breaking into a trot. After all, most of them had never said more than a word or two to Sidd. He was "that monk guy." He had been carted into their midst just the week before—like an unpacked piece of furniture. They surrounded him, shouting happily at him, but he was escorted off the field more as if they were an armed guard.

The Cardinals stood on the top step of their dugout gazing out toward the goings-on as if watching some sort of display with which they had not been involved in any way at all.

Debbie Sue and I went home after the game. We thought of waiting around near the clubhouse entrance to try to get to Sidd.

"You don't think he needs us?" she asked in the car.

"He must have a hundred shepherds by now," I replied.

"We're going to lose him, Owl," she said after a while. "We've moved him from one institution into another."

When we reached the apartment we turned on the Mullins' television set just in time to see a camera move in for a close-up of Sidd on the pitcher's mound. They were recapping the game. The particular segment we saw was in slow motion. His long face, slightly worried, filled the screen, as if we were being given his image to memorize for posterity. The muscles of his cheeks worked slightly, sucking on something within. His mouth opened and we had a brief glimpse of a white peppermint Life Saver encircling the very tip of his tongue. The camera pulled back hastily, as if the intimacy of his chewing habit was not to be dwelt on.

XIV

DEBBIE SUE HEARD Sidd's steps coming up the stairwell and she ran to meet him. He came in looking somewhat harried. His shoulders sagged.

He looked at me as if I were somewhat responsible for the rigors of his afternoon, or more particularly what he had gone through in the locker room afterward.

"I was not informed," he said. "I had an idea that one dressed and went home."

He sat down in a chair and looked out at the river.

"You pitched the perfect game," I said. "You did the equivalent"—I felt awkward using the reference—"of reaching Nirvana—bodhicitta. It's the ultimate. Turn on the television and you'll see."

Debbie Sue hung over his shoulders. "We're so proud of you, Owl and me. We saw your peppermint a little while ago. It was on ABC."

"I did not find the Mets a particularly affectionate group of people," Sidd told us. "The conversation I had with Mr. Johnson about how to hold the bat was the only one I had until the end of the game. I felt like a leper. I said to Mookie Wilson, 'My congratulations to you on your home run.' He had just hit the ball over a fence in the sixth inning. It put the team ahead by three runs. I put my fingers up like everyone else when he came into the dugout so that I could bestow a high-five salute to him for doing such a thing. He turned away."

"The creep!" Debbie Sue said.

"That's a famous tradition," I told him. "If a pitcher is on the way to a no-hitter, none of his teammates talk to him. That's what was happening."

"The Mets were all huddled at one end of the dugout."

"That's right. Quite natural."

"I will have to apologize to them and to Mr. Mookie Wilson for not understanding this."

I asked what had happened in the locker room.

"I was carried about in there as if in the motion of a great wave," Sidd told us. "There was a considerable amount of shouting and popping of flash bulbs and the stretching of microphones toward me. Some people were trying very hard to get me to Kiner's Corner. What, may I ask, is Kiner's Corner?"

I explained that Ralph Kiner was a famous home-run hitter who once played with the Pittsburgh Pirates. I said, "His corner—actually it's spelled with a *K*, which is . . . well, it's just spelled that way—is a little studio under the stands where Kiner interviews the stars of the game. The stars sit in there with their uniforms on and tell him what happened."

"Doesn't Mr. Kiner know what happened?"

"He does. The star is there to reinforce what Mr. Kiner knows. There is considerable curiosity about heroics in this country."

"I never got to Kiner's Korner," Sidd said. "Instead I was pushed along in the locker room to a tub of ice cubes. They wanted to put my arm in there. 'Sit down on this stool and put it in.' I stuck my arm in there. It made them all feel much happier. It was unbelievably cold and uncomfortable.

"Ronn Reynolds came by and he put his left hand in the ice. We smiled at each other. He said a very pleasant thing. He said it was the greatest moment of his life, even if someone else would have to cut the meat on his plate that evening. I thanked him for his sentiments. I could barely hear what he was saying for all the shouting. Most of the people wanted to know either how I felt or how my arm felt."

"How *is* your arm?" asked Debbie Sue.

"It is still cold from the tub of ice cubes," Sidd said. "That is the worst thing about pitching that I have experienced so far—to have my arm plunged into a tub of ice cubes."

We took him over to the television set to show him what an impact he had made. By chance, Davey Johnson was on the station we tuned into— a repeat of an interview he had given in his manager's office not long after the game. He was seated at his desk in his undershirt.

"I might pitch him every other day," he was saying.

"What about his arm, Davey?"

Johnson shrugged. "He says his arm is cosmically in tune. I gotta believe him. They tell me Satchel Paige pitched a hundred and sixty-three games in a row—pitched in the Negro leagues 'by the hour,' as he used to say. Maybe my guy can do the same."

"Did you see Johnson after the game?" I asked Sidd.

"He came by the ice tub," Sidd said. "He was

241

very pleasant. He said, 'Nice game, kid.' He asked me if I could perform again on Thursday. I said it was up to him. He also asked after my arm."

Debbie Sue knelt in front of the set and shifted to the public broadcast channel. The *MacNeil-Lehrer Newshour* was in progress. MacNeil was saying in his introduction, "Throwing a baseball is the sequential snapping of shoulder, elbow, and wrist. Throwing with one hand very likely produced the very first lateralization in the human brain, long before humankind developed language skills. Humankind had to *knock down a rabbit* before he could talk about how he wanted it served. Therefore," MacNeil went on, "throwing something is an ancient skill concentrated most commonly in the left hemisphere of the brain, and one that has not markedly advanced over the millennia. There have been no great leaps forward until the phenomenon of Sidd Finch. Tonight we will be talking to Dr. Ernest Caroline, a sports sociologist from Carnegie Polytech." The doctor's face appeared on a screen behind MacNeil, who spun slowly to listen to him.

First we had a view of Sidd himself on the mound, a glimpse even of his peppermint; then the camera pulled back to allow the hoist of his delivery to show in the frame; then in a sideview we saw the pitch itself. In the slow-motion replay the ball was possible to see. It moved against the slow haze of a motionless frieze of faces in the stands with a speed that was quite foreign, a streak against the background that seemed rather from a glitch or a malfunction in the television set.

"What we have here," Dr. Caroline said, "is a most curious and possible deranging influence on baseball. Something will have to be done, but, frankly, Robert, I'm not sure what. It's the kind of discrepancy you get in Little League baseball when one of these great tall twelve-year-olds turns up—all elbows and a great, whippy arm—who can deliver the ball down the shortened chute of a Little League pitching alley, a third shorter than the regular distance—like a *bullet*. It gets the kids coming up to bat just about whimpering, scared half to death. These big overgrown phenoms can strike out twenty-one kids in a seven-inning Little League game, even *more* because the catcher'll let the occasional third strike slip by, which'll get the batter safely down to first. They go on, these terrors, decimating the League until the authorities come in and see what's going on. What they do is take these kids and move them up to the next level, where the distance from mound to plate is less generous. The problem with Finch is that he's already at the highest level—the major leagues. There's no place they can send him up to. . . ."

Robert MacNeil did not seem especially perturbed. His large, pleasant face filled the screen and we watched him shift to a baseball historian— from Cooperstown, I believe: "Mr. Deane, you have heard Dr. Caroline speaking from a sociologist's point of view. Do you find his testimony disturbing?"

243

"I would have to admit," Mr. Deane said, "that Mr. Finch put on a startling show, to put it mildly. A lot depends on whether he can duplicate it. But you must understand that there's been tinkering from the beginning to get the balance between pitcher and batter exactly right."

"Would you explain?" MacNeil asked.

"Well, in the earliest days of baseball—the mid-nineteenth century—the pitcher, who incidentally was also called the 'pecker' or the 'feeder,' had to throw the ball underhand. The batter could ask to have the ball thrown exactly where he wanted it. Before the first pitch the umpire would ask him whether he wanted the ball high or low and this would be indicated to the pitcher. It wasn't until 1884 that pitchers were allowed to throw overhand, and not until 1887 when this practice of the batter calling for what he wanted—a 'fat pitch'—was discontinued. Did you know that Walt Whitman, of all people, was very upset when the curveball came into being at the turn of the century?" We watched MacNeil's eyebrows go up.

"Yes, pitchers simply got tired of serving up the ball, and began in their frustration to practice deception—curving the ball and so forth. It outraged the old gentleman. He deplored such a thing as morally reprehensible and unfair. 'I should call it everything that is damnable,' he wrote. Oh, there've been all sorts of changes. The original distance between the mound and the plate was forty-five feet. Pitchers could get a man out by hitting him between the bases with the ball. 'Plugging a man' it was called. The spitball was out-lawed. Aluminum bats aren't allowed in the majors. So the tinkering goes on . . . to keep that extraordinary balance provident. It may be that Finch will require some kind of adjustment—I can't imagine what, frankly."

"I see," said MacNeil.

The historian was having a good time. "Did you know," he said, "that in 1886 a rule had to be passed restricting the first- and third-base coaches to boxes near their bases? Up until then the coaches could range down the line and practically perch on the opposing catcher to scream things into his ears. The St. Louis Browns had a pair of coaches who were famous at this—Charles Comiskey and Bill Gleason. These guys would come down their respective baselines and the catcher'd get it, hot and heavy, in both ears, from about ten feet away."

"Think of that!" said Robert MacNeil. "Well, now we'd like to shift to Providence, Rhode Island, where we will be talking . . . "

Debbie Sue leaned forward and turned the channels. We found a number of baseball people on the programs. Indeed, one of them was a St. Louis Cardinal who had actually batted against Sidd. He said the experience reminded him of Joe Garagiola (an ex-Cardinal himself) grousing to an umpire after striking out against a fastball pitcher, "Ump, that pitch *sounded* off the plate to me. Your ears are bum, that's what!"

Most of the players interviewed couldn't really comment on the situation because they hadn't seen

Finch pitch, except maybe a couple of innings repeated on television. Their jaws worked slightly on gum. They shifted in their chairs. I heard one say that Finch's rotator cuff was going to solve the situation. "His arm is going to explode out there on the mound, that's my guess. A guy's muscle structure just won't take that strain time after time. There's going to be a big pop! The guy's arm will hang straight down, and afterward he won't be able to pick up a coffee cup."

The major networks had managed to corral two high baseball officials—Commissioner Peter Ueberroth, and Bob Brown, the president of the American League. Brown, a former third baseman with the New York Yankees in their glory years, was arguing that Finch should get out of the National League and come over to his.

TV Anchorman: Why is that—if I may ask?—that you would want him in the American League?

Brown: He's too dominant a force in the National League. In our league we have designated hitters. They bat for the pitcher—who is traditionally worthless at the plate. That would establish a type of equality.

TV Anchorman: Do you really think so? The guy's struck out every man he's faced.

Brown: He wouldn't have an easy time with our players. I'll guarantee that. Of course we'd have to check to see that Finch isn't using a mysterious Tibetan *sap* on the ball.

TV Anchorman: I beg your pardon?

A small smile played on Brown's features. The

sportscaster apparently had no idea he was being mildly joshed. He leaned forward and continued earnestly.

TV Anchorman: Have you seen Finch pitch?

Brown: Can't say that I have.

The sportscaster then put a series of "What if?" questions: "What if the balance between the pitcher and batter really *was* upset?"

The president—somewhat more seriously, it seemed to me—began talking about regulations the leagues could initiate if there really were problems.

Brown: Let me give you an example. The Texas Rangers have a pitcher, Greg Harris, who is ambidextrous. He's actually a natural right-hander, but off the left he can throw a pretty good fastball—timed in the low eighties by one of those radar guns. The Texas coaches told him he could throw left-handed in a game if he could get that fastball up in the high eighties. In the meantime they designed a special mitt for him, with a thumb on either side. The League came down with a rule about all this—that Harris could switch from one arm to the other in the middle of a game, even in the middle of an *inning*, but not during an at-bat. The rule was that Harris had to decide which side he wanted to throw off when the guy stepped into the batter's box. I'll tell you something I'll bet you didn't know. Harris is an ex-Met. Yup! The Mets seem to spawn these strange pitching freaks. . . .

TV Anchorman: What about Finch?

Brown: In the case of Finch we could rule [that

owlish smile appeared again] that Buddhist monks from Tibet, or from that general area, must move back four feet. We'd require the clubs to build little mounds back there—just for Buddhist monks . . . I believe they call them stupas.

Brown pointed out that even in modern times adjustments to perfect the balance between pitcher and batter are made. "Remember in sixty-nine when the pitcher was dominating?" he remarked. "That was the year Bob Gibson had a 1.12 earned run average and Denny McLain won thirty-one games—the first time since the thirties anyone had a record like that. The authorities lowered the pitching mound from fifteen inches to ten and they cut a couple of inches off the strike zone both at the bottom and the top. The American League brought in the designated hitter. The next year the batting average went up twenty points. So why not a stupa back there for Buddhist over-achievers . . . ?"

Commissioner Peter Ueberroth, with his suave, matinee-idol manner, seemed cool and completely unruffled by the furor. He had been quoted in the *Sports Illustrated* article as saying that he would have to see Sidd Finch to believe him. Now that he *had* seen him, what did he have to say?

"Well, frankly, now that I've seen him . . ." the Commissioner replied laconically, "I believe him."

"What are you going to do about the situation?"

The Commissioner was very forthright. He mentioned the regulation in his powers that allowed him to do just about anything in the "best interests" of baseball.

"I'd bring that option into play. If Finch keeps this sort of thing up, I'd be inclined to mandate a trade from the Mets to the last-place team in their division," the Commissioner said. "At the moment, let's see, that would be *Pittsburgh*. A minor-league player to be named later would be part of the deal. It always is. So Finch would go there. Pittsburgh's performance would improve, and their attendance, which is about a third of the Mets, would increase dramatically."

His questioner was aghast. "The Mets management . . ." he stumbled. "Your powers as Commissioner . . ."

"If you're asking me if I have the power to do this, the answer is yes," the Commissioner said. "I'll tell you something else that I would see done. The Major League Scouting Bureau is based in Irvine, California. I'd recommend the establishment of a branch in the Himalayas. It may well be that in terms of supplying talent, the Himalayas will become the Dominican Republic of the major leagues!"

It was obvious that, like Bob Brown, the Commissioner was having fun with his interviewer. He is noted for his puckish actions on occasion. On the day of the major-league draft he gave an extra choice to the New York Yankees that allowed them to pick a mysterious George F. Will, who turned out to be the famous conservative essayist ("He's forty-three and bats right, very right.") . . .

a prank that did not go down especially well with the baseball fraternity, and especially the scribes, who feel that baseball is a religion and should not undergo ecumenical fiddlings, especially of an irreverent nature.

"You think I'm kidding around?" the Commissioner was saying. "Hell no. I've got the best interests of baseball at heart. I've got a lot of options. I intend to exercise them."

All evening long television pulled in analysts—ranging from medical specialists trying to explain the mechanics of Sidd's delivery to representatives from extreme religious cults who announced that their karma was just as powerful as Finch's and that their people could throw a baseball just as fast if *that* was what was important in life, which, of course, it wasn't. They were scornful—it was a dereliction of values.

The last show we watched was *Nightline*. Billy Martin came on, his small angry face filling a huge screen beyond the host's, Ted Koppel's, shoulder. Martin, who was playing in a golf tournament in Phoenix, said that the answer to Finch would be to have him solidly plunked in the ribs with a pitch when he came up to bat. "That'll do something to his concentration, I'll guarantee. Watch him on the mound the next inning and see that fastball fade. . . ."

Koppel turned on his swivel chair and said into the camera, "We have heard Billy Martin say he would knock Finch down. When we come back we will find out to what degree he would carry such measures. . . ."

The effect of all this on Sidd was not clear. He had listened and watched intently, barely aware of Debbie Sue's ministrations. Perched on the arm-rest, she occasionally leaned over to rumple his hair or knead his arm muscles. One of the few times he turned away from the set was to ask if the Commissioner truly had the right to send him to Pittsburgh.

"I am content with the Mets," he said, "although I know very few of the personnel and have yet to refer to anyone by their first name. I know very little of Pittsburgh, except that Mr. Kiner of the corner once played with that organization."

"Yes," I said. "I think the Commissioner was having fun . . . keeping his interviewer a little off balance."

"Do you think I will have to pitch four feet back?"

"They were kidding."

"They are worried, though. I can tell."

The next morning the same sort of thing appeared in the newspapers. The Finch story was on the first page of *The New York Times*. One of the *Times* writers referred to Sidd as "mysterious as the Yeti, the Abominable Snowman, who is said to prowl the bamboo thickets of the Himalayan highlands." A multitude of photographs accompanied the stories, though, oddly, many of them seemed taken on the fly—strange, fuzzy photographs of Sidd, his head turned half away, or his eyes half closed, or the picture a bit out of focus, so that he seemed almost as anonymous as a gangster hiding behind his fedora. The New York *Post* described Sidd as the "Kathmandu Fireballer." The *Daily News* called him both "the Buddhist Bolt" and "Shoeless Sidd."

Debbie Sue looked up from the papers and announced she had come up with a nickname for Sidd. She would not tell us, ducking her head and giggling. It was too personal and silly. Finally she fessed up. It turned out to be "Debbie Sue's Sidd."

"What?"

"That's what the radio announcer would say— '. . . coming up to bat, "Debbie Sue's Sidd.' " Well, it's better than 'the Buddhist Bolt,' " she said defensively.

The Mets driver came for Sidd at 9:00 A.M. We heard the horn down on the street.

"They're giving me fielding and batting practice this morning," Sidd said. "I am going to learn the signals—what it means to 'go to the mouth' and such matters." He looked at the newspapers on the dining-room table. I caught sight of a tabloid headline that read "Mom Toppled Off Cliff." "I'm not sure about all this," he said.

"Not many people make the first page of *The New York Times.*"

"Maybe it won't change things," Sidd said. "I can come back here after every game. You and Debbie Sue can have your tetrazzini. We can set up a table by the window and watch the river traffic."

"I don't think it will work out that way," I said. "It's not that simple."

XV

THE METS MANAGEMENT called at noon. Jay Horwitz asked if I would drive out to Shea Stadium to see them. They had some important news to tell me, which they thought best to do in private.

"Isn't Sidd out there?" I asked.

"I'll say he is," Jay replied. "He's out taking fielding and batting practice. He can't seem to do anything halfway. His peg to first—once he gets control of the ball—goes at that same god-awful speed. Lots of yelping down there."

As I drove out to Shea in my sister's car, I turned on the radio to find every talk show along the length of the dial pulsating with speculation about Finch. There was an edge to many of the conversations—an indication that people were worried about what he was doing to the inherent structure of the game. One listener (calling in from Tucson, Arizona) had a suggestion. Wouldn't it be possible to *outlaw* a pitch that went over, for example, 125 miles an hour? With a speed-gun monitor, a signal would be flashed from the center-field scoreboard to the umpire that would alert him to the presence of an "overspeeding ball," as the listener put it; the umpire would raise an arm

253

and that particular pitch would be disallowed. If the pitcher persisted in "overspeeding," the umpire could penalize the pitcher by calling a ball. The talk-show host said, "Hmmm, that's interesting, Tucson."

He reminded his audience that the listener's idea had precedence: the spitball, a doctored pitch that slipped and swerved, was outlawed in the 1930s as being too difficult to hit. The rule had a rather touching "grandfather clause" proviso—that pitchers who relied on the spitball as a major part of their repertoire were allowed to continue throwing the pitch until their careers were over. A few pitchers continued to throw the spitball, doctoring it in some way, though it was done, of course, surreptitiously. But it was important to remember, the talk-show host said, that there was a difference here. Sidd Finch's pitch, though apparently *totally* unhittable, *hadn't* been doctored. He hadn't spit on the ball, or notched it with a razor-blade tip sewn into his glove. What he did was legal. He just wound up and threw the thing! Thus if anything was to be outlawed, it would have to be the whole apparatus—Sidd Finch *himself*.

The next caller was from Portland. First, he praised the program. "Ed, you've got a great show there." Ed thanked him and said, "Now what's your question, Portland?"

The listener from Portland said that first he would like to make a comment. He agreed that legislation within a sport was usually the way to handle problems of this sort. In basketball the three-second rule had kept the big guys from parking under the hoop. Controlling a superforce, the kind of guy Sidd Finch was, was simply a matter, in basketball at any rate, of moving lines and setting up time zones. "You normalize these guys."

"And what's your question, Portland?"

"Well, Ed, with this guy Finch we got a problem."

"Yes."

"Let me make a further point, Ed."

"Go right ahead, but keep it short, Portland."

"Let's take hockey. Suppose you found a guy whose body shape—a kind of very fat turnip-shaped body—really plugged up the goal mouth—"

The talk-show host interrupted to say there was a rule that limited the width of the leg pads in hockey; whatever the shape of the goaltender, it was still likely that his skills would be a matter of agility and quickness of hand—eye reactions rather than bulk.

The listener persisted. "Ed, I respect your judgment." His voice had a faint strain of New York in it. "But I know a circus fat guy, six hundred and fifty pounds, who would plug up a goal mouth just by squatting there. Or suppose he was one of those very big Japanese sumo wrestlers. Those guys could lie down in front of the nets. Ed, they could go to sleep out there—"

"Thank you very much, Portland." The talk-show host sounded tired. He was saying that all sports had regulations that barred anything obviously detrimental to the spirit of the game . . . such as a sumo wrestler lying in front of a hockey goal. That was what baseball had done about Eddie Gaedel, the midget who weighed sixty-five pounds and stood three feet seven inches. "He wore the number ⅛ on his jersey. I'll bet not too many of you remember that," he said. He apparently prided himself on his fund of sports trivia. "He came up to bat for the St. Louis Browns in a game against the Detroit Tigers in August 1951. Bill Veeck, who was then the St. Louis general manager, was the guy who engineered all this. The pitcher was Bob Cain. How's that for the old memory bank? Walked Gaedel, whose strike zone must have been about five inches, or four straight balls. He trotted down to first base and they sent in a pinch runner for him. Bet not too many of you guys out there know that the base runner's name was . . . Jim Delsing." He stopped briefly for effect. "Now, what the league then did was to disapprove Gaedel's major-league contract on the grounds that his participation was not in the best interests of baseball."

There was a long pause for commercials, and when Ed's program came back on he had a listener from Syracuse, New York, on the line.

"Hey, Ed, I like your program."

"Thanks, Syracuse. It's always good to hear from Syracuse."

"Ed, you were talking about Eddie Gaedel, the midget?"

"That's correct."

"I'll bet you didn't know that right here in Syracuse, Eddie Gaedel came up to bat for a *second* time. That's right . . . in a sandlot league."

"No. I didn't know that. What happened?"

"Struck out on three called strikes," the voice from Syracuse announced proudly. "That little strike zone of his didn't bother the pitcher in the slightest. Gaedel was furious. They say he turned around to the umpire and shouted at him, 'You're the worst umpire I ever hope to see.' "

"Is that so? Well, you sure flummoxed ol' Ed!"

"Ed, I have a comment to make about this guy, Sidd Finch?"

"Go right ahead, Syracuse . . . ."

"Why isn't it a pertinent fact that the guy is not only English, as I understand it, but a *Buddhist*. He worships some kind of Himalayan *saint*. I'm not saying that's the same as doctoring a baseball with spit—"

"Hey, hold on there, Syracuse. What you're talking about now impinges on a guy's First Amendment rights. . . ."

"But, Ed. This guy hasn't sworn to uphold the Constitution of the United States. He's probably not even got a green card that allows him to work here. He's a tourist. A *Buddhist* tourist—"

The radio host was quick with the Syracuse listener for his prejudices and clicked him off. Commercials came on again, followed by a call from Fort Lauderdale.

"Yes, Fort Lauderdale."

"Ed, may I produce a scenario? This guy Finch

pitches, let's say, and wins eight games in a row—perfect games, eighty-one pitches, all that . . . what's it going to do to the *gate?* It's going to drop off. The fans, even the greatest of them—Mets fans—aren't going out to see a row of games that look . . . well, like forfeitures."

The radio host disagreed. "I disagree, Fort Lauderdale. They'll come to watch Finch so they can tell their grandchildren they watched the greatest pitcher who ever lived."

"Hell, Ed—excuse the profanity—it's odds on that their grandchildren *will* see this guy pitch. Don't these Buddhist guys up there in the mountains of Tibet live to be a hundred years old, eat yoghurt, and carry pianos around on their backs? That's what I hear. We may have this guy Finch screwing up the game for thirty or forty *years.*"

"He'll have his day in the sun, Fort Lauderdale," the talk-show host said. "Every once in a while a guy comes along who dominates a sport—a Nicklaus or a Palmer in golf, or a Manolete in bullfighting, or a Jim Clark or a Jackie Stewart in the Grand Prix, or a Joe Louis or a Muhammad Ali in boxing . . . and it enhances a sport to have these guys emerge and control the roosts for a while. Correct?"

"But, Ed, this guy's a spook. He's like a machine. Coming out to the ballpark'll be like buying tickets to see a machine gun setting out there on the mound."

"It's an interesting point, Fort Lauderdale, but I disagree. Fans will come to see who gets the first

258

hit off him. Some will come to see the first guy *he* hits. The first home run. The first guy he walks. They want to see the strategy used against him. They want to see how the hitters behave. He can't do this forever."

"Something's going to get him long before that," the listener said. "It won't be baseball. It'll be the institutions, the tradition guys, the Establishment. . . . I'll bet they're working on it right now. . . ."

"Thank you very much, Fort Lauderdale."

A call came in from Duluth.

"Ed, what about that bare foot. As I understand it, a baseball player in the major leagues is required to wear a proper uniform out onto the field. A pitcher can't go out there wearing a green bowler."

"Yes, Duluth. The newspapers commented on that today. The Mets apparently went to the National League offices to get some kind of dispensation about that bare foot. Their reasoning to the offices was this: to put a shoe on the guy might throw off his balance, the timing, and maybe a Cardinal would get himself blown away. Simple as that. Or the umpire. Or some poor guy sitting in the stands behind the plate turning and asking his girl for some mustard. Bop! That'd be the last thing he'd ever see—a little mustard squeezing out onto his hot dog."

"The league allowed it?"

"He's the biggest thing in baseball, Duluth."

"Well . . ."

"The Cardinals may appeal the case up to the Commissioner's office. One story we read was that Steve Garland, the Mets trainer, was going to paint a blue shoe on Sidd's foot."

The last caller I heard was from St. Louis. He asked, "Ed, remember the House of David teams—the guys with the long beards? They were good ballplayers and great entertainers. Sort of like the Harlem Globetrotters? They did these incredible fielding drills in which they whipped an invisible ball around the infield. Right?"

"Yesss . . ." the announcer said.

"You couldn't believe they didn't have the ball—a great act."

"And your point, St. Louis?"

"That this guy, Finch, doesn't actually throw the ball. He palms it somehow."

"Well, now . . ."

I clicked off the dial.

Coming off the Triborough Bridge I suddenly had a clear image of what Sidd was doing to the game. It was what the listeners were suggesting—he was changing the properties and the essence of the ball itself. It struck me how often the ball *is* inspected during a game, as if anyone who touches it has to make sure the ball has *not* changed its properties. If the ball disappears over the fence, another, like a youngster's dream pinball game, emerges from a black sack at the umpire's side. He looks at it and gives it to the catcher, who rubs it briefly, and after a glance fires it out to the pitcher; *he* looks at the ball and rubs it with both hands, his glove dangling from its wrist strap, and then, as he stares down at the catcher for the signal, his fingers manoeuver over its surface feeling for the comfort of some response—yes, this time it will do exactly as he wishes! Who has not seen a shortstop handling an easy ground ball—two big hops and there it is for him to look down into his glove and seem to read (*National League, Chub Feeney, Rawlings,* whatever) before plucking it out and zipping it across the diamond to the first baseman who, of course, in turn inspects it. If the last out of the inning, the first baseman lobs the ball nonchalantly to the first base umpire who cannot resist taking a peek too, just to be reassured, before he rolls it out to the mound where the opposing pitcher, emerging from his team's dugout, will stride up the slope of the mound to bend and pick it up for *his* inspection and then comfort his fingers with its texture.

Football players do not have this kind of kinship with their ball. Most of the players don't even touch the thing during the course of a game. It sits stolidly on the grass. The center comes up over the ball from the huddle and barely giving it a glance turns it under his hands; his eyes are staring across the line of scrimmage at the unpleasant visage of the nose guard opposite. A defensive tackle is so uncomfortable with the ball that if he chances to pick it up on the practice-field he tends to throw it end over end to get rid of it.

Basketball players do not look at the ball. They are taught not to. Look downcourt. Look at the rim of the basket. Look at the midriff of the defender. The thing *planking* off the wooden floor to the palm and back is simply a piece of luggage to be moved from here to here, and then tossed to another porter, so that he too can hurry it down the floor.

Tennis players have been told since infancy to keep their eye on the ball, but they have no true affection or interest with the ball itself. Tennis balls are not kept on the mantelpiece. Too many of them around. Who cares? Golf balls are illusive and small; they infuriate; they are whacked into the bushes; they buzz off like yellow jackets.

But Sidd had done something to the ball of baseball—at least in the one game he had pitched. He had removed all its familiar associations. When the ball got into his hands, it was almost impossible to see; the comforting sounds it normally made were removed: the easy slap of the ball into a fielder's mitt, the cork sound of the bat against the ball. Suddenly a phrase from his April Fool's Day letter to the Mets came to mind: the ball had become a *thing*—what was it?—"of Chaos and Cruelty."

At Shea I had a short visit with Frank Cashen—chatting mostly about Sidd Finch and his state of mind in New York. He told me he was having a terrible time with Sidd's reluctance to say anything to the press. The requests had been voluminous, obviously, from every quarter of the media. He had tried to let Sidd know that the situation could be controlled. Dwight Gooden had gone through the same problem the year before. Jay Horwitz, sitting right beside him, had helped him through the press conferences. The arrangement could be the same. Sidd wouldn't even have to *speak*. Jay would speak for him. "Sidd Finch likes New York. Sidd Finch is going to visit the Statue of Liberty," and so forth. If Sidd wanted to say anything, he could pass Jay notes. (I thought of Jay reading a series of koans to the press.)

"How did he react?" I asked.

"He said he wouldn't. He was very polite and apologetic," Cashen said. "I had the sense he felt part of his spirit could be talked away—the way, you know, certain tribal people feel they lose part of their souls if you snap their picture? He was scared of being asked about his pitching. Disruptive maybe. It'd be like asking a pro golfer whether he breathes in or out when he swings."

Cashen grinned and ran his hand through the close crop of his hair. I noticed he was wearing a beaded copper bracelet.

"When he gets harassed he says these weird things, doesn't he? We'd finished talking about the press. He looked at me and said, 'The ass looks at the well; the well looks at the ass.' "

"Hmmmm."

After my chat with Cashen, I was ushered in to see a security agent named Bill F. Scott. We talked in a small airless office somewhere in the innards of the stadium.

"Mr. Temple," he said, "we've had a report

from a source that we have to worry about a little bit."

"Oh?"

"It's of concern since Sidd Finch is staying with you. The report, in brief, is that an argument broke out last night in a social club in Astoria—Abe's Fish and Stream. It's a mob hangout. The guy we're worried about is a big hood, a three-hundred-pounder, named Al 'Big Cakes' Caporetto. There are two things to remember about Al—or Big Cakes if you prefer."

"Al," I said. "I prefer Al."

"First, he's crazy about the St. Louis Cardinals. He either came from St. Louis or did a couple of jobs there, during which he picked up this passion for the team. He wears a Cardinals cap, they say, even on the job. Tassels on his Italian shoes. Second, he tends to flare up—a quick, violent temper. He has a reputation, a very well-founded one, for being a compulsive hit man."

"A compulsive hit man?"

"A guy who gets overenthusiastic and tends to blow away more people than he's supposed to. He's not considered very reliable by the capos. A maverick."

"What happened in Abe's Fish and Stream?" I asked.

"He and a guy named Noodles McGuire got into an argument."

"Noodles?"

"That's what they call the guy," the security agent said. "Hardly any flesh on him. Turns sideways and you can hardly spot him. Record as a cat burglar. Very wise-ass guy with a high voice like a rasp."

"What was the problem?" I asked.

"The argument was about Finch."

The security man explained that Caporetto had apparently read the article about Sidd in a three-month-old *Sports Illustrated* he'd picked up while having a haircut. After piecing his way through it he had announced hotly to the barber that the contents were a fraud. He had repeated his feelings to a table of his kind at Peter's Pizza, a hangout in the Red Hook area of Brooklyn, and later at Abe's Fish and Stream in Astoria. It was there that Noodles McGuire, who had heard through the grapevine that Finch had rejoined the Mets organization and was going to pitch that afternoon, taunted him into betting a substantial amount that Finch was not only for real but was going to pitch a couple of shutouts in a row.

"The odds on two shutouts in a row are huge, of course," Scott said. "If Caporetto loses the bet when Sidd pitches this Thursday—he stands to lose a bundle, not only to Noodles, but a real big one to the bookies."

"What does this have to do with Sidd?" I asked.

"Well, the word we get is that Caporetto might try to tamper with Finch's performance. He boasted he was going to take matters into his own hands."

"Nothing much I can do about that," I said.

The security man leaned over his desk. "At

worst he might try to damage Finch on home territory—where you're staying."

"Shouldn't you move him to a hotel?" I asked. "Where we're living—the Mullins apartment—is not exactly a fortress."

The security man suggested such a move would attract more attention. "Moving guys in and out of hotels," he said, "is a security nightmare. Too many people around. Your street is quiet," he pointed out. "A dead end. Just the kind of place we like. We'll put a security man down in front of your apartment house. It's no more than a precaution. After all, this guy Caporetto has no idea Finch is living there."

"Should I say anything about this to Sidd?" I asked.

"You're kidding me! No, no, nothing!"

From the urgency of his voice I guessed that he knew something about the catastrophe in the enclosure at Huggins-Stengel back in April. Sidd was obviously not to be put under any mental pressure. "I want you to understand that everything's under control," he said firmly.

"That's fine," I said. "I'm very glad to hear it."

On the way out of the parking lot I spotted Sidd by the clubhouse entrance, waiting for his ride home. I stopped the car and leaned out the window to wave at him. He grinned and said he would tell someone inside that he was going back to Manhattan with me.

266

He got into the front seat and folded his hands in his lap.

"How did practice go?" I asked.

"I managed a foul in the batting cage," he said with a grin. "Around the field the Mets players clapped their hands. The one they call Mookie Wilson shouted, 'Hey, man!' In the batting cage I thought of Sadaharu—how he thought of the ball as something to eat—the wolf devouring the rabbit. I thought of ma, the space between the pitcher and the batter that one must control." He shook his head. "But it was of small avail. I have no appropriate mantras or ngags for hitting a baseball. I craved the sanctuary of the dugout. It is clever that designers of ballparks have put in dugouts like burrows into which one can duck to hide one's shame."

"Did they teach you how to steal a base?" I asked.

Sidd laughed. "That is against my tantric principles. I do not believe I will put myself in a position to do such a terrible thing."

Bill F. Scott, the security gentleman, telephoned me later that afternoon.

"Did you drive Sidd Finch home?"

"Yes," I replied. "Piece of luck. I happened to see him waiting for his driver."

"So we understand. Did you take an evasive action on the way back into Manhattan?"

"I beg your pardon?"

"Did you go up one ramp and down another, run a light or two to shake anybody . . . ?"

"Why no."

"Hmmm."

"Are you telling me we were followed?"

"It's a possibility. Finch's regular driver follows a whole procedure to lose guys—the press, for example. Just in case."

"I drive a fairly nondescript car," I said. "It's my sister's. It's awfully easy to lose in traffic."

"That's a relief. Any distinguishing features?"

"It's a rather dusty station wagon. It has an old George McGovern sticker on the back window, come to think of it, and an *I Brake for Whales* on the rear bumper. That's about all."

"What about the license plate?"

"Actually, it's one of those personalized plates," I admitted. "It says SALTY IV. That's the name of my father's yacht."

The security man sighed. "Well, we'll hope for the best," he said. "The chances are big, very big, that you weren't followed. But if you were, you sure didn't make it rough for them. You could have tied a dozen tin cans to the bumper."

"I'm sorry."

The security agent said, "Well, if you get a phone call from a guy with a muffled voice who says that if Finch pitches on Thursday he'll get himself turned from a right-hander into a left-hander, let me know, will you?"

"Absolutely."

XVI

THE NEXT MORNING, after Sidd was taken off to practice at Shea, and Debbie Sue left to take a river trip around Manhattan on the Circle Line, I called an old friend and writer, Gay Talese, to ask his advice about Al "Big Cakes" Caporetto. I could not rid my mind of the security agent's account of the three-hundred-pound "wise guy"—the current term for a mobster—the threats he had made in Abe's Fish and Stream Club, and the chilling fact that he was known as a compulsive hit man! Talese had won a Pulitzer Prize for his study of the mob, *Honor Thy Father*. He was astounded to hear from me. "My God, it's been ten years. I heard you've been in"—he paused, and I had the feeling he was going to say "sanitarium," but he shifted at the last—"in the East," he said vaguely. He wanted to plan a dinner and "catch up on things." I said I would look forward to that.

In the meantime, I had a favor to ask. Without referring to Sidd by name, I asked Gay how the mob would deal with a major-league pitcher who for a complexity of reasons had to be shut down . . . how would they see to it?

"You mean like how they got to Robert Redford in *The Natural?*"

"I guess so."

269

Gay thought for a moment.

"I've been doing other things," he said.

"Yes, I know," I admitted.

He cleared his throat, and after mentioning the obvious possibilities—bribes and financial inducements (as in the case of the Chicago Black Sox), harassment, telephone threats, the intimidation of relatives or lovers, that kind of thing—he said that the mob would probably contact one of the third-world union people.

"Who are they?" I asked.

"In baseball they're the guys who hold fairly specialized low-grade positions—sub-grounds-keeper stuff. The guys who paint the foul lines and come out with the steel mats and haul them around to sweep the base paths halfway through the sixth inning. Whoever puts the rosin bag out behind the mound. The guy who drives the pitcher in from the bull pen in the golf cart . . . *those* are the guys you have to watch. They can be reached."

"You mean they might put poison in the rosin bag?"

"Exactly. Doctor the rosin bag with something that cramps up the pitcher's fingers. He picks it up, toys with it, and his fingers are like steel hooks for twenty minutes. Or driving the pitcher in from the bull pen. For thirty seconds they've got him defenseless, sitting there in the front seat with his baseball glove in his lap."

"You mean they'd simply drive out of the park with him?"

"Why not? They'd turn and head for the left-field exit, where some accomplice—another third-world union guy—would swing open the gate and they'd be sailing through the parking lot before you could say 'scat.' They'd shove the pitcher in the trunk of a Chevy in one of those body-shop alleys behind Shea and be off to Hoboken."

"Hoboken?"

"That always seems to be on the itinerary in this kind of thing." Gay laughed at the other end. "I'm being a little overdramatic."

"You don't think they'd simply break the pitcher's arm?"

"That's a little Little Caesarish," he said. "These mob guys tend in most cases to be fairly low-key. In the case of your hypothetical pitcher, they'd get some guy to close a car door on his fingers. Hey, how about this guy Sidd Finch? Twenty-seven strikeouts! You going to Shea on Thursday?"

"I'm going to try, Gay," I said.

"I wouldn't miss that one for anything!"

Not minutes after my conversation with Gay Talese, the doorbell rang. I had just started a desultory game of solitary pool on the Mullins table. The cat, Mister Puss, was sitting on the window seat. The river moved by in the background. His ears perked at the sound of the bell. Through the intercom system I asked who it was. Scroggins, Scraggle, some such name.

I buzzed him in, but I kept the apartment door locked and looked out the peephole to see who was coming up the stairs. Anyone over two hundred pounds I decided to keep out.

The man appearing in the peephole seemed harmless enough—stout but small, carrying a tan suitcase—obviously neither Big Cakes or his shadowy nemesis, Noodles McGuire. Nor did he remind me of a "third-world union" man. I let him in.

He looked around.

"Am I the first?" he asked.

"I beg your pardon?"

"The bubble gummers haven't turned up yet?"

His name was Tom Scranton. To my astonishment, he knew that Sidd Finch was living in the Mullins apartment. Before I could find out *how* he knew, he had his suitcase open.

"Got some items here that'll interest you and Sidd Finch," he said. "Sidd's going to be contacted by lots of people wanting his endorsements. The sportswear people are going to contact him. So are the shoe people, the bat and glovers, the bubble gummers, you name it. My line is gimmicks—dolls that bounce on the back shelves of cars, state-of-the-art things like that. Right?"

I said I was not really in a position to answer for Sidd Finch.

He was reaching in his sample case. He pulled out a mug in the shape of a face.

"Are you familiar with toby jugs? A hundred years ago it was a big Dutch and English item. Right? Just about every *king* had his likeness done as a toby jug. Henry the Eighth. Charles the First."

"You'd like to do Sidd Finch as a toby jug?" I asked.

"Right on! We're looking to the kids' market," Scranton said. "A kid's more likely to drink his milk if it's out of a Dwight Gooden or a George Brett mug. An adult, a guy sitting at a bar ordering up a rye and ginger ale, wants to drink out of a *glass*, not a mug that looks like a face. Right? But a kid's different. Look, he drinks right out of the top of the guy's head." He demonstrated. He smacked his lips as if the mug contained a liquid. "The whole item retails for $10.95." He held it up. "This one's a Fernando Valenzuela, but you get the general idea."

I explained that I couldn't speak for Sidd. I wasn't his agent. As far as I knew, he didn't even have an agent.

"Besides, Mr. Scranton," I went on, "I don't think Sidd believes in the kind of worldly goods you've got there in your suitcase—the toby jugs, the little wooden bats. To be frank, Sidd just doesn't care about income. He gets through life with a beggar's bowl and a long stick."

"I've read about all that," Scranton said. "If this guy's only got a bowl and a stick, he's going to want to improve his life-style, right? The perks. The fast cars. The Nautilus equipment. The stereo. He's got to have a roof over his head. Give Finch a credit card and you'll see what happens.

"Possibly."

Scranton asked if he could leave a few samples for Sidd to look over. "Compliments of the com-

273

pany." He left me the Valenzuela mug, a miniature bat, a few dolls (I recognized a Gary Carter model), a catalog of the various items his company offered, and a business card.

"You sure the bubble-gum guy hasn't been here yet?" he asked. "He's usually on hand before the signature on the contract is dry."

"No," I said. "Sidd doesn't chew gum. He's a peppermint man."

After Scranton left I called up Smith, the Mets security expert, to tell him I'd had a visitor.

"What?" He seemed agitated. "Did you let him in?" he asked.

"He seemed harmless enough," I said. "A small man carrying a sample case. But what surprised me was that he knew Finch was living here. He knew the address."

"What's the guy's name?"

"Scranton," I said. "Tom Scranton. He sells mugs that look like faces."

"Just a sec," the security man said. He was apparently looking in his files. "Scranton's okay. He's a Mets licensee. He's on the 'Need to Know' list."

"Who else is on the . . . 'Need to Know' list?" I asked.

"About twenty or so, I'd guess."

"Twenty!" I said in astonishment. "I thought this was supposed to be a secure location."

"Well, there's Mr. Cashen. Mr. Doubleday. The personnel department. Tickets. Sidd may want some comps. The coaches . . . Steve Garland, the trainer . . . people who might have to get in touch with him for one reason or another."

I could not resist asking, "Does the guy who puts the rosin bag out on the pitcher's mound . . . does he know?"

"What's that? Listen, not to worry," the agent said cheerfully. "We got an operative watching your place. Relax. I'll tell you who else is on that list."

"Who?" I asked.

"*You're* on it."

"Oh. Well, I'm very glad to hear that," I said.

When she got back from her boat trip around Manhattan, I told Debbie Sue about Big Cakes. I put it simply: that the Mets security people had warned us to be on the lookout for an "overemotional gambler" (I didn't use the words *mobster* or *compulsive hit man*) who had bet too much on the Thursday game coming up. He might try to influence Sidd, perhaps even with physical harm. He was a huge man, over three hundred pounds. Wears a Cardinals baseball cap. Hard to miss. If she saw anyone like that, she should . . . well, keep Sidd away from him, and let me know. Sidd was not to be told anything about this. The Mets hadn't; their thought was that his frame of mind might be disturbed.

Debbie Sue's eyes widened slightly at all this, but she seemed very collected—*cool* was the word—and I was surprised. It struck me that a nineteen-year-old girl confronted with the possibility of dealing with an overemotional three-hundred-pounder bent on harming Sidd would produce more of a reaction. She nodded and started telling me about her trip around Manhattan. Looking up at the Mullins apartment as the Circle Line boat went past, she told me she had spotted Mister Puss outlined distantly in one of the windows. She startled a number of people sitting on the slatted seats around her by shouting out his name.

"Oh, Owl, it was funny," she said. "Over the public address system the Circle Line guide had just finished telling us all the famous people who live in the big apartment houses just down from the Mullinses'—Greta Garbo, J. Paul Getty, Johnny Carson, Gloria Vanderbilt, Henry Kissinger, and everybody, and that Frank Sinatra once had a penthouse on top of the building opposite . . . and all of a sudden here came the little black apartment house where we live and there was Mister Puss looking across at us. I could see him clearly. I shouted at him, "Mister Puss! Look, it's Mister Puss!" All these people around me cried out, 'Who? Who? Mr. Who?' "

When Sidd got home from practice that afternoon, Debbie Sue twirled him around. "How did it go? Did you bean anyone?" But then she startled him by saying she was going to put a disguise on him. We were planning to go out that night—our first evening on the town.

"Why must we do this?" Sidd had asked.

"I don't want you stared at," she said simply.

Sidd sat in a chair opposite her. I sat and

watched. It was a wonderful time for her—being utterly in control of him, tipping his chin, asking him to stare at the ceiling, while she applied various eye shadows, paints, ointments, and powders she had collected from the Mullinses' bathrooms. Sidd complained—but mildly. He looked vaguely like a clown when she had finished. His faintly melancholy looks were emphasized by eye shadow; his cheeks were brightly rouged. She settled a pair of dark glasses on his nose. We went to a Japanese restaurant. People stared at him, not because they recognized the Mets' newest star, but because he looked vaguely like someone prepared for Halloween.

Once, during dinner, Debbie Sue nudged me. "See that man over there?" She pointed surreptitiously at a man sitting alone at a corner table in the recesses of the restaurant.

"Yes."

"How much do you think he weighs?"

I looked and said about two hundred pounds.

"How about that guy over there?"

Sidd didn't seem bothered by Debbie Sue's interest in what people weighed around the room. From across the table he asked me, "Whatever happened to the small man with the bow legs?"

I went through a moment of confusion.

"The gentleman from Burma who could hit home runs."

I suddenly understood he was asking me about the dream I had described to him in Florida. "But that was just a dream, Sidd. Yes. A Burmese batter with a silver bat came up to the plate and really socked one off you. The ball went up over an elephant in the bull pen in left field."

"There's no reason why there shouldn't be someone in baseball like that," he remarked.

"There're millions of Burmese," I said, grinning at him. "The law of averages . . ."

"Mr. Johnson would like me to pitch again on Thursday night," Sidd said. "He is apologetic, but what he calls his rotation is 'shot'—as he put it. It's the last game of the Cardinals series and he feels that having pitched once against them successfully, I might be able to do so again."

"What did you say?"

"I told him I was prepared. The arm—"

I interrupted to ask if he wasn't worried about having a bad day. I shuddered to think what that might be like with a ball that traveled at that rocket speed. "After all, Sidd," I said, "most athletes have . . . well, good days and bad ones . . ."

He nodded. "It is difficult. There is a test in the Himalayas where the *trapa* sits in a snowfield and his tumo is judged by how much snow he melts around him. I knew of a very cocky trapa sitting down in a great snowbank near Tang Tin, which is a mountain in western Tibet, to show everyone his stuff, and nothing happened. They all stood around while he tried to get his tumo-heat going, straining hard, and imagining himself as a charcoal fire, and finally he looked very fragile and small, shivering there in the snowbank. It was not his day."

278

"So it can disappear," I said. "I mean once you learn, it's not necessarily with you always."

"I'm afraid so," he said.

We turned on the television when we got back to the Mullins' apartment.

"Lordy, it's Smythe," Sidd said. He dropped down in front of the set. "He was at Stowe with me."

The screen was showing a haughty face listening to a question. A microphone appeared near his mouth; he looked at it nervously. A tongue flickered out to wet his lips, which appeared faintly rouged. "Calls himself Finch now, does he? Used to be Hayden Finch. His father was related to Sir Philip Sidney. Of course, Hayden was adopted. Played the French horn in the woods, I do recall that. Left school early. Something about his father dying in an airplane crash. Never spoke to anyone. We always thought he was stuck up. Or stuttered. Never answered any questions. I remember him saying 'I'd rather not say.' Don't recall what was being asked of him."

A master appeared on the screen wearing a tweed coat. "Hopkins," Sidd whispered to us. "Taught Classics." The master smiled brightly. "He was a clever boy. Rather independent Fink-Hadden was . . . oh, Finch . . . yes Hayden Finch. Quite a good musician. The oboe, was it? Oh yes, French horn. He tended to play the wrong compositions at practices, as I recall, which made him somewhat . . . how would one say? . . . unsteady. Not one to play in the school orchestra. An athlete? I can't say really. He wasn't one of the great athletes we've had here because I'd remember. Colin Shellington, the great Irish miler we had here, or R. M. Bartlett, who won four caps on that splendid English rugby team back in the fifties. Hayden Finch was certainly not of that calibre. Oh, a *baseball* player? Well, that explains why his name doesn't spring to mind . . . we don't play baseball at Stowe. Or do we? Never have to my knowledge."

The BBC announcer appeared and talked about Sidd's father—mentioning the mysterious airplane crash in the Himalayas (an aerial view appeared showing the general area where the plane had disappeared), the tragedy of his wife, Edwina, a line or two about her famous scarab brooch collection, and then, of course, an account of her fall (once again an aerial panorama appeared showing the fatal peak in the mountain chain).

We had a brief scan of the house on Denbigh Close. Their reporter had rung the bell. No answer. The camera peeked through the windows. The furniture within was covered with shrouds. Neighbors were interviewed and said that the house had been deserted for years. Sometimes, for hours on end, they said they could hear a Hoover whining through the place.

"Do you suppose your model train is still in operation?" I asked Sidd when the program was over.

His eyes lit up. "Oh, I suspect so. Everything

was to be kept as it was. The sheets over the furniture can be whipped away. The cleaning lady is required to go down to the ballroom. She is supposed to go to the electric panel and push the appropriate switch to keep the train set operative. It must be the worst moment of the day for her. Everything starts up. The lights in the farmhouses go on. In his caboose the Mr. God of All He Surveys is carried along for two or three feet, at which point it's all right for her to cut the switch and hurry back upstairs."

That night after supper Sidd began talking about Dennis Brain, the famous French horn player who had performed in his father's house in London. He described a composition Brain often played in concert halls—Mozart's horn Concerto in E, which is notorious for stopping abruptly in midflight.

"It's quite odd," Sidd said. "It's unfinished— this marvelous piece of work."

His father had described a performance of the concerto in London's Jubilee Hall where Brain had sat in a chair out in front of the orchestra. After a series of brilliant violin and oboe passages, the horn enters heroically, suggesting great things to come. But then in the middle of an intricate and wonderfully florid passage, the horn *stops* . . . like a breath cut off. In that abrupt silence, Brain stood up from his chair. He smiled. He shrugged his shoulders and then turned and, carrying his horn, walked off the stage. It was that shrug of his that Sidd's father remembered so vividly: it seemed to suggest not so much bewilderment as an acceptance that the composer had the right to do such things.

Debbie Sue wanted to know why Mozart hadn't finished the concerto.

Sidd smiled as he shrugged *his* shoulders. "Who knows. Mozart left a lot of unfinished pieces . . . but what is so strange is that this one is so obviously a masterpiece."

He asked us if we would like to hear the last notes. Debbie Sue went up the spiral staircase to bring down his horn.

I have vivid memories of her, instant portraits, as if flashed on a screen from a carousel projector. She is always in half-light in these flashbacks, as if the magic of her would dissolve in a bright glare. No matter. One of the recurrent images is of her on the circular stair that night. She seemed to be guided by the gold instrument in front of her, holding it as if the coils were quite foreign to her; she handed Sidd the horn almost in relief.

"There!"

It took Sidd a relatively long time to prepare the horn to play . . . so different from the instantaneous action he gave to his other skills—pitching a baseball or producing his sounds of mimicry. He took it and blew emptily through the mouthpiece.

"Do horn players have to warm up?" I asked.

"Horn players are usually the first to arrive at the concert hall," Sidd said. "My father told me Dennis Brain warmed up for over an hour."

"You don't do that?"

"Well, not for an hour."

"You're like the English tennis player. The one who said, 'I don't knock up.'"

Sidd smiled. He raised the horn to his lips.

The fragment lasts only three minutes or so—a theme, and then a trill that trails off, and sure enough, just as he had described it, it stops terrifyingly . . . as if the player had been run through and toppled off the chair.

"You *ache* for more, don't you?" he said, placing the horn on his lap. "It stops on a dominant, which is the *a* of *amen* without the *men* after it."

Debbie Sue's lips were half parted. "I don't understand," she said.

Sidd smiled . . . very much as Dennis Brain probably had on the stage of the Jubilee Hall. "There's a saying of Buddha," he said. " 'Be earnest in cessation although there is nothing to cease; practice the cessation although there is nothing to practice.' "

XVII

THE BACK OF the Mullins apartment looks down on a mangy alleylike garden. A fire escape lets down into it. It is not quite clear how Al "Big Cakes" Caporetto got onto the fire escape—perhaps by hooking the bottom ladder down somehow, or being given a leg up onto it by an accomplice. In any case, he got into the Mullins apartment from the fire escape landing opposite the dining room.

He squeezed his bulk through one of the windows and dropped to the floor, upsetting a large brass candlestick in the process. It fell on the rug, bounced, and rolled noisily across the bare floor before fetching up against the baseboard.

Debbie Sue heard it. She was lying, half awake, in the big bedroom upstairs. Her first thought was that Sidd was practicing one of his domestic sounds in the next room, an odd one to be sure, an object rolling on a bare floor. Then she realized that Sidd was beside her, lying on his back, his thin nose aloft like a sail. Someone else was downstairs.

The window shades were up. The two enjoyed the morning sunlight streaming in from across Queens and the river. At night they liked the half-light from the streetlamps along the East River Drive below, a soft, silvery light that shimmered on the ceiling and made their bodies—often the sheets thrown back in the summer heat—glow. Debbie Sue could see the cat on the window seat. His head was poised, fixed: he, too, had heard whatever was down the spiral staircase below. . . .

She nudged Sidd. He stirred. She whispered, "Sidd, something's downstairs."

His eyes snapped open. She could see his eye-lashes flick in the light.

"What?"

"Something's downstairs in the back. Something fell off onto the floor. It made a clatter."

"It's the cat," he whispered.

"No, look."

Sidd raised up on his elbows. On the window

seat the cat's outline against the night sky was as stiff as if sculpted. "He hears something," he said. "It must be Robert coming home. Maybe he's in the kitchen getting something to eat. What time is it?"

"It's two in the morning. Sidd, let's go and see."

He groaned. But he swung his feet to the floor, pulled on his shorts, and the two of them, Debbie Sue in her man's shirt, crept along the corridor to look down the well of the spiral staircase.

Sidd felt Debbie Sue's fingers tighten on his shoulder. Her breath popped in his ear. Crouching to peer down the stairwell, he could see the length of the living room. He could make out the bulk of a man, his shadow huge on the carpet, moving slowly, like a widening pool, for the foot of the stairs.

Debbie Sue called down, "Owl?"

The figure started. His face shone vaguely under the brim of a baseball cap tilted up.

Debbie Sue sputtered softly. "It's not Owl, it's Big Cakes!"

"What?"

"Frighten him," she whispered. "Make a sound."

Sidd's throat was dry. His mind was vacant. Later he thought what he *might* have produced— the scream of an elephant. The click of a rifle bolt being drawn back. The hissing of a fuse. A police siren. Instead, clearing his throat, he worked up the sound of a taxi horn—an old French taxi he had heard once in Kathmandu.

Below, the man jumped. His shadow wavered on the carpet. They could see his head turning in the faint light coming through the riverfront windows. Then Sidd did the click of a refrigerator door opening and closing, following that with the sound of a carpet sweeper being drawn back and forth over a rug. He did the sad warble of a mountain dove. He finally produced a gunshot, but it was the sound of a rifle fired far in the distance, its echo in the ravines dying prettily away. There was very little reasoning for his selection—it was like the aimless humming of someone walking nervously down a dark alley.

The barrage of sound—as if from a turned-down television set being flipped from station to station—seemed to have little effect. The shadowy shape paused at each sound, but continued to move toward the foot of the stairs.

"Throw something at him," Debbie Sue whispered. "Wing him!"

Sidd whispered, "The best remedy for all obstacles is to meditate on Voidness."

Debbie Sue punched him sharply on the arm.

Sidd was continuing, "Milarepa suggests that one should regard all enemies as passersby on the road."

Debbie Sue whispered, "That guy wants to *hurt* you!"

" 'The angry fist never strikes the smiling face.' "

"Sidd!"

They could see the thin gleam of a flashlight hunting for the spiral staircase, finding it, and they knew the intruder was on the way up.

"Throw something," Debbie Sue whispered again.

Sidd reached out in the semidarkness, his hand patting swiftly across a tabletop. His fingers closed briefly around a book of matches, then a tiny picture frame that he knew contained a baby photograph of a Mullins child.

"Quick!"

His hand, sweeping back across the floor, touched what at first he thought was the bulk of a wastepaper basket, pliable, though, and liftable. His fingers gripped into whatever it was and with a grunt he picked it up, cradled it in his palms, and tossed it down the stairwell.

A yowl went up as the man reeled backward into the living room. A lamp went over. Sidd and Debbie Sue scuttled down the corridor back into their bedroom. Sidd slammed the door.

"Lock it!"

"There's no lock," Sidd said, feeling up and down the side of the door.

"What did you throw?"

"I threw the cat at him," Sidd whispered. "I hit him in the chest with Mister Puss."

"It won't stop him," Debbie Sue said. "He's coming up after us."

Someone else was in the apartment. Noodles

McGuire had let himself in about five minutes before Caporetto. It had been a simple enough matter to tail Big Cakes from Abe's Fish and Stream in Astoria to the East Side of Manhattan. While Big Cakes was reconnoitering in the back-alley garden, Noodles pushed all the buttons of an intercom in an entryway just up the street and got himself buzzed in. He could hear the intercom behind him squawking, "Come on up, Betty." He hurried up the several flights out onto the roof. There he crossed over the adjoining roofs to the last building on the block, where the Mullinses lived. After a quick look at the dark river and the lights of Queens beyond, he jimmied open the roof-entry door and hustled down to the top floor of the Mullins apartment. The name was below the peephole. With a quick manipulation of a credit card and a thin tool of his own devising, he let himself into the darkness of the apartment. He sniffed. A cat. Somewhere a cat was in the place. He smiled. He himself was a cat burglar. For him the excitement of his profession was not necessarily that he made off with jewelry from a bedside table, but that while doing so a head would stir restlessly on the pillow just inches from his hand. A couple on the bed . . . even more exhilarating! He was very good at his trade. He checked out his sneakers. He cleared his nostrils with Afrin Nasal Spray so that his breathing was as quiet as a bird's. When he jimmied his way into houses that were empty, he was disappointed. There was no challenge. He wrote notes and left them in place of what he had lifted. On the piano he played "Chopsticks" loudly in the dark.

The reason for his presence in the Mullins apartment was out of the ordinary. He had heard that Big Cakes was boasting around Abe's Fish and Stream Club that he was going to take care of the Buddhist monk, like, "personal." No guy was pitching two shutouts in a row, not against the Cardinals anyway. Not with the kind of money *he* had bet. Someone asked how he was going to do anything about it. Caporetto, who'd had a few beers and was never one to keep much to himself, said that he had gone out to Shea after practice and had tailed the pitcher home from the ballpark to a dead-end street on the East Side. He'd seen him moving around in the windows of the second floor. No problem at all. Finch was holed up in the apartment of some guy called Mullins. He'd gone to the entryway and looked at the buttons.

Noodles knew something of Big Cakes' working habits—that he carried a hunting knife and a large .357 Magnum on the job, both of which he could secrete on his vast bulk without their being noticeable. Noodles himself, because of his slender physique, on rare occasions carried a small-calibre pistol, barely the size of a ladies' handbag derringer. Anything larger would have puffed out his suit as if he were carrying a squash.

He had the little pistol with him in the Mullins apartment—a very sensible precaution with Big Cakes on the loose, since he was well known in their crowd for surges of rage, often unprovoked.

At a lunch counter, sitting over a plate of waffles, Big Cakes would wheel his stool around to stare at someone up the line reading a tabloid over a cup of coffee. Others in the vicinity who knew of these eruptions would sidle off their stools. The man drinking his coffee would hardly be aware of what was moving up the counter until he felt a touch on his shoulder and turned to look into Big Cakes' moon-cratered visage and hear, "I don't like your *hat*, mister."

Often the man at the counter would not be wearing a hat. It didn't make any difference—anything to get a confrontation going.

Noodles had never shot his little pistol at anybody. The term "to waste someone" made his lip curl. It was one of the reasons he despised Caporetto. His job for the Mafia, which he prided himself on for its relative subtlety, was to get into the houses of those marked for extinction and leave the traditional message—a fish wrapped in a newspaper—to indicate to whoever woke up that he had a very short time to live. In *The Godfather* he would have been the man who tucked the horse's head into the marked man's bed. Indeed, Noodles was often asked in Abe's Fish and Stream if he could have pulled off *that* caper, sneaking into that fancy Hollywood house with a horse's head, quite a bulky thing to lug around, and everything and put it between the satin sheets, with a man asleep in his bed, without *help*. He had asserted scornfully that he worked alone, and that while he wasn't interested in the business of *getting* the head, whatever was delivered to him to deliver, he would deliver.

Noodles had let himself in on the second floor of the Mullins duplex. He looked in on Debbie Sue and Sidd—the excitement stirring to see their forms under the sheets. He saw the cat on the window seat, the triangle of his ears against the vague light from the East River Drive. Animals in a house were among the terrors of his professional life, but the cat, a very large one he could see in the shadows, seemed to accept his presence.

A minute or two later he, too, heard the clatter of the candlestick falling over in the dining room below, the stirring of Debbie Sue and Sidd in their bedroom, their soft voices in discussion, and then from the shadows he had watched them creep along the corridor for the stairwell.

The strange sounds floating back startled him somewhat, especially the carpet sweeper being drawn back and forth, as if down on the first floor Big Cakes had taken it into his head to clean the place.

He could see Debbie Sue and Sidd crouched at the top of the stairs, whispering to each other with increasing nervousness. Down the corridor he saw the cat's languid approach, the abrupt movement of one of them, and then the yowl erupting from the stairwell and the crash of furniture below. He watched the pair skitter back along the corridor, and he heard the slam of the bedroom door and even Sidd's forlorn complaint from within that there was no lock to keep out whoever was below and coming up for them.

At the head of the stairwell the bulkish form of Big Cakes emerged as if from a trap door. Swiftly he started down the hallway. For Noodles McGuire there was no question what had to be done. He aimed his undersized pistol and squeezed off a single shot that hit Cakes in the upper thigh, tripping him up and dropping him to the floor. There, bellowing with pain and rage, Big Cakes rolled onto his side, and reaching for his shoulder holster, he fired two shots from his .357 Magnum at an angle up into the ceiling—hardly aiming at Noodles, barely visible in the gloom, but simply *reacting*, firing off the shots as he might deliver himself of a couple of angry shouts.

Al "Big Cakes" Caporetto's evening must have seemed so uncomplicated when it started—just a question of hanging around until one o'clock or so in the morning before getting into Finch's apartment. He had cased it—a walk-up flat with easy access up the fire escape in the back. Once in, he thought how simple to intimidate the guy . . . a matter of showing the weirdo the .357 Magnum or the glint of a knife.

It *had* started easily—getting onto the fire escape and climbing into the apartment through a rear window. Wiggling in had been a problem—a candlestick going over as he dropped to the floor. But even if the Buddhist came downstairs to see what was going on, so much the better. Wait for him. A wrench of the arm. Maybe draw a knife across it.

But then out in the darkness of the living room, scouting the place, looking for the stairs leading up to the bedrooms, he must have felt his senses begin to cave in. First, a mysterious question drifted down from above: "Owl?"

Then the loud eruption of a taxi horn close at hand, the old-fashioned kind that Harpo Marx used to honk. It made him start. Then the soft, inexplicable click of a refrigerator door opening and closing somewhere in the room. A carpet sweeper! The sound of a bird. A distant gunshot. He took out a small pocket flashlight and sailed its beam around the room—paintings, a large clock, a bookcase, a piano with a vase of flowers. It picked up the circular stairs. He headed slowly for it.

On the bottom step he paused, waiting for another sound so perhaps he could identify what was going on. A radio somewhere? Nothing. Perhaps the vaguest sound of whispering at the top of the stairwell—mice claws skittering on the floor above? He touched his suit to feel the comforting bulge of the .357 Magnum. He aimed the flashlight beam up the curve of the stairs.

With his first step he had only the barest glimpse of the shape flying down the stairwell toward him, a monster-film manifestation preceded by four outstretched sets of claws. Accompanied by a terrifying shriek, it attached itself with a concussive force to his lapels. The blow sent him reeling back. A standing lamp went over. A glimpse of a row of teeth just inches from his face. He toppled back over a coffee table, clearing its surface of cigarette cases, ashtrays, and picture frames. Whatever had attached itself to him dropped off and scurried away, its claws scrabbling on the wood floors. Upstairs, a door slammed.

All of this might have intimidated anyone else . . . who might have thought he was in some kind of booby-trapped spook house. But Caporetto, puzzled though enraged, hurried toward the circular staircase, climbed it, and started down the corridor. (He had heard a door slam.) The monk had to be cowering in one of the bedrooms.

At the end of the corridor a shape moved against the window—the Buddhist's, Caporetto first thought, but then he realized it was too slight, too thin, the profile too ratlike, and just as he realized he was looking at *Noodles McGuire,* of all people, the instantaneous spit of flame and the soft thunk of the silencer accompanied the murderous bite of a bullet into his leg. He staggered. His leg gave way. He reached for his Magnum and fired off a pair of random shots. He half rose, and then fell again. His shoulder crashed up against the street-front window and buckled the frame.

Down in the street, the security man hired by the Mets to watch the entrance to the Mullins apartment was stretched out in the front seat of his car about to bite down on a sandwich.

It was two in the morning. He had been given a checklist and description of the people in the build-

294

ing, along with a picture of Al "Big Cakes" Caporetto, complete with Cardinals cap. It had been an uneventful night. No one had gone in the entryway since eleven, when the schoolteacher who lived on the fourth floor of the walk-up had let herself in with a key. Robert Temple, who was staying in the Mullins apartment, had gone out around ten and had yet to return. Finch and the girl had been in all evening.

When he heard the commotion from the Mullinses' second-floor apartment—the yelling, the muffled sound of gunfire, and then the crash of glass as one of the street-front windows burst out and sent a few panes splintering to the pavement below—the security man's first impression was that a domestic squabble had broken out. But then the *severity* of it hit home—gunshots, windows breaking, and so forth. He dropped his sandwich. He jumped out of the car and ran across the pavement into the entryway. Faced with a locked front door, he frantically pushed the buttons on the intercom-system panel, hoping someone in one of the apartments above would buzz him in. No such accommodation. His only recourse was to step back and, with a short running start, spring the door open with a shoulder block.

His success at this—the door, which was relatively flimsy, gave way with a crack—caught the attention of two patrolmen in a squad car that had just parked at the foot of the street. The two had taken the tops off their cardboard containers of coffee. They looked over in time to see what looked like the most blatant kind of break-in—a man launching himself full-blast at an entryway front door and snapping it open. They could see his form advancing up the stairs. They put their coffee containers down quite carefully on the lip of the dashboard and reached for their revolvers.

I had gone out that night. Gay Talese had called at noon and suggested dinner at Elaine's, a literary hangout up in the East Eighties that I had heard a lot about. It did not sound like the kind of place— in my reclusive frame of mind—that I would enjoy very much.

The restaurant—a narrow defile with a bar on one side and round tables set along the wall on the other—opened up in the back into a larger room decorated with memorabilia and works by people who apparently went there. Framed book jackets, *Paris Review* posters, Richard Avedon's famous photograph of his dying father, paintings and so forth, including a curious mural of fuzzy nymphs standing in a purple pool. Talese, who is a small, dapper man, was engulfed by the proprietress, Elaine, who came out from behind the cash register to embrace him. I stood by and waited. I thought what a rare gesture between owner and customer, probably not indulged in since Toots Shor used to pummel and embrace the more famous of the athletes who came into his place.

We dined in the defile, practically under the overhang of the people standing five deep at the bar. They stood with their drinks, talking among themselves, and watched us order. At our table nobody looked at the people standing at the bar—apparently it was bad form to be seen standing there—although occasionally we looked up to see who was coming in through the door from the street.

We sat at a round table that almost immediately filled up with Gay's friends. It was hard to tell whether he had invited them or they just sat down there as a matter of course. No matter. I had a much better time than I thought possible. A certain amount of the talk was about Sidd Finch. A lot of them were going to the game the next night. I never let on that he was staying with me. I didn't say much. I said the Mets surely were worried about his rotator cuff. Everyone nodded.

I left Elaine's at two in the morning. The place was still lively. At the table a novelist from the Midwest, Jim Harrison, was talking about shooting at tennis balls with a bow and arrow. I thought I'd walk home, but after a few blocks I hailed a taxi.

The end of the Mullins' block was crowded with squad cars—their circling red lights illuminating the building fronts in quick strobe flashes. An ambulance maneuvered down the street. In it, I was to discover later, was Al "Big Cakes" Caporetto, handcuffed and his leg bandaged. Noodles McGuire had been taken away in a squad car, along with the security man from the Mets, who spent a couple of hours at the precinct station before he was able to establish his identity. On the

297

stairwell, hearing the footsteps pounding up behind him, he had turned and shouted "Freeze!" at
the two squad-car policemen, frightening them into
dropping their guns.

Nobody who lived on the block seemed to know
what had happened. A few residents had come out
of their buildings, standing in the warm summer
night in their sleeping apparel, bathrobes and such,
and gossiping—the drift among them apparently
that a big drug bust had taken place down at the
end of the street. "Who would have thought the
Mullinses!" I heard someone say.

It took me a while to talk myself back into the
apartment. Debbie Sue flung her arms around
me. "It's Owl," she said to the policeman at the
door. "He's mine." She pulled me into the apartment and shut the door. She showed me the bullet
holes and where Big Cakes ("He was here, Owl,
he actually was—a *huge* man") had bumped up
against the windows after being shot in the leg at
the end of the second-floor hall. She was very
proud of her performance. "Oh, Owl, I haven't let
on about Sidd. They don't know. Sidd threw Mister Puss at the fat man in the dark."

"Where *is* Sidd?"

I half expected her to say that she had hidden
him somewhere in the apartment—settling him in
behind a row of clothes in a closet . . . "Owl, I've
put him in the cleverest place"—but she did not
say that at all.

"Owl, I don't know. He's gone. He's totally
disappeared."

Sidd had not had an easy time of it. After the gunshots the apartment began to fill with unknown people, many of them shouting "Freeze!" He went out to the apartment stairwell. People were coming up. He retreated to the roof. He tried to let Debbie Sue know where he was—leaning over the parapet and lofting down the sound of the Tibetan long trumpet, the tungchen. By then his throat was completely dry from the taxi-cab horn, the refrigerator door, and the other effects he had tried in the Mullins apartment.

Up there he felt a certain exhilaration wearing so little. He had on just his underwear. It was a warm night. His bare feet were sensitive to the surfaces he crossed—the tar paper of the roof, the iron of the fire-escape steps that took him down to the garden in the back, the earth there, cool and moist, and then the texture of the cement floor of the underground garage he let himself into next door through the back entrance. He hid in there, listening to the cars, dozens of them in their stalls, just the faintest occasional click of an engine cooling off. Sometimes there were footsteps, the echoing sound of a car door slamming, the engine turning over.

The garage entrance was on York Avenue. After waiting among the cars for almost an hour, Sidd ventured out to see what was going on. He trotted out in his underdrawers, his arms pumping, so that anyone glancing at him would take him for a predawn jogger. He looked down Seventy-second.

The street was still throbbing with activity—the twinkling rose glow of the police beacons like a bonfire opposite the Mullins apartment house.

He retreated to the garage and wandered down the lines of cars. He found an unlocked tailgate and climbed into the back of a station wagon. A blanket in there smelled vaguely of dog. He curled himself up in it—his notion that when he awoke the ruckus would have calmed down and the police cars gone. He would leave the garage and trot down the street to the end, turn in the entry, ring the buzzer downstairs, and hope that someone in the Mullins apartment, preferably Debbie Sue, would be upstairs to let him in.

In the back of the station wagon, he pulled the horse blanket up to his chin and, exhausted, fell asleep instantly.

It was a fitful sleep—a night of distant bells, voices calling from station platforms, a small nightmare about being shanghaied by the crew of a Chinese junk, a storm at sea. . . .

He was awakened by sunlight streaming through the windows of the station wagon. Startled, he sat up to find that the car was in an outdoor parking lot off a highway. A sign on a nearby shop read "Tuxedo Park, New York." It took him a moment or so to realize he had been driven there earlier that morning by a car owner unaware that he was carrying along someone curled up in the horse blanket in the rear of the wagon.

Sidd climbed over into the back seat and waited

300

for an hour for the owner to return. His hope was to try to explain things and get some help getting back to New York. The car clock on the dashboard showed a little after noon. The driver never returned. Sidd found a pad and pencil in the glove compartment of the station wagon and wrote the following message:

"I have taken your horse blanket. I have your license-plate number and should be able to return into your hands the aforementioned blanket when it is no longer an item of necessity to me. My apologies for this unforgivable act of purloining (just temporarily, I must assure you) your horse blanket."

He stepped out of the car and arranged the blanket, a faded green military color, so that it hung from his shoulders not unlike the robes he had worn as an aspirant in Tibet. The smell of dog was not quite right, but there was something almost familiar and nostalgic about the feeling of the coarse wool against the bare skin of his body. Hunching its folds into a proper conformity around his frame, he started off for the highway.

It took him over an hour to hitch a ride. He knew that he did not present a figure that inspired trust—tall, barefooted, and in a blanket that gave him the appearance of someone who has just escaped a hotel fire. The cars sailed by, their drivers staring fixedly ahead. It was a question of patience. He rubbed one bare foot against another. He said a few ngags. He rearranged his robes. Finally a man in a pickup truck stopped. A dog was in the back. He stood up with his front paws on the side panel, his body shaking from the wagging of his tail. The driver leaned across the front seat and opened the door.

"Hop in, Father," he said.

After they had started off the driver said, "I have given rides to lots of people in this truck. It's almost a hobby, so it's a pleasure to have a member of the cloth," he said, looking over. "There's no one at home but me and the dog. That's Ralph in the back. The wife left fifteen years ago because she said I was too much of a gabber, always talking, even, she said, in my *sleep*. Well, I *like* talking and I like meeting people. I even go out looking for hitchhikers. I look for them the way *they* look for rides. I slam on the brakes. These guys climb in. I've had some interesting ones. Eskimos. An artist who painted nothing but peaches. An evangelist. A retired six-day bicyclist. A guy who once played the calliope in the Clyde-Beatty Cole Bros. circus. I had a foot fetishist once—a guy who leaned over and began admiring my shoe, which was pressed down, you know, on the accelerator. I was delivering a diesel generator to Falmouth, Mass., down on the Cape. I let this guy off just this side of the Canal. Didn't like him. I told him I was turning off just down the line. I never did anything like that before, or since, to one of my passengers. When he got down on the pavement he asked me one last favor. He kept looking down at my shoes. He wanted me to *kick* him."

They drove along in silence for a while. "Are

you from a monastery around here?" the driver asked. "What's the order? A Carmelite or something?"

Sidd felt the thing to do was to tell him everything . . . perhaps the driver would get caught up in the spirit of the occasion and drive him all the way to Shea Stadium.

"My name is Sidd Finch," he said.

The driver smiled and introduced himself. "Tom Smarts." Apparently the name Finch had no discernible impact.

"I'm supposed to be working for the Mets against the St. Louis Cardinals tonight," Sidd went on.

"You're the team chaplain! Well, I'm not a baseball follower," the driver said. "I'm into antiques." He went on to say that for someone of his limited means, antiques was a hopeless passion. He had one good piece in his house—a gilt eighteenth-century chair—but the rest of the stuff was Danish modern.

Sidd listened politely. Then the driver said, "I take it that the Mets will have you in there before the game to lead them in *prayer*. Is that it? The Mets need divine guidance? They'll all gather around you in the corner of the locker room?"

"I guess that's what *would* happen," Sidd said. "I've never—"

"So this is your first time out," the driver exclaimed. "Your first pregame service! Quite a day for you."

The dog kept peering in the back window of

the cab, his tongue lolling, and staring through the glass at Sidd. Very likely he had caught a whiff of Sidd's blanket as he was climbing into the truck. The driver looked over. "My dog's taken quite a liking to you," he said. "Do you keep dogs at home?"

Sidd shook his head.

"What's your order?" the driver asked. "I hope you don't mind my asking." He looked him over. "It doesn't look as though they allow you very much in life. Not even shoes."

"I'm what they call a trapa," Sidd said. "Which is an aspirant Buddhist monk."

"For God's sake!" the driver exclaimed. "Is that right? How many Buddhists do they *have* on the Mets?" he asked.

Sidd said, "Perhaps you would let me explain." He began with his religious training in the Himalayas, and how by lung-gom and pegging rocks at snow leopards he had learned to throw with speed and accuracy. He talked about his tryout with the Mets, and his uncertainty about baseball and his future.

From time to time the driver beat the palm of a hand in a rapid tattoo on the steering wheel. "Well, doesn't that beat all?" he said.

Sidd did not describe what had happened in the Mullins apartment the night before—since it was so unclear to him—but he said that, because of the various circumstances, he had fallen asleep in the back of a station wagon that had deposited him just hours before in Tuxedo Park, New York, and how this very night he was scheduled to take the mound and *pitch* against the St. Louis Cardinals.

The driver smacked the steering wheel. "Well, doesn't that . . . To think I thought you were a *priest!* I've had all kinds of people up here in the cab with me—did I tell you about the calliope guy and the foot fetishist?—but this is the *climax!*"

The upshot was that Mr. Smarts drove Sidd directly to Shea Stadium. He said he was going to lock Ralph in the cab, try to buy himself a ticket, and see a baseball game for the first time in twenty-five years.

Sidd's appearance at the locker-room door created a stir. The players looked up from their locker stalls to see him walk in barefooted with the horse blanket wrapped around him. Mookie Wilson leaned out from his stool and whispered to Ray Knight, "He's not only got the worst body I ever saw, but the man *dresses* real bad. . . ."

XVIII

THE METS TELEPHONED us a little after three that afternoon to say that Sidd had arrived at the ballpark. He was in the clubhouse and wanted us to know that he was okay. The man on the phone could only tell us that Sidd had been in Tuxedo Park. He didn't know why. Yes, he was pitching that evening as scheduled. The Mets had tickets for us that we could pick up at the press gate.

That morning Debbie Sue had been frantic.

"Where the hell is he? The thing is—Sidd doesn't know how to *do* anything," she'd complained. "He doesn't know enough to pick up a phone and call collect. He doesn't know our number here. He doesn't know how to call Information for the Mullins number." She had stared at the phone.

"He knows enough to get along," I'd assured her. "He got along in the Himalayas."

Debbie Sue had snorted. "Tumo-heat isn't going to help him out in the streets. He went out of here practically naked. . . ."

Debbie Sue and I left for Shea about six o'clock in my sister's car. We turned on the radio. The happenings the night before were mentioned in brief on the news programs. The day's tabloids had described it as some kind of Mafia in-family squabble: both of the men arrested were low-echelon mob figures. Why the shoot-out took place in an East Side apartment was still under investigation. Caporetto's police record got much more play than Noodles McGuire. It was mentioned that he had been arrested for aggravated assault in an Astoria coffee shop. None of the papers or radio stations made any connection between what happened in the Mullins apartment and Sidd Finch.

His association with baseball, however, was a main topic on the car radio. The announcement that Sidd was going to pitch on Thursday caused a mild stir. Usually pitchers work on a rotation of four to five days between outings. Johnson told

306

reporters that his rotation was shot . . . in need of a respite. Sidd was an exceptional case: he was willing to pitch and buy time for the rest of the staff. Debbie Sue paused at the station on which two ex-ballplayers were chatting about Sidd's fastball. One of them was saying that speed wasn't that important. Rex Barney, for example, threw the ball well up in the hundreds, a terrifying thing to see from the stands, but it was easy to hit because the ball didn't move. It was a hard *dart*. You could get away with something like that in the minors, but if you throw it, two strikes and three balls in the majors, that hard dart would get itself thumped. Robin Roberts, on the other hand, threw in the nineties, but his fastball jerked around on the way in, and you could almost feel the wood of the bench on your ass because that was where you were going back to. They talked about Barney and Roberts and some of the others with a kind of nostalgia. "Yeah, Rex," a voice reminisced. "If the plate was located high and inside, he would have been a thirty-game winner."

Johnny VanderMeer's name came up. He had pitched two no-hitters in a row for the Cincinnati Reds, considered, along with Joe DiMaggio's fifty-six-game consecutive hitting streak, to be the most unassailable records in baseball. *Now* look . . .

"How do you think Sidd'll pitch?" I asked Debbie Sue over the chatter of the car radio.

She didn't answer for a while. "He must be rattled," she said finally. "What's in Tuxedo, any-way? Why do you think he went there?"

"It's a very posh community about an hour upstate," I said. "The tuxedo—the dinner jacket—gets its name from the place."

"Do you think he *knows* anybody in Tuxedo?" she asked. "He wasn't wearing *anything* when he left the apartment."

She was obviously flustered.

"You're not jealous?"

"I don't like him running off like that."

The traffic was heavy. A number of the parking lots around Shea were already filled. "They've come out in force," I said. We drove under the subway trestle looking for a place to park.

"Up there's where you get the Number Seven back to the city, isn't it?" Debbie Sue asked.

I was surprised. "You're getting to be quite the New Yorker," I said.

We parked by the tennis stadium. She took my hand as we walked toward Shea. "Owl, you've been the best thing that ever happened to us," she said. "Look!" The Goodyear blimp was drifting low over the ballpark, the hum of its motors audible, the lights of the "Skytacular" faint in the soft mist of the night. I thought back on the morning Smitty had telephoned in Pass-a-Grille. Perhaps he himself was up there piloting, the big wheel alongside his seat, and thinking of the leather bag and Stottlemyre leaning out that early spring day and dropping the baseballs.

Our seats were behind the Mets dugout, about thirty rows back. We caught a glimpse of Sidd. He came out of the dugout and looked back into

at the plate briefly while the infielders finished throwing the ball around the horn—as we used to say—and then one of them lobbed the ball underhand to Sidd so he could proceed. The whole character of what we were watching changed. It wasn't that what was happening was uninteresting, or lacking in intensity. Sidd's half of the inning was so quick—at least in the earlier part of the game—that one strained to capture what was going on . . . as if to imprint a glimpse of an incredible treasure before the door closed on it.

Some concentrated on Sidd—the whirlwind delivery, the tip of the sock dangling high above his head, the catapult action, the ball that stretched like a silver thread into Ronn Reynolds' glove—trying to divine how it all worked. Others watched Reynolds—because it was at his position that the power of Sidd's delivery was most noticeable—as if the catcher had been hit by a jolt of electrical power . . . knocking him back toward the umpire, who often put a hand out to keep Reynolds upright. We studied the batters' attitudes—some of them wondrously cool, as if nothing untoward was happening, gazing out at Finch with their jaws working evenly on gum or whatever, swinging the bat menacingly over the plate, as if it were almost a surety that they could poke the next offering up into the left-field seats. Others were more shaken. After the first pitch zipped by, they stared in bewilderment, first at the plate, then back at the catcher; they watched the ball, its properties now defined as it was arched back to Finch. They looked over their shoulders into the dugout, where the faces of their teammates lined along the top step were as non-committal as a jury's; they inched away from the plate in spite of themselves; their rear ends stuck out more prominently.

The game went into the seventh inning without either the Mets or the Cardinals able to score.

As in his first game, Sidd looked increasingly exhausted as the innings went on. He paused for longer intervals between pitches, waiting for the energy to flow back in. Once refreshed, his body swayed, his leg, the dusty sock at the end of it, rose stiffly toward the night sky, and the delivery—mesmerizing to watch—uncoiled and the ball tore for the plate. There was no question of pacing the pitch itself. It was as if any slackening or shift in how the mechanism functioned would damage the whole.

The Cardinals tried to throw off his timing. Just before Sidd's leg started that awesome hoist into the sky, the batter would back out. The umpire called time. The Cardinal stood with his back to Sidd. After the bat boy had dashed out with the chamois cloth, he would dust off his bat handle with slow, infinite care, as if polishing a piece of antique furniture.

It struck me as a terrifying strategy, since the consequences could well affect Sidd's *control* rather than his speed. Dr. Burns had warned us at the Huggins conference in March that it was essential never to disturb a lung-gom in the process of his work. What was it that he had said—that a devil

312

would shake the lung-gom and deprive him of his senses?

To do this with Sidd could well mean that his pitch would once again become a "thing of Chaos and Cruelty."

The memory of what had happened—the rip in the canvas backstop, the ricochet off the iron pipe into the alligator pond—scared me so much that I thought of somehow getting a note to Whitey Herzog, the Cardinals manager, to warn him that this tactic was endangering his batters. My fingers itched to write. I could dash off what Mike Marshall had said: "We're talking death here." I nudged Debbie Sue.

"Have you got a pencil?"

"What?"

"And a piece of paper? I've got to get a note to the Cardinals."

Debbie Sue stared at me. "Oh, Owl, you're kidding me. You've decided to write? Right at this moment . . . ?"

Just then a great roar went up from the crowd. Vince Coleman, the fleet Cardinal outfielder, who was leading off in the seventh inning and had two strikes on him, swung late and missed a pitch that was, incredibly, slightly off target—hitting the side of Ronn Reynolds' catcher's mitt, twisting it cruelly on his wrist, and bouncing off at right angles toward the third-base seats. Coleman, though a strikeout victim, was free to run on a dropped third strike. He lit out for first, made a wide turn, and reached second with a nifty slide—the first base runner of the game for the Cardinals.

"Sidd's control's going," I whispered.

Debbie Sue was staring ahead, her hands twisting in her lap.

The next batter was Willie McGee, the switch-hitting outfielder. I remember Coleman down at second drawing on a pair of red golfing gloves, which he wears to protect his hands on slides, arms outstretched for the bag.

It was obvious he was going to steal third. Sidd had no idea how to hold him at second base. He peered bleakly back over his shoulder once or twice and then, with a full windup, he delivered his fastball past McGee. By the time Reynolds had extricated the ball from the pocket of his catcher's mitt, Coleman was standing down on third, the crowd howling, knowing that despite Finch's mastery, he was in danger of falling behind in the game if Coleman could get home to break the scoreless tie.

"He's going to go," I whispered to Debbie Sue. "Right now." We watched Coleman inch down the base path toward home plate, his red gloves bright as he poised them off his hips.

I could see Sidd's lips moving on his ngags, a flash of white—perhaps a peppermint on the tip of his tongue—and then his stockinged foot twitched and rose in the air.

Coleman broke for the plate.

Ronn Reynolds shifted his glove from the inside corner to the ground on the third-base side of the

I looked over to wonder aloud to Debbie Sue what had happened. Her seat was empty.

Jesse Orosco finished up the game. Pendleton looped a single over second base, the first time a ball had touched a Cardinal bat, but then Porter hit a two-hopper down the line to Ray Knight at third, who threw him out at first. That won the game for the Mets 1-0. The crowd noise had not varied since Sidd had walked off the mound—a strong and steady buzz of bewilderment.

In the melee of reporters in the back corridors, I managed to find Jay Horwitz. His large, melancholy face seemed to float among the shoulders of people shouting at him. He disengaged himself and we shuffled ourselves through the crowd into a corner. "No sign of him," he said to me. "He got back in the clubhouse, grabbed that weird green blanket, and was gone. The clubhouse boy saw him. Davey Johnson saw him just for a second in the corridor. There's nothing in his locker except a bunch of hangers. His 'batting' shoe was found under the dugout bench."

"What was he doing in Tuxedo Park?" I asked.

"Damned if I know," Jay said. "He came into the clubhouse this afternoon with his head stuck through that blanket. No money. No nothing. He had a helluva time talking himself into the stadium. Somebody finally recognized him. Where's his girl?"

"She disappeared in the ninth inning," I said. "I turned around and she was gone."

plate. It must have been a terrifying moment for him—trusting that Finch could readjust in the middle of his delivery and throw the ball to a different target.

The ball hit the pocket of his glove with a wallop and stuck. He yelped yet again, not so much from the pain as from the excitement.

The umpire, leaning over his shoulder, could see the mitt at the corner of the plate, the white of the ball in it, and one of Coleman's red gloves sailing into view like the flick of a tongue. He pumped his right hand up in the air. Coleman was out. Sidd got McGee and Herr on strikes, and the inning was done.

Perhaps conscious that their pitcher was fading (although he got himself safely through the top of the eighth), the Mets got a run in their half of the inning. A walk. A sacrifice. Then Ray Knight, pinch-hitting, socked a ball deep into the gap in right center and was thrown out trying to stretch the hit into a triple. The run scored in front of him.

Debbie Sue looked at her watch. She seemed subdued. I nudged her and said that Sidd had only nine pitches to go. For the top of the ninth inning that enormous crowd rose from their seats as if standing for the national anthem.

Whitey Herzog put in a pinch hitter for the twenty-fifth man at the plate—I've forgotten who the fellow was. You could look it up. A left-handed batter. Like almost all those in the lineup who had preceded him, he took three quick-swinging strikes, as if he had been ordered to get his bat into the strike zone where a chance connection between it and the ball might occur. I noticed he was peeking back, quite illegally, to try to see where Reynolds was setting the glove for a target. Two outs to go.

I don't recall the twenty-sixth batter either. I kept staring at the twenty-seventh waiting in the on-deck circle—perhaps because I knew he was almost surely destined to be the final out of the game. He was Terry Pendleton, pinch-hitting for the Cardinal pitcher who had come in during the Mets' little flurry in the eighth. Pendleton wears two black gloves and a guard on his right forearm. One knee was on a pad to keep his pants leg from getting dusty. He was swinging his bat, weighted with an iron ring, with a nonchalance that belied the fact that twenty-five of his teammates had struck out before him and the twenty-sixth was about to do so, flapping his bat jerkily and futilely as the third strike streamed by him. The crowd noise at the twenty-sixth strikeout was immense. Pendleton seemed hardly aware as the twenty-sixth strode by him on his way to the Cardinal dugout. He stood up and pounded the handle end of the bat on the ground to dislodge the iron ring—as if ridding his bat of a giant parasite. He leaned over and, with his bat between his knees, dusted the bat handle with the chamois cloth. On his way to the plate he never glanced up at Sidd until he had settled himself carefully in the batter's box.

As every schoolboy knows, it was at this point that Sidd, after a long look down at Reynolds and Pendleton, bent over and placed the baseball next to the pitching rubber, putting it there very carefully, even fastidiously, as if it were as delicate as a seashell. He then took off that decrepit black glove of his, stuck it under his arm, and walked off the mound. As he headed for the Mets dugout, the first assumption was that he had something to ask Davey Johnson or Mel Stottlemyre. I myself thought he was going into the dugout to get himself a Band-Aid, or perhaps replace his sock. When those who could see into the dugout saw him disappear into the tunnel leading back to the locker room, they must have guessed he was rushing back to the lavatory.

We waited. The umpire came out behind home plate and peered into the Mets dugout. Seated back in the lower box seats, I could not see what was going on in there, but I was told later that the first indication of something untoward was when the Mets on the bench began streaming back under the stands, presumably to find out what had happened to Sidd. Out beyond the right-field fence two pitchers began getting ready. The quick movements of their arms flashed above the fence. The stadium crowd, their bewilderment a loud hum, must have come to the conclusion that Sidd, pitching at that incredible speed inning after inning, had finally done in the rotator cuff or whatever. He was hurt.

For a while I stood in the back of the interview room, where a throng of reporters were shouting at Davey Johnson.

"You saw him after he walked off the mound?"

"That's right. Back in the corridor behind the dugout."

"Davey, what happened? What'd he say?"

"I asked him what the trouble was. He shrugged. His shoulders went up and down. He apologized. He said he would call me. It seems to me there was a girl standing close by. They ran off down the corridor."

"Davey, what did you do?"

"Well, if you want to know the truth, I watched them go. Off into the sunset."

"Davey! Davey!"

"I don't know what else I could've done. You expect me to *tackle* the guy? We got the game. We got Orosco in the bull pen. One out to go. What's the big deal?"

"He had a perfect game, Davey!"

"That's his concern. For me, it's a practical matter."

"Davey! Davey!"

"Any guy that leaves me with a 1-0 lead and one out to go, and he wants to go boating in Central Park, I say okay."

"Hey, Davey. He's gone *boating* . . . ?"

"I didn't say that. I was—"

"Is he coming back?"

"He didn't say."

"Davey, any idea it was going to happen . . . ?"

319

Johnson nodded slowly. "I had an idea. But I didn't know he had such a dramatic sense of timing."

I left for the parking lot. I looked for Debbie Sue. I stood by the car as the parking lot emptied, half expecting to spot her striding across the asphalt with Sidd in tow.

I worried about her. Although resourceful, she was scatterbrained enough to get into any number of fixes. No sight of her. The parking lot stretched off toward its boundary fences, symmetric pools of light under the lamp standards, until finally just a few automobiles were left here and there in that vast landscape, seemingly abandoned, as if their engines had been lifted during the game.

I drove back to the city and let myself into the apartment. I walked through the darkness to the library to turn on the television set and see what news there was of the night game . . . or Sidd. *Nightline* was on. Its host, Ted Koppel, was talking to a high-ranking Egyptian.

The phone began buzzing in the darkness.

"We've been calling and calling!" My pulse jumped at the sound of Debbie Sue's voice. She was with Sidd. She said they were waiting at Kennedy airport to board a flight to London. "I've disguised Sidd," Debbie Sue said. "He's wearing a huge pair of black glasses."

"London?"

"Isn't that wild?"

She apologized for deserting me at the game. Hand in hand, they had run through the parking lots, down the lanes of cars, for the subway, the Number Seven, which they had taken into Manhattan, Sidd enveloped in his blanket. At the subway entrance they caught a taxi to the Mullins apartment, where they had picked up their belongings, the French horn and so forth, and after saying good-bye to the cat they had hurried out to Kennedy.

"It was funny in the subway going into town," Debbie Sue said. "Sidd was sitting there with his blanket and his baseball uniform on, one baseball shoe and then his white sock on the other foot. No one seemed at all bothered. Everyone looks straight ahead in New York subways, don't they, Owl?"

"Yes," I said. "They're scared of looking down the line and seeing someone dressed like Sidd."

I asked why they hadn't let me in on it. I could have driven them directly to the airport with their belongings already in the car.

Debbie Sue said that I mustn't be upset but that it was their adventure. It was an act of independence that they had to do on their own.

Sidd came on the phone. "Namas-te," he said softly. I had to move the receiver closer to my ear to hear him. "I hope we have not caused you too much consternation."

"Well, you startled everyone," I said. "I hear you threw Mister Puss."

"I regret to say that he was the only implement I was able to find," Sidd said. "I did not throw him overhand. I sort of shoveled him down the stairwell."

He told me something about his adventures to and from Tuxedo and about Mr. Smarts, the Good Samaritan driver who had taken him to Shea.

"He was very accommodating," Sidd said. "He picks up everybody. Calliope players."

"What about the Mets?" I asked.

Sidd said that he had spoken briefly to Davey Johnson in the corridor and then he had called him up from the Mullins apartment. "They put me through to him," Sidd said. "He was still in his office. He was surprised. He said, 'Hey, where'd you go?' I told him that I was going to the airport. I gave him a couple of mantras to use for the season next year. They should do very well, the Mets, perhaps not this year, but there is a karma that I suspect will lead them to a championship. I told him I had given a mantra to Ray Knight, and also one to Ron Darling, the pitcher who had studied Zen and knew exactly what I was talking about."

"What did he say to all of this?" I asked.

"He listened, quite carefully, I think. Then I told him that if he needed me the following season, in 1986, I would entertain the notion of coming back and rejoining the team. He laughed and said that was very thoughtful of me but that he would try to get the team off to a very good start so that I would not be needed. Perhaps the World Series. I think he wants me to return to my studies . . . or whatever."

"Did you tell him why you walked off the mound?"

"No."

"Did he know you weren't going to stick around?"

"Oh, I think so," Sidd said. "I think he knew I wasn't going to be a permanent fixture."

Debbie Sue came back on. She said the plane was boarding. They would call me from London. "Owl-love, we're going to turn on the trains. Sidd's buying a suit."

XIX

I STAYED IN the Mullins apartment for a few days—Mister Puss and I. Then I arranged for the school-teacher living in the apartment upstairs to come in and feed him until the Mullins family came back from Botswana. I also told the superintendent he might want to do something about plugging up the bullet holes in the second-floor ceiling. Then I went to Marblehead for a weekend of sailing with my family aboard the *Salty IV*. My father carried his unlit pipe upside down in his mouth, still in place as he told me to trim the genoa just a tad. We sat in the galley at night, comfortable in some quiet harbor.

My father had watched the second Cardinals game on television. He could hardly believe Sidd had been a kind of ward of mine.

"He *stayed* with you? Why don't I know these things?" he asked. "You should have invited them aboard for a cruise."

Across the dial of the portable radio there was still a lot of chatter about Sidd, especially why he had walked off the pitcher's mound. There was even talk of an official inquiry.

"Why would they want that?" my sister asked. She poured us coffee into mugs decorated with bright yacht-club flags. I wondered if Mr. Scranton, the toby-jug man, was still planning on a Finch model.

"Sorry?"

"Well, I was curious . . . why an official inquiry?" my sister repeated.

"Some people may have pressured Sidd in some way," I said. "It's hard to believe he'd do such a thing on his own—leave baseball like that."

"What kind of people?"

"The Establishment, for one—the baseball crowd. After all, he was upsetting the balance of the game. Then you've got the bookmakers. Maybe even the Mob. Those guys didn't like him hanging around. Even the umpires can't be happy. With him, they have to rely on intuition rather than judgment—on their ears more than their eyes. The fact is, for baseball, Sidd was the worst kind of pariah."

"So you think he was pressured out of the game?" my father asked.

"I don't think so," I said carefully. "Anyone who's gone through the rigors of that lung-gom training would be pretty stubborn."

I told them a story about Milarepa's obduracy, which Sidd had mentioned enough to us to make

324

me think it meant something particular. It was about Milarepa visiting a monastery from which the monks—who didn't like him, to put it mildly— came running out and beat him savagely. "Go a-way! Go a-way!" They thought they'd gotten rid of him, but no, they looked around and there he was *inside* their temple. Once in, they couldn't get him out. He wasn't going to move until *he* wanted to. It was as if he had suddenly become a huge piece of sculpture. They put ropes on him, and a long line of monks, all sweating and heaving, like a tug-of-war game, just couldn't get him to budge an inch along the temple floor. They finally gave up. He sang to them and a lot of them became his disciples.

I told them that when Sidd finished the story, he made the sounds of the monks grunting and straining as they tried to haul Milarepa out of their temple.

My sister was fascinated by Sidd's skill with sounds. She bemoaned that she hadn't gone to the Himalayas to learn such a thing rather than spending three months in The School of the Museum of Fine Arts in Boston to paint.

I nodded. "It's really uncanny. He could sit down here with us in the galley and flutter his throat muscles in some way, and you'd swear from the squeak of oarlocks that someone outside was rowing by in the night. He could have made a living at it. A cabaret act. He could have put together a routine of his best sounds—taxi horns, tubs emptying, a glass breaking on the floor, the echoes of trumpets, things like that, and then the audience'd call up requests. 'Do a golf ball dropping into a cup.' "

"That doesn't sound like the sort of thing he'd do," my father said with a smile.

"I agree." I was embarrassed. "I never mentioned it to him. It's the last thing he'd do."

"Did you ever ask him why he walked off the mound?" my sister asked.

"No. I never really had the chance," I said. "But he would have answered almost surely with a koan, which is a kind of puzzle that can't be solved logically. He left a koan for his roommate when he quit Harvard. The note read, 'How do you get the live goose out of the bottle? There, it's out!' "

"But there's got to be a practical reason," my sister insisted. "It would have been a perfect game."

"Perfection seems to have its problems," my father said. He was reminded of buying an Indian blanket in the Southwest. He had praised its perfect symmetry, but the Indian who had sold it to him shook his head and told him that the practice was always to weave a few mistakes into a blanket. Perfection meant trying to match the gods, and it was important not to do that. Arrogance.

My father began tapping the bowl of his pipe into the palm of his hand, an unconscious and somewhat inconsequential habit since he hadn't smoked the thing in years.

"That's an interesting idea," I said. I told them

that Sidd seemed fascinated with unfinished works of art—his preoccupation with Dennis Brain and the Mozart horn concerto, and how he played it for us the night before he pitched at Shea.

"He once said that there were a great number of ways to reach *tharpa,* or supreme liberation," I said. "Sometimes one achieves tharpa by *not* reaching the goal. Sometimes there are more important goals than the one that is visible. *Not* to give oneself the twenty-seventh K is a possibility."

"What's a K?" my sister asked.

"A strikeout. It's what you put in the little box in a scorecard."

"The twenty-seventh K," she repeated. "That's a nice title for a book. Your book. Why don't you write something about all this?"

"Don't badger him," my mother said, somewhat to my surprise.

"Maybe he'd find out why Sidd behaved the way he did," she commented.

"Perhaps Sidd should write the book," my mother said. "Or Debbie Sue."

My father asked if I had seen Sidd and Debbie Sue after the game.

I described how I had sat next to Debbie Sue but that she had suddenly disappeared during the ninth inning. I looked around and she wasn't there. She had gone to meet Sidd. They must have decided what they wanted to do a few days before.

"I had no idea what they were up to," I said. "I thought I'd find them back at the apartment. They telephoned from the airport just as I walked in the door."

I described how after our phone conversation I had wandered through the apartment into their bedroom. Sidd's Mets uniform was laid out on the front-room bed—the baseball shoe, a single one, propped up, its toe toward the ceiling. Debbie Sue's work. It gave me quite a start when I first saw it. A note lying on it. A koan! I thought. The note said—and it was in Sidd's monastery writing—*"Please Return to Nelson Doubleday."*

"He's gone secular," my sister remarked with a grin. "What are they doing now?" she asked.

"They're in London," I said. "Sidd's going to buy a suit."

"Do you think he has any regrets?" she asked.

"He felt very strongly about the game," I said. "I think he wanted to stay in it. He kept asking me about players who had been overwhelming forces—Babe Ruth, Henry Aaron, Joe DiMaggio, Ted Williams, Sadaharu Oh . . . a guy called Steve Dalkowski, who threw the ball faster than anyone until Sidd came along. I don't think he wanted to be on a pedestal by himself."

I said, "I'll tell you something that has occurred to me once or twice. During the game I noticed Sidd occasionally glancing at the outfield scoreboard. I assumed he was doing what pitchers often do—checking on the count. But then I realized that such things were of small practical value to him. Perhaps he was checking on the time! There's a digital clock out there."

"Why the time?" my sister asked.

"They had to catch a plane to Europe," I said. "The last Pan Am flight for London leaves at one. They had to get back to New York, pack up in the Mullins apartment, say good-bye to the cat, and get to Kennedy airport. Maybe Debbie Sue said to him, 'Now, Sidd, I want you to stop doing whatever you're doing at ten-thirty *sharp.*' "

"That's the most farfetched reason I ever heard!" she said.

"He stopped pitching right on the half hour," I said. "I happened to notice."

"A coincidence."

"I'll give you a more plausible possibility," I said. "That is, that Sidd suddenly realized he was losing it—his control, his concentration. So he put the ball down and walked off the mound rather than endanger anyone. It had happened once before in Florida. And here was Coleman, the Cardinal base runner, nagging him . . . waving two red gloves and doing his best to disconcert him. In fact, I got so frightened that I nudged Debbie Sue and asked her for a pencil. If you can believe it, I was going to try to get a message into the Cardinal dugout to warn the manager to calm Coleman down."

My sister was incredulous.

"You were going to start *writing!* Right there in Shea Stadium?"

I said I didn't know that I actually would have done it—but I was certainly frantic enough to *try.*

"Well, what happened?" my father asked.

"It turned out to be of no matter," I replied. "Coleman tried to steal home and Sidd threw him out with an unbelievable peg. And Debbie Sue didn't have a pencil."

Outside in the darkness, a little outboard went by, a dinghy or a small raft, perhaps, barely audible, so lowpowered that I imagined its propeller being about the size of a teaspoon.

My mother cleared her throat and said she had a suggestion to make.

"Perhaps he simply did it for *love*," she said. We stared at her. Such intimacies, even the mildest forms, were not in her nature to discuss. "Perhaps she's the kind of girl," she went on, "who would insist on some proof of his love—you know, show me that you love me by walking off the pitcher's mound."

My father laughed and said *he* would never have done such a thing.

My mother peeked at him over her glasses. "There was a time . . ."

They grinned at each other as we laughed. "That's not so improbable," I said. "I know Debbie Sue hated the idea that she had to share Sidd with a million or so Mets fans."

A faint breeze outside stirred a loose halyard abovedecks. It touched the mast with a faint metallic clank. It made me remember the bell at the Rongbuk monastery at the base of Mount Everest. I wondered when such sounds would stop bringing back memories of Sidd and Debbie Sue.

My father asked my sister what *she* thought.

She leaned back so her face was in the shadow. "Well, I think," she said in mock solemnity, "that he walked off as an exercise of will. Just to show he was in control. He was sort of de-institutionalizing himself. Throwing off monkhood. Baseball." She leaned forward out of the shadows of the bunk and gave me a glance. "Maybe he was telling *you* something . . . how easy it is to be in control—either to start or stop something."

"Don't badger him," my mother said again, quite gently this time.

I went from Marblehead to Boston and took a flight to Florida. I arrived at the bungalow in the late evening. The stuffed animals in their rows startled me. I had forgotten them. I turned the fans on. The sultry August heat stirred in the rooms. I cranked open the louvered windows. The frogs were booming out in back.

Perhaps I could start by writing about the man who rose up above Pasadena in his deck chair, vainly popping at the weather balloons with an air pistol to stabilize his flight—now *there* was a chronicle.

Or closer to home. Sidd Finch. I could start with that first phone call from Smitty asking me to go flying with him in the Goodyear blimp. Perhaps it was too conventional a beginning—a phone ringing in a darkened bungalow—but at least it was worth trying. I walked out to the side porch. The typewriter was sitting on its bamboo table, the paper parchment-colored and curled. I pulled it out and rolled in another. What was it Sidd had prompted me to say? The card on which he had written out the mantra was under one corner of the typewriter. "Living ripens verbal intelligence"—that's what it meant, wasn't it? *Om Ara Ba Tsa Na Dhi.* I repeated it a few times. My voice sounded faint and a little frightened in the emptiness of the bungalow. I cleared my throat and gave it a firm reading. I drew out the *Dhi* and let it tremble in the air. My fingers floated above the keys. . . .